AGROUND

Book Three in the
Wheels and Zombies
series

By

M. Van

AGROUND

Book Three in the
Wheels and Zombies series
By

M. Van

42Links Publishing

Visit:
www.42Links.net

Cover design by Shezaad Sudar
Edited by Book helpline

ISBN: 978-90-824472-5-5

Prologue

It had hit New York first, and from what I had learned, it might have been deliberate. They had tried to contain it, but the Mortem virus, as it came to be known, swept through the population like a plague. It struck as fast as a bullet and then coursed through the veins with every heartbeat and nestled inside the brain. Once infected, your body became a vessel for an entity forcing you to feed on the flesh of others, unable to stop unless every cell inside had turned to dust. People fled, running for their lives. They ran from a certain death brought on by a virus that wouldn't take their lives.

Part One
Hope Kills

1

"Come on, Ash. Get your butt up there." My arms trembled as I felt the dumpster under my feet waver. Ash grunted, and I couldn't suppress a smile. Fortunately, Ash wasn't a heavy burden to lift—the scrawny fourteen-year-old kid was still too damn skinny, although I kept giving her all the carb-rich foods we gathered on the road.

"Push me up some," Ash said through clenched teeth.

"Use your arms already."

With a groan, her weight lifted from my arms as she pulled herself up onto the roof of a building, and I heard her land with a thud on the other side of the ridge. "You okay?" I called out with a chuckle before I flung my backpack after her. There was another thud followed by an *oomph*.

"Hey, watch it."

Unable to stop laughing, I gripped the drainpipe to lift myself up onto the roof. Not that long ago, I would never have been able to lift my own bodyweight to climb onto a roof, but it seemed that allowing myself to be bitten by a zombie has significantly improved my physical condition—even though, it wasn't by choice.

I swung my legs over the ridge and rolled onto the tar roof next to Ash. An army of stars reached out over our heads and lit the night sky as we lay on our backs, panting. Ash gazed up at the sea of shimmering dots, and I embraced this rare moment of her being silent for once. Her blue eyes reflected silver in the gleam of the half-moon.

"You like that, huh?" I said as I watched her crack a smile.

"We never got to see that in the city." Her voice was soft—small even—as if it came from the girl she was supposed to be.

I got to my feet and looked around. A few lights still illuminated the gas pumps that belonged to the gas station underneath my feet. In the distance, waves crashed on the beach, and the ocean looked brilliant under the starlit sky. The world seemed vast, as if it were endless. The sight reminded me of home and the vacations I had spent with my parents and siblings when I was a little girl. Although the beach in Scheveningen could never match in size what I was seeing here, that didn't mean I didn't miss that little speck on the map called the Netherlands. It was still my home.

I stood over Ash and watched her endless smile for a minute before I grabbed her arms and yanked her up.

"Hey, watch it," she said, but I ignored her as I lifted her over my shoulder. Her strength had improved, but she was still a tiny thing, barely five foot two. Her legs hung limp as I held her to grab the pack with my free hand and walked to the other side of the roof.

I knew she would have kicked my ass if she'd gotten the chance or had legs to use. She didn't appreciate my ferrying her around like this. If I had learned one thing the past year, it was not to underestimate Ash, but I also knew I could go a long way with her.

"Don't do that," she said as she slammed her fist into my upper arm after I sat her down. I had to bite my lip to contain my smile.

"Sorry, old habit," I said and rubbed a hand through her messy blond, almost white, hair. Ash jerked her head and scooted away from me in annoyance, but I had an idea to soften her mood. I pulled the M4 from my backpack—our own personal carbine assault rifle, at least I presumed that was its name. Ash narrowed her blue eyes and grinned at me like a kid on a sugar high. I shook my head, clicked out the magazine from the rifle and started to fill it with the .223-caliber rounds that came with the weapon. Thirty rounds later, the magazine clicked into the rifle.

Ash nodded as she crawled to the edge—her legs sliding along the tar roof. I took in a deep breath, followed in a crouched position and lay down next to her, the rifle tilted over the edge of the roof. Ash's grin evaporated after one glance over the parking lot below, and the sight made my stomach turn.

The lot had been empty when we'd gotten here.

It had seemed safe enough to leave Ash's wheelchair behind, and she'd clung to my back as we'd strolled into what was left of the shop. The place had been gutted, but we'd found a couple of bottles of water, two soda cans, and a box of salted crackers in a plastic bag stuffed underneath the counter as if someone had stashed them there but had never come around to retrieve them for whatever what reason. I had been shoving them in my pack when Ash had spotted our first visitors.

Unwilling to face them, we'd decided to exit the shop at the back and had figured the roof to be our safest bet. Although our conditions kept us from being touched by the virus that had swept the country, facing the people who had contracted the disease felt threatening. It's strange to think that the cancer we both suffered from, and that would have surely killed us, had saved us from turning into zombies. More than that, it had saved our lives. It also meant that if we had wanted to, we could walk out of here without the zombies being bothered with us, but what I saw on the street and the parking lot below made my blood run cold.

In any other point in time, it would have sounded weird and shameful, but I had grown accustomed to the decrepit bodies drained of life. The sheer mass of this group wasn't anything I hadn't seen before. Other than the army of infected we had to plow through during our escape from the lab in Florida, we had been fortunate enough to avoid the masses. We knew these giant parades of zombies existed, and had once brushed the edge of a big group, but we'd kept our distance because even though they couldn't infect us, that didn't mean they couldn't cause us harm. I had seen zombies in agitated states that didn't seem to care about what they caught between their teeth.

Body after body lumbered down the street. The moans rose in unison to a chilling hum. I stopped counting after I reached twenty-five. There must have been over a hundred of them. Shoulder-to-shoulder, creatures that used to be human beings filled the parking lot in slow, steady stream. Dirt and blood coated mutilated bodies that pressed against our Knight. The armor-plated truck, our trusted vehicle, had aided our escape from a lab located inside a US military base in Florida and had since become our home. The tank-like vehicle, known as a Knight XV, was a force to be reckoned with, constructed with fiberglass, ballistic steel, and armored glass all around. It weighed tons, and had we been in it, I don't think we would have had any trouble mowing our way out of this place.

Broken fingers clawed at the truck as the zombies pushed each other in a continuing flow. I started breathing through my mouth when the foul smell of decaying bodies wafted up to where we lay on the roof. In a sideways glance, I noticed Ash's mouth stood open as well. She seemed fascinated by the march of the walking dead.

I figured the amount of zombies didn't have to spoil my plan to get some target practice and placed the stock of the rifle to my shoulder. Peering through the scope, some of the distinctive features of the zombies became clearer. In their filthy clothes, most of the zombies looked alike from a distance, but through the rifle's scope, a flowery dress or a red baseball cap returned some humanity to them. They shuffled their zombie shuffles and moaned with their heads raised to the sky, sniffing out their next victim.

Set to single shot, I aimed the rifle and pulled the trigger. My body flinched as the bullet left the barrel. It wasn't the forehead shot I had been going for, but a bullet through a zombie's ear gave the same desired effect. The other side of its head splashed open, and the body fell limply to the ground. Some of the zombies reacted to the sound, flailing their arms and releasing those guttural sounds.

Ash gave me a nudge and looked at me with an eagerness that made me a bit nervous. Though she wouldn't allow me to call her a kid, she very much was, and this probably wasn't good parenting, but then I wasn't her mother. I was just a tourist from the Netherlands who got stuck in the United States during a zombie apocalypse. After our chance meeting, I'd promised myself to take care of her, although I was aware of the fact I might suck at it. Shooting guns might not be a proper upbringing for a fourteen-year-old girl, but then it wasn't as if these were conventional times, and she needed to be able to take care of herself. I passed her the rifle.

"Keep your finger off the trigger until you're ready to fire," I said in a low voice. She rolled her eyes at me and scowled. I raised my eyebrows and edged back in defeat.

"I'm just saying."

I followed her line of sight as she picked her target. My mouth opened to warn her, but I was too late, and a metal clank followed the loud shot into the night sky. With my mouth open, I glared at her. The sight of her cheeks going crimson made my day.

"You shot the Knight," I said in disbelief. "You actually shot the Knight." She nervously glanced at the truck and then at me. At that point, I wished I was someone who could hold a straight face, but I lost it and snorted out, laughing. She punched me in the shoulder, and I rolled onto my side, still laughing.

"I think the armored vehicle will survive," I said.

Ash frowned, but I could tell she tried to hide a smile.

"Ass," she said, raising the weapon to her shoulder again. Attracted to the shot and probably our laughter, the zombies had moved closer to the side of the building and glared up at us. Ash aimed and fired. A zombie struck in its shoulder fell backward on its ass.

About half a dozen shots later, she started to get the hang of it. I fired off a couple of rounds myself before I emptied the chamber and clicked on the safety.

I yawned and rubbed a hand over the aching muscles in my neck but kept my eyes on the shuffling parade of zombies. The few that had stood gawking at us from the ground had long since rejoined the larger group and resumed their shuffle once we'd stopped firing the weapon.

Similar to the group we had encountered before, this parade seemed to be heading northwest, but it looked as if it would be a while before they all got on their way. Some, like the ones that had been watching us, strayed from the pack like curious children exploring their surroundings.

"I think we should stay up here for the night," I said as I watched a zombie's leg snap in half. Its dilapidated body, which, from the looks of it, had endured a number of assaults, crashed to the ground, and I shuddered at the sight. The thing, dragging a dead dog on a leash, didn't seem fazed and struggled on by clawing at the pavement.

Ash released a long breath and eyed me sideways.

"Do we have to?" she said. I ignored the whining in her voice.

"Well, I for one don't want to go down and disturb them," I replied.

"You're such a wuss," she said and huffed in frustration as she scooted back from the edge. I knew Ash well enough to not take the bait if I didn't want to get into a lengthy debate; besides, if she didn't argue the point on her own, she probably agreed. The fact Mortem didn't affect us and the fact that the infected rejected our smell didn't mean the zombies wouldn't attack us. If they became upset or agitated, it was possible they'd confuse us for a meal.

I watched the slow-moving parade for a moment. It seemed as if these large groups of zombies had some sense to follow the fleeing population. From a group of travelers on the run, we had learned that heading west would be our best bet to survive. They had told us that the military had attempted to keep the Mortem virus isolated on the eastern side of the country and had set up a border along the Mississippi River.

Although we hadn't made a definite decision on what our plan would be, we had followed the traveler's advice. Because of our special ability to avoid becoming zombies, we weren't much on the run from them. This had led us to travel between waves for a while, stuck between a throng of people fleeing the carnage and the growing number of infected that followed. It led us through abandoned towns or, in some cases, towns where folk had dug in to defend their homes. Most people, though, tended to flee west or north, probably unaware of the zombies following their meals. I guessed the zombies weren't that eager to let their food source get away.

Scooting from the edge, I grabbed my pack and removed a sweater. We were somewhere on the Gulf coast and, if I wasn't mistaken, not that far from New Orleans in midsummer, and it was still hot outside, even though the sun had set hours ago, but the sweater would work as a pillow, and I handed it to Ash. I lay down next to her and used the pack as a pillow for my own head.

"This isn't too bad," I said as I watched the remaining light of a long burned-out star.

"I guess so," Ash said under her breath. "Wow, did you see that!" Her arm shot up pointing a finger at the sky.

"Make a wish," I said, smiling.

2

I woke to the sound of birds and felt grateful it wasn't the growls of the walking dead. A pinkish-red light spread across the sky, warming up the air, although it hadn't lost much heat during the night.

My eyes fell on Ash's wild mop of hair that seemed to have a life of its own, and I subconsciously rubbed my own wild mop of hair. My hair had grown longer than it had in a long time. It probably wasn't wise to let it grow much longer, for it gave the zombies something to grab, but chemotherapy had kept it short for long periods of my life, and it felt nice to have it back.

Ash had settled herself in the crook of my arm, still peacefully asleep. It made me smile, because this was one of the rare moments I got to see the kid she was, so eager to hide from me at other times. When we'd first met, Ash had told me she was sixteen, but I had found out that she had actually been thirteen back then. She hadn't looked a year over twelve, so I hadn't believed her for even one moment. She always gave me this tough-chick routine and could barely hold up the wall she had built around her. I knew Ash's mom and dad had blamed her for her sister's suicide, and I knew her sister had done it to save Ash from a life as a guinea pig, but I wondered if Ash believed that. I wouldn't want to think of the burden she carried around with her if she believed anything else than that her sister loved her so much she didn't want Ash to become the lifesaving vessel to her sister's disease-ridden body.

I kissed the top of her head and whispered near her ear, "Wake up, sunshine."

Ash growled and dug her head deeper into the crook of my arm. "One more minute," she said.

I grinned at her reaction, but my back ached, and the backpack wasn't much of a pillow. I scooted out from under her, replaced my shoulder with the pack and got to my feet.

At the edge of the roof, the moans of a few undead that hadn't left with the procession from the night before greeted me. There weren't a lot, but enough to make a stroll to the car unpleasant, and I picked up the M4. I had reloaded it last night for good measure and placed the stock against my shoulder.

"Ash," I said in a raised voice as I clicked off the safety, "you better wake up, or you'll regret it."

She waved a hand and rolled to her side. With a grin, I took aim and caught sight of a short, stubby guy with a bald head in a blue polo shirt. I focused on my breathing, placed my index finger on the trigger, released my breath, and pulled the trigger. The gun crackled, shocking birds and other animal-life around awake, including Ash. The bald head in my sight exploded at the back. In the same moment, Ash shot up and glared at me. Her eyes were wide, and I was pretty sure I had gotten her attention.

"What the fuck? Mags!" she exclaimed. I laughed, took aim, and pulled the trigger again.

I didn't take me long to get rid of the remaining zombies and get ourselves down from the roof. The can of soda and box of salted crackers we had found inside the shop hadn't been much of a dinner, and I was hungry.

Up close the Knight looked as if it had received a mud bath, except that the mud had been replaced with blood and other gunk. Fortunately, the truck stood on massive wheels that nearly reached my waist, and considering the fact I was a solid six feet tall, that meant they were big. For that reason, the opaque, bulletproof-glass windows reached high over most zombies' heads, so I didn't have to do any cleaning in order to be able to look outside.

We had changed the interior somewhat after we'd inherited the truck. We had removed the backseats, except for one, to make room for Ash's chair and a mattress we had picked up from a Wal-Mart. Along with a bunch of blankets, pillows, and some other stuff, it made for a cozy home. Every time I stepped inside the mega-SUV, it made me feel grateful Mars had handed me the keys.

Special Agent in Charge Rodrigo Marsden was one of the FBI agents who had helped us escape Dr. David Warren's lab in Florida. Mars and his partner, Angela Meadow, had worked undercover at the time to learn about the doctor's plans. They had been the ones to break us out, and Angie had even gotten herself shot in the leg during the escape.

The thought of Dr. David made a cold shiver run down my spine, and I shuddered. Pushing the thought of him from my mind, I tried to focus on preparing oatmeal for breakfast, but now Mars kept interrupting my thoughts, and I sighed.

Ash sat in the open door of the truck, eating the oatmeal I had prepared, while I loaded the gas cans we had filled before the zombies had showed up. Ever since we had gotten a hold of the truck, I'd been a bit neurotic about fuel. The thing drank it like a hippo eligible for an AA meeting. I knew it ran on biodiesel, but what did I know of that, so I collected fuel everywhere I could.

After that, I was keen to get on the road. The zombie procession had unnerved me, and the stink of the ones left behind pierced my nostrils. Still, there was one thing I wanted to do before we left the coast.

My skin tingled where the sun threatened to burn it, but my body welcomed it. After spending too much time trapped in the basement of Dr. David's lab, I had regained a new appreciation for the sun. I had become a lizard feeding on its energy.

"Are you ready for this?" I said, my trusted Timberland boots buried in the sand. Ash hung off my back, and I stood next to the Knight parked on an endless stretch of beach.

"Shouldn't we take off some clothes?" she muttered next to my ear. I glanced down. Like Ash's, my clothes were limited to military-style cargo pants and black T's, either long or short sleeve, thanks to a pawnshop I had the sense of raiding at the beginning of the outbreak and to Mars who had managed to help us keep our stuff. Not that I minded, I liked comfortable.

The beach around us seemed empty except for some bulges in the sand. I pushed the thoughts of half-buried bodies from my head.

"I don't want to be caught by something running around half-naked on a beach," I said and then dropped the backpack loaded with guns and ammo onto the sand.

"Yeah, but a machete."

"I don't know what this infection does, might affect water life—what if we're attacked by zombified jellyfish?" I said with exaggeration in my voice, but I knew the blade carried my confidence.

"Yeah, I'll make sure to watch out for those," Ash said, snorting a laugh. I left the unstable, loose sand behind and stepped into the surf.

"Actually, these clothes stink; they could use a wash," I said as I waded into the deep blue to give Ash's feet their first shower of seawater. She shrieked, and her grip tightened around my shoulders.

"Don't let me drown, okay?"

I turned my head to her and rolled my eyes.

"Yes, I'm sure I won't let you drown," I said. Without warning, I dropped us neck deep into the water. Ash squirmed on my back. "You were the one who wished we could have gone swimming back in Neponsit," I said.

I couldn't stop grinning. It was beautiful, and the water felt like heaven. Ash's arms clung around me. She yelped as I tried to shrug her off, clinging tighter to my body. "Don't be a baby, Ash," I said, loosening her grip. With my feet placed solidly on the ground, I had no trouble to keep her head above the water. Water splashed violently where she beat her fist at the rolling waves. I had to close my eyes to keep the salt from stinging.

"Don't flap around like a lost puppy," I said. "Wave your arms through the water. Let it carry you."

"That's easy for you to say," she said, spluttering water. I ran an arm through the water to show her what I meant. She started to mimic the movement. It didn't take her long to get the hang of it.

"See? You don't need legs to swim."

Her eyes widened, and she broke into a smile. I grabbed her when she went under, splashing water at me. She coughed, her expression sour as she spat out the salty water. However, the smile that followed was unambiguous.

"Try this," I said and held a hand at the back of her head. She gave me a wary look, and I rolled my eyes. "Trust me already." I scooped up her legs to let her body float on the water. The biggest smile caressed her face as she squinted against the sun before she closed her eyes. Without a word, I let her go bobbing along the water.

"This is great," she said, opening her eyes. Panic set in when she realized I had let go. She tried to jerk up. Her head went under, but I had her within a second.

"Ass," she sputtered.

I couldn't contain a laugh. "Had enough?"

"No way, help me," she said. "Just tell me when you let go."

I raised her to the surface.

"You got it?" I asked. She nodded, and I let go. "You're on your own." I settled in beside her with a hand on her shoulder, to be sure.

The blue sky resembled a wonder, containing a purity that these days seemed hard to find on earth. The water caged my hearing. The only thing left was the blood rushing through my veins accompanied by a rhythmic heartbeat. Except for the grip on Ash's shoulder, I felt disconnected from this world and free. The world around me was gone. The madness of escaping labs, bandits, and zombies was gone. I felt at peace, and as it did often in a moment of silence, my mind wandered to that certain agent of the FBI, and I wondered what he was doing right now. It took me a while to recognize the sound I heard until I feared it was too late.

3

I jerked up in an instant, fixated on the sound. Ash did the same, heavily blinking and cursing under her breath.

"What?" she asked confusedly as she grabbed hold of my arm. My hart hammered so fast in my chest it started to hurt. It didn't prevent me from a nervous chuckle.

Without explanation, I guided Ash arms around my neck and started waving my arms through the water—frantic to get to the shore.

"My phone, it's ringing," I said. Ash didn't reply, and I figured she understood the significance.

As soon as I reached shallow-enough water, I nearly dropped Ash and sprinted to my pack. Water dripped down off my face and clothes as I dropped to my knees next to the pack and jerked it open. By that time, the phone had stopped ringing, but the fact it worked at all might mean there was still a signal out there.

My wet fingers grabbed hold of the slippery gadget and started to work the buttons. Adrenaline coursed through my veins, and the added tremble in my hands didn't help with operating the thing.

A year ago, I couldn't have imagined abandoning my phone for over five minutes, but I guessed the interest in the bells and whistles of modern technology faded when they weren't in our daily lives. It showed too, because I couldn't unlock the screen.

"They must still have a signal in this area," Ash said as she crawled across the sand to get to me.

"Ya think," I replied. The added retort I had thought of faded when it started to dawn on me. I had a voicemail. I was still pushing buttons when Ash came up next to me and started to wipe the sand from her hands.

"Give me that," she said and in the same instance pulled the phone from my hand. "We changed the code six days ago to somethin' we could both remember so I could use your playlist after my iPod died, remember?" I clenched and unclenched my fists and drew a breath to calm myself.

From my peripheral vision, I could see Ash staring at me. I cleared my voice. Her eyes had gone wide, but she bit her lip as if she didn't know what emotion to show.

"You have two hundred and forty-nine voicemail messages and about five dozen mails," she said. "The last message is from a minute ago."

As if my brain could not comprehend the information, I just sat there, watching the phone in her hands. She held it out as if I should take it, but I couldn't move. Her thumb moved over the screen.

"Don't," I said abruptly. She peered up at me with a nervous glance.

"Don't you want to know who——" she started to say.

"I'm pretty sure I know who," I said, cutting her off. With trembling fingers, I took the phone. The little red circle over the green icon indicated the two hundred and forty-nine messages. It wasn't a hard guess whom they had come from—my family, my mom, dad, brother, and sister. But I supposed they would think I was dead. If it hadn't been by the hands of the mindless infected zombies, they knew the cancer should have killed me by now.

"Call them," Ash said in a tiny voice.

"They're better off thinking I'm dead," I replied in a shaking voice without taking my eyes from the screen.

"They obviously don't think you're dead or else they wouldn't be callin' you every day," she said. My throat closing up kept me from replying.

"They don't know," Ash added. "Don't you think that's probably worse?"

I shrugged, unsure what to say.

"Call them," she repeated.

The sun had reached its peak by the time we had dried up and changed clothes.

I needed to get a handle on myself if I didn't want to turn into a blubbering mess while I called home.

Ash didn't understand my reluctance. My

relationship with my family was strange at best. For years, I had tried to push them away. I hadn't wanted them to see me wither away like a fallen leaf. Of course, that had been a stupid idea, and it hadn't worked.

The heat rose inside the cabin as I sat behind the wheel, holding the phone as if my life depended on it. Ash watched me with encouraging eyes as I took in a breath and pressed the number on the screen.

The phone seemed to connect after some static sounds and was then reduced to a simple dial tone. It took a while before the other side picked up and even longer for a tentative trembling voice to answer.

"Hallo." Tears started to roll down my cheeks at the sound of Mom's voice. I had to force myself to choke out the next word.

"Mam." The shock in Mom's voice was evident when she couldn't construct a sound sentence.

"Oh God, oh God," she almost squealed and then started shouting for my dad. In between, she jammed question after question. *Are you okay? Where are you? What happened? How can this be?* The language I hadn't heard or spoken for almost a year flooded my ears. I had even stopped thinking in Dutch. But with every feeling I had held hidden over the past year emerging, my mother's words sunk in. I had become a blubbering mess in a mere five seconds. Ash squeezed my hand. Grateful, I glanced at Ash and could see the tears in her eyes.

It struck me that all this time I had buried any thoughts of the existence of my family, because I thought they'd be better off by thinking I was lost. Ash had no one left, and I never even considered what she must have thought of me when I had abandoned mine so easily.

Mom had switched the phone to speaker, and I heard the relief in my dad's voice, although it didn't take him long to switch to his business persona. He ordered Mom to calm down and reminded me the line might disconnect any second. He turned the topic to planning an exit strategy. At that point, I too switched my phone to speaker. In the middle of my dad asking where I was so he could send a private jet, Ash spoke up.

"Huh?"

I smiled at her, and before Dad could ask who that was, I introduced Ash and requested he speak English.

"Ash," he said in a questioning voice.

"Hi Mr. ..." Ash started to say before she faded off and looked at me with furrowed brows. "What was your last name?" she whispered. I mouthed her the name *Vissers*, but it deepened her frown.

"Never mind," my dad said impatiently. "Tell me where you are." I switched app and glanced at our position. As we'd traveled, I'd occasionally managed to find an Internet or a GPS connection to help us find our way.

"We're somewhere south along I-10, I think."

"Don't think. Know, Margje," Dad replied. Ash's brows shot up. I shrugged it off with a shake of my head.

"Later," I whispered, and then told Dad, "About an hour's drive east of New Orleans." In the background, we heard him clicking on his keyboard.

Dad was the epitome nerd when it came to electronics. If it used electricity—preferably with a keyboard and a display—then he would know how to use it. Combine that with the business-like thinking he had inherited from his mother's side of the family, and you had an entrepreneur who had built a company producing computer parts that could rival the best.

"Then you're probably nearby Stennis International Airport, or Diamondhead, and that's why you've gotten a signal, but it won't be any help getting you out—both airports are out of commission," Dad said after a while. "I need you to get to Jackson. I'm not sure how yet, but I will find a plane to get you out."

Ash gave me an incredulous look that made me smile.

"Can he do that?" she asked in a small voice.

"You bet I can," Dad's voice came over the speaker.

"You heard him," I said.

"So that was your family," Ash said. I looked at

her with a faint smile as I helped her put on the heavy boots and added the load-carrying system to our military camouflage outfit. The latter was more of a vest to help carry the primary load of a soldier, like ammunition, canteens, and grenades. On the road, this getup turned out to be our best bet for staying out of trouble. People kept their distance or treated us with a little bit more respect while roadblocks set up by law enforcement or the military became a mere inconvenience.

Ash huffed as I clicked her leg holster in place and tugged at her vest. This getup restricted her movement even further, but we had to make sure we looked the part if we wanted to reach Jackson.

"Yeah," I replied. I wanted to say more, talk to Ash, see how she felt about all this, but my body felt emotionally drained. Dad had been right, of course —the call was cut short before we could get into anything too personal. Mom had managed to squeeze in some *I-love-yous*, *be-carefuls*, and *come-back-safes*. She also said she would keep calling every night as she had done the past year. I felt so guilty over the fact that I hadn't even tried to get in touch with them. My reasons seemed so stupid and selfish now.

My mind remained stuck for a moment as I watched a sea gull land on a half-buried corpse. It started picking at the lifeless form, and I wondered if animals would be able to contract the virus by eating leftover bodies or even zombies. The thought made me shudder, and I snapped out of it.

I glanced sideways and noticed Ash staring at me. It wasn't hard to read the curiosity on her face.

"What?" I asked.

"You really think your dad will find a way to get us on a plane?" I turned at the subdued excitement in her voice. She was trying to play it down, but those big blue eyes of hers told she wanted it to be true.

"If there's anyone that can do it, it's him, and even if he can't, he'd find another way," I said, trying to convey confidence. "It might take longer, but I wouldn't put showing up on a boat past him."

"I think he might be pointin' us in the wrong direction if he's plannin' a boat ride," Ash said.

"Well, you're the one who told me to be more positive—so I'm positive."

She grinned and handed me a pair of aviator sunglasses. I took them eagerly.

"Nice," I said. "Where did you find these?" She pressed a similar pair on the brim of her nose and smiled.

"Back in the shop." She smirked as she inspected them in the side mirror. We had changed into the army fatigues given to us by Mars to support our fake army IDs, and the sunglasses gave the ensemble an edge. I flipped the key, and the Knight roared to life.

"Ready," I asked and glanced a final time at the ocean and all its beauty.

"Ready," Ash replied. I released the brake and pressed down on the gas when Ash startled me.

"Wait, stop!"

My foot slammed on the brake while she scooted closer and jammed the phone in front of my face. With her in the frame she yelled, "Cheese." Before I could adjust my face, the phone clicked, and the image displayed wasn't one of my prettiest. I frowned at it and then at Ash.

"Yeah, we better do that over. You look like you ran over a puppy," she said. She threw an arm around my shoulder and tried again.

I looked at the picture for a second and smiled. I hadn't seen a sincere smile on my face for a long time. Our hair—still short for certain female standards, aviator glasses, and army-green jackets made me think of brothers in arms. Well, more like sisters in arms, but with a bond that could have been created on the battlefield, and maybe it had.

"Now, we have our own *Thelma & Louise* picture," Ash said with a smile as she scooted back into her seat. I raised an eyebrow at her.

"You saw that?" I asked, sounding suspicious.

"Yeah," she replied, drawing out the word, "why?"

"No reason," I said with a shrug. "Just that it's old. I think I might have been your age when it came out."

"So what? You're saying you're old?" I poked a finger into her shoulder.

"Smart ass," I said. Ash grinned and shook her head.

"They had this patients' lounge back at the hospital," she said. "It had this old VCR with about four tapes, and that was one of them. I must have seen it about twenty times." I reached out and pulled my hand over her head.

"From watching old movies to zombie-killing badass," I said and set the Knight in motion.

Warren

Dr. David Warren sat in his office overseeing the small space that he had become forced to call his laboratory through the connecting window. The cramped lab could barely hold the one technician he had been assigned, let alone give him room to work or even think. On an improvised table set up as a workstation in the corner of his office, a centrifuge dinged and stopped spinning. He had been forced to move some of the lab's equipment inside his own office. Except for his desk, all nonessential furniture pieces had been removed from the tiny space and replaced by tabletops filled with the limited research equipment at his disposal.

The lack of resources had dampened his mood for weeks, along with the results he had been searching for. *How could he find what he was looking for if they didn't permit him the use of a proper lab?* He sat back in his chair and glanced at the papers scattered across his desk. The failure at the Florida research lab that had resulted in the building blowing up and most of his samples vaporizing had hurt his progress more than he would have liked to admit. Though he had been granted the opportunity to lead the FMDT—the Federal Mortem Defense Team—the government that had appointed him the job had also tightened the screws. Extensive testing privileges had been evoked, and he had to find a way to get back on track.

His head perked up at the sound of the phone ringing on his desk. A familiar number popped up on the display, and he recognized it as the White House phone number. He grinded his teeth, already feeling the anger coursing through his veins. The phone rang several times before he stretched his arm to pick it up.

"How can I help you, Mr. Doyle?" he said in a condescending manner. Silence hung on the line for a moment as if the caller hadn't expected an answer. Considering the fact that the same number had alone this morning called Warren's number six times before he decided to pick up, it could have been expected.

"Dr. Warren," an elated voice came over the other end of the line. "How relieved I am to finally speak with you. We feared there might have been another incident when you didn't return our calls."

The voice on the other end of the line belonged to Trenton Doyle, White House Chief of Staff—a man Warren had no patience for.

"Please get to the point," Warren said, feeling annoyed. "I'm busy here."

"The president would like an update on your progress."

Having sat in his office for the past hour brooding over his lack of progress, Warren wasn't in the mood for government games, and Doyle had caught him at a moment where he couldn't filter his thoughts.

"You can tell the president that if he wanted results, he shouldn't have impaired my research to the point where it has become insignificant," Warren said in a clipped voice. He knew this wasn't the person he should have vented his frustration at if he wanted to be taken seriously again, but as before, his work had become shunned to the point that it seemed unnecessary, even if deep down they all knew they needed him.

"Dr. Warren, I know it is frustrating for you, but we cannot allow another incident as we had in Florida—many men and women died in that failure. The program had to be reduced in size."

"You want a solution to the Mortem virus, and you want a way to enhance our military capabilities. The only way I can do that is to be able to conduct my research the way I see fit," Warren said. "With more resources—"

"Your resources vanished when our financial backers left, because of the fact that your virus is destroying our country—no one of sound mind would want to be associated with that. The only reason you are still on our payroll is to find a solution to the Mortem virus. After that, you may count yourself lucky if we don't shoot you for treason."

Warren drew in a breath, trying to calm himself as Doyle continued.

"We are willing to expand your lab and funds,

but not as long as you keep your research heading in the same direction as it has been."

Drawn to a noise in the lab, Warren glanced out through his observation window and saw the large man approaching his office. William stopped in the open door and knocked as if Warren hadn't seen him. Warren indicated he was on the phone and imitated a chatting mouth with his hand.

"We cannot allow you to experiment on new subjects, as you like to call them. They are human beings, for God's sake," Doyle said, but Warren barely paid any attention anymore to the man speaking on the phone.

His curiosity drew him to William, who now stood bent over at his desk, writing something on a piece of paper. With the priorities focused on his research, he had appointed William to take care of the operational duties that came with being the head of the FMDT. Now, he was eager to learn why William had felt the need to visit him in person at the lab while his job would usually take him all across the country. William held up the paper, and Warren read it: *Possible contact subjects 101 and 102, location confirmed within one-hundred-mile radius.*

Warren sat up in his chair—he felt exhilarated.

"Mr. Doyle," he said, "what if I can promise you the results the president is looking for within three weeks and I need only two things?"

The line fell silent again as if Doyle had to think it over, but Warren already knew how to win him over. William had just returned him his salvation.

"I'm listening," Doyle said.

5

The road stretched out in never-ending asphalt while we weaved around abandoned cars. The Knight easily dispersed with vehicles blocking the road as I notched and eased them out of the way. It made me feel uneasy, and I felt the muscles in my shoulders tighten as I clenched the steering wheel. Ash didn't seem to be bothered even when some of the cars we passed contained dead drivers or passengers. The bite of a zombie was enough for most people to turn into one of them, but I guessed even the Mortem virus couldn't sustain a body after brutal onslaught. It felt strange to me that both Ash and I had been given a chance to survive. We had both been bitten at one time and hadn't turned.

Trees flashed past the armored glass on both sides as the sun started to make its descent.

We followed the I-10, crossed over onto I-12, and switched to the I-55 near a place called Hammond. The place looked like ghost town. We hadn't overtaken any zombie parades as far as I could tell, so I hoped people had fled instead of hunkering down, thinking they could survive the horde, but because many houses looked boarded up, it was hard to tell. We didn't stay to prowl.

The road stretched on, with nothing to be seen but trees, trees, and more trees. Ash had dozed off, and I had caught myself nodding a few times. Soon, we would have to stop. I didn't know what was worse: the tenacity of a busy road or the boredom of an empty one. To keep myself distracted, I was thinking of a way to get Ash behind the wheel. Maybe a stick would do the trick—the Knight was an automatic after all, but I dismissed the plan. In the wake of a zombie apocalypse, I shouldn't throw all sanity into the wind.

Still, it became hard to focus on driving. The conversation with my mom and dad raked through my mind. Mom had sounded exhilarated over the phone even when I tried to apologize for the way I had treated her the last few years. How I'd acted back then hadn't been my proudest moment, and I'd felt relieved that part of the phone call had occurred in Dutch, which meant Ash hadn't understood a word. In my defense, I had been dying at the time I'd acted out like that, and the only way I had been able to think of that would soften the blow for my family had been to push them away. For her, all this had seemed forgotten, but not by me.

While awake, Ash had asked if I wanted to listen to the voicemail recordings; it wasn't as if she could have understood any them and I would have needed to translate them, but it seemed a waste now. Everything had changed. We had a real possibility of seeing each other again, and listening to my mother's heartfelt messages would mean looking back and not ahead.

We stopped at a gas station in a place called Terry. The place looked like a stronghold managed by the Terry Police Department. They had secured this one gas station and maintained it, guns raised. The message surrounding the Mortem infection spreading fast and heading their way had been clearly received. Dozens of cars stood in line, waiting in turn for a chance to fill their tanks while their owners hovered around their vehicles. Some people waited patiently inside their cars while others honked their horns or shouted profanities. It seemed only a few of the cars were allowed near the station at a time because about two dozen stood waiting on a nearby parking lot under the watchful supervision of the Terry PD.

It turned out a massive vehicle like the Knight caught some attention, and a pair of officers approached our truck. We hadn't used the IDs Mars had provided us in Florida much, but this seemed like a good time to test them. Wearing sunglasses and military caps, we mimicked being soldiers as best we could.

"Let me do the talking, okay," I said to Ash as the two officers approached. She pulled a face in disgust.

"What? Why? You sound even worse than Arnold Schwarzenegger," she said.

"I do not," I replied, resenting her comment. Ash was always pushing buttons, testing how far she could go, but today I wasn't in the mood. Besides, with two officers on their way to interrogate us, I hardly thought this would be the right time.

"Well, maybe not Arnold, but definitely Jean-Claude."

"What are you talking about? Those guys aren't even Dutch," I said as I pressed the button to lower the window. Before she could retort, I added, "Ash, please shut up."

"Good evening and welcome to Terry," the first officer said. He had to look up at us sitting in the Knight. Relieved Ash kept her mouth shut, I bid the officers a good day.

"We have business in Jackson but would like to make a pit stop before we head into town," I said in my best US-sounding English and showed the man our credentials.

The officer who had spoken lowered his sunglasses and peered over the brim at the plastic cards I held out. He was an older man and the years as a cop showed on his face. The hair poking out from under his hat reflected silver in the sinking sun. A woman in uniform, also sporting shades, held a drawn gun but kept it pointed at the ground.

The man looked from the cards to his partner. "Looks okay," he said as he handed her the cards. "Call them in." The woman holstered her gun and pulled on the radio pinned to her shirt. The woman spoke into the radio, and as she walked off, the man leaned a shoulder against the door. Even with the shades on his face, I couldn't deny his concerns as he gazed up at me.

"Do you need to refuel?" he asked, returning his gaze to the line of cars waiting for a chance to fill up. "We are low as it is, and we're trying to give everyone a fair chance to reach the Mississippi before the clusters hit."

I kept my face devoid of any reaction. It wasn't that hard, hiding my eyes behind the shades on my nose. As a supposed member of the US military, it probably wouldn't come across well if the man could read the ignorance on my face, although I could imagine what he tried to convey with the word *clusters*. He meant the large groups of zombies that might be parading in this way. The mention of the Mississippi River reminded me of what those travelers had told us about the river being used as a border to contain the virus.

The officer expectantly looked up at me, waiting for my answer. I was always on the lookout for fuel for this beast of a truck, but as I watched the line at the pumps grow, I figured those people needed it more than us.

"We won't take up any of your resources," I said, "although I wouldn't say no to a cup of coffee." For the briefest moment, his lip twitched into a smile.

"Have you seen any of the clusters on your way in?" he asked. I glanced at Ash who had her jaw set in a tight line. It was somewhat amazing she'd been able to keep her mouth shut for this long. She nodded in support. I turned back to the officer. He didn't need a positive tale—the man needed the truth.

"The last ones we came across headed northwest, not far from New Orleans," I said.

"It sounds like the ones you're describing won't be the problem. We've got a massive cluster coming in east of here," he said. "That's why we're trying to get everyone across the river as fast as possible."

The man let out a long breath, lifted the hat off his head, and wiped a sleeve along his face.

"I should have forced them to leave," he muttered. It sounded as if he were talking to himself, so I hesitated to respond. The reply that came from Ash startled me.

"Who should you have forced to leave?" she asked in a low voice. I was afraid the man would recognize the voice of a young child, but he didn't seem to notice. From our high vantage point, I didn't think he'd get a good look at her. The man placed the hat back on his head.

"My wife," he said in an exasperated voice. "You see, our boy serves in the forces as well, and she wouldn't leave without us."

"There is still time," I said, not knowing what else to say.

"Maybe," he said under his breath as he watched the female officer return with our cards.

"The IDs check out," she said, handing the

cards back to me. "Sign in with the officer over there. He'll show you where to park. Stay in your vehicle until the officer says you can come out."

I frowned as my eyes followed the woman's pointed finger to a small section of a nearby parking lot. Two officers stood guard by the area, carrying shotguns.

"It's just a precaution," the man said. "We don't have ways to check for the virus, but we figure if you don't change in the next fifteen minutes, you're good."

"Right," I said and felt relief that there wouldn't be any physical inspection. This meant there wouldn't be any risk that the bite marks that Ash and I both had would be discovered.

We said our good-byes and wished the two officers the best. I huffed out a breath.

"Hadn't thought about the possibility of quarantines, did ya?" Ash said with a twang of arrogance in her voice.

"Did you?" I bit back.

With a smirk she said, "Nope and I'm glad we didn't."

"Why's that?" I asked as I glanced at her.

"Because I don't think it would have come across well with the officer if we acted like nervous wrecks." She had a point. Still, we should have thought things through before we had emerged on this journey to find an airport that would probably be crawling with military personnel. However, risks were necessary if I wanted to find a way home.

After our fifteen-minute stint sitting in an overheated truck—as I refused to turn on the air-conditioning even though Ash begged me to—the two officers allowed us to exit our truck. Knowing better than to offer help, Ash maneuvered her chair out of the truck and climbed in before we headed for the station. Inside, we were surprised to see the man sitting behind the cash register still demanded cash. Fortunately for us, Mars had managed to return all our stuff Dr. David had confiscated while he had held us captive, including my old travel backpack that had contained my ID and traveling money. In Florida, we had found a bank with a working ATM, and I maxed out all my credit cards. We were still on the run from Dr. David and had no idea how far his resources went, so we didn't want to leave too much of an electronic trail—for as long as that would even be possible. The cash was meant for cases just like these.

I had to admit we must have looked odd to the people hanging around the gas station, with our tank-like vehicle and army fatigues. It wasn't that the folks around weren't used to the military—no one even looked up when a huge convoy of military truck and jeeps tore by the station. But I guessed it wasn't often that they encountered a five-foot-two active soldier in a wheelchair who looked like a twelve-year-old. If I had thought it would be of any use to try and talk Ash into staying in the truck, then I would have, but she had the stubbornness of a mule. Besides, with our new pair of aviator glasses and a scowl on Ash's face, it seemed that they had bought it. At least no one asked any questions, and the coffee had been worth the stop. I had about three cups in record time and already felt the jitters when we heard that first shot being fired in the distant.

I glanced down at Ash, who sat in her chair next to me. She must have heard the shot as well, because she glanced up. I peered out the window, leaning on the standing bar where we had confiscated a spot as I tried to get a better visual of the sides of the building.

All I could see were the people, who had been filling up their vehicles and busying themselves around the station, stopped in their tracks. A man refueling his sedan shifted his head frantically from left to right before his gaze got stuck facing our direction or whatever it was that was happening behind the building. The man dropped the hose without replacing it on the pump and bolted for the driver side of his car. A woman and two kids sitting inside the car had their faces glued to the windows. The kids were crying, and the woman turned to scream at the man.

Without a word, I abandoned my cup of coffee and ran for the other side of the shop.

"What's goin' on?" Ash shouted at my back. I

didn't reply, and I also ignored the attendant who shouted at me for entering a restricted area as I shouldered the door full force and stepped inside a breakroom. On one side of the wall, there was a small kitchenette and a basic table, along with a couple of chairs that stood in the middle. Wrappers and empty cans of soup covered the tabletop. It seemed as if someone here had no shortage of supplies. I rushed to the window where the view was obscured by blinds and yanked at the cord.

The attendant, who by now had started shouting profanities, had followed me inside the room. He stopped as I pulled open the blinds and caught a first glimpse at what was happening outside.

"Oh, shit," fell from my mouth, and I heard the words echoed back to me by the attendant.

What looked like a fifty-yard-wide wall of bodies tightly pressed together shuffled toward us. Nothing seemed to stop them. Not a single object presented an obstacle. They lumbered on across the field parallel to the road Ash and I had used to get here, and it wouldn't be long before they reached the gas station. Hands clawed into nothingness. Noses frantically sniffed the air as if they hadn't already known what they would find here.

A patrol car flashing lights passed by the window and stopped between the building and the oncoming horde of zombies. Two officers stepped out carrying shotguns. They took a stand behind the car while others arrived in a similar manner. Four more cars joined, forming a wall of their own—anything to stop the zombies from reaching the station.

"What's wrong?" Ash said. I turned to the door where she had maneuvered her chair—a grim expression on her face. I shook my head, which I knew to be enough to assert it wasn't good, as the first shotgun burst made me flinch.

It must have freaked out the attendant, because he screamed and then bolted for the door, nearly knocking Ash off her wheels. Ash released the doorpost she had clung to, not even calling names after the attendant who'd rushed past her. The screams of the attendant added to the panic that had ensued inside the shop. Distraught shouts and screams, along with stuff crashing to the ground, served as background noise to the gunshots outside.

"What do we do?" Ash asked as I returned my gaze to the window. I took a moment to watch the officers lose their claim on the makeshift fence of cars. The zombies already started to squeeze past the vehicles or clamber over them. The officers retreated, still firing their weapons. Among them, I saw the elderly officer who had talked to us before. He had taken a position in the back of a pickup truck that gave him a high-ground advantage over the zombies edging closer. Even from this distance, I recognized his fear from the way he frantically tried to reload his shotgun and dropped a couple of shells, but he quickly composed himself and fired his weapon with accuracy, like the seasoned officer he exuded to be.

"Mags," Ash said. Her voice brought me back into the tiny room, and I faced her.

"We do what we always do," I replied.

"Lay low, take what we can," Ash said. I nodded in agreement.

6

Ash stayed behind me as I made my way from the small lounge to the attendant's desk inside the shop area of the gas station. The doors to the shop stood wide open, and the sounds of terror in the form of screams, weapons fire, and accelerating car engines wafted inside. The shop itself looked deserted as I spotted a sales rack for bags.

"Stay here," I told Ash and, without further explanation, rushed to the rack. Most bags were too small and useless for what I needed, but a shoulder bag looked up for the job. I swung it over my head and rejoined Ash at the counter.

Ash casted a dark gaze out the window where the zombies had breached the perimeter set by the officers. Everything seemed to have turned to shit in just a few minutes.

I jumped at the crash outside the shop as an old, beat-up truck slammed into the station wagon of a man who was still filling his vehicle with gas despite the threat of zombies. The driver's side door to the truck swung open, and a man dressed from head to toe in denim tumbled out of the truck. The owner of the station wagon still held on to the hose of the pump, and he looked as if he wanted to scold the man in denim, but when a woman in a brightly colored dress dropped down from the truck, sinking her teeth into denim man's throat, he dropped the hose and ran for his life. Highly flammable liquid poured from the hose as the woman's head flung up, her jaw stretching as if her life depended on it. Blood ran down her dress while the denim man gurgled for his last breath.

The station wagon man ran for the shop. His screaming attracted the attention of some other zombies, and they started lumbering after him. Sneakers squeaked on the tiled floor as station wagon man stopped in search of a place to hide.

Ash tapped me on the arm as I watched the man decide whether to hide behind an empty rack that once seemed to hold potato chips or a refrigerator box.

"Get the door," Ash said with enough urgency in her voice to get me moving. I hurried behind the counter. There had to be a switch or a button to close the automatic doors and lock them. I searched the desk but found nothing until my eye fell on a key sticking in a panel that sat mounted to the side below the register. As I turned the keys, the doors started to slide close.

"Are they locked?" Ash shouted, pointing out the obvious. "They're motion detected."

The zombies' jaws had already dropped, noses flaring in expectation of sinking their teeth into station wagon man's flesh. With the doors closed, I gave the key another turn, and I felt it click into place.

The first zombie slammed its face into the glass door. The black oily substance that had replaced its blood splashed and spread onto the glass. Loud thuds followed as the remaining zombies plowed against the doors. I could hear the glass crack and knew those doors wouldn't hold them for long.

"Check him," I said to Ash as I made my way to the canned goods.

As far as food was concerned, Ash and I were in good shape. Because the zombies ignored us in most cases, we didn't have much trouble loading up on supplies in overrun shops that weren't accessible for regular people. The back of our Knight piled over with mostly nonperishables, but these days I didn't take any chances and took whatever opportunity I had to stock up on food.

The shoulder bag was already starting to get heavy when a hand grabbed my ankle. I screamed in a panicked reaction and jerked back. My heart pounded in my chest as I pulled my handgun from its holster.

"Please don't," a frightened voice came from under the lowest shelve.

"What's wrong?" Ash shouted from the other side of the shop. Gun raised, I stepped back to get a better glimpse of the person hiding under the shelve. Ash repeated her question, and I heard the tires of her wheelchair squeak on the tiles as she drew closer.

"I'm fine," I answered but kept the gun aimed in

the direction of the voice.

"Please," that same frightened voice said as I watched the middle-aged woman who came with the voice crawl out from underneath the shelf. I made room for her without lowering the gun. Ash's chair stopped by my side, and we exchanged a glance while the woman climbed to her feet.

"Suzanne!" a man's voice exclaimed. Ash and I both turned to see station wagon man rush around a couple of racks right into the woman's arms.

It took the man and woman a moment to notice we were still watching them. Not to mention the zombies pounding on the doors. It took them long enough that I decided to holster my weapon—I didn't think they'd be turning into zombies after all that time.

I noticed the open-toed slippers on the woman's feet, along with the pink tracksuit she wore. The station wagon man wore a dark-blue tracksuit along with matching sneakers, and I wondered if they had even realized the world had gained a zombie problem.

"Mags," Ash said, "this is the guy hiding behind the refrigerator box."

The man composed himself, taking deep breaths while he took the woman's hand before he turned to me.

"Richard Shaffer, but call me Dick," he said, stretching out a hand. Ash made a noise that came close to mocking the man. As I raised my hand to shake Dick's, I smacked Ash in the head. Not hard, but enough for her to notice. Dick eagerly shook my hand before he pointed at the woman.

"This is my wife, Suzanne," he said, clinging to the woman.

I nodded and then pointed at the zombies knocking on the doors. These two wouldn't stand a chance if we didn't get out of here.

"We need to get them into the Knight," I told Ash and moved around her wheelchair. The front of the shop didn't provide another way out, so I returned to the small lounge. Through the window, I noticed the row of patrol cars that now stood abandoned. The zombies, along with the officers who had survived the first onslaught, had moved on. A single figure stood waving its arms as it tried to free itself from where it had gotten stuck between two cars.

A side door caught my attention, and I went to it. I tested the handle, and the lock clicked open. Easing the door open to a crack, I peeked out. The brewing dusty air hit me like a brick. Hanging out in an air-conditioned gas station made the outside air hard to breathe.

I stuck my head out the door and could just catch a glimpse of the Knight. The sight of it made me sink to my knees, the task of getting to the truck overwhelming me. Two or three police officers had barricaded themselves inside a different truck parked on a strip of grass between us and the Knight. They fired rounds out the window. The truck itself stood surrounded by zombies two rows thick. A couple of zombies stood clawing at the door of a restroom building that stood apart from the main gas station.

Shots were fired from high above, and it seemed as if someone had taken refuge on the roof of the station and was attempting to take out as much as they could. The zombies besieging the truck holding the officers took most of the hits.

Other folks tried to flee as they sped away in various vehicles.

"Mags," Ash said as she rolled her chair into the lounge. As I glanced at her, the corners of her mouth instantly dropped. She knew me too well. Rolling closer, she removed the sunglasses and narrowed her eyes at me.

"They won't be able to get out," I said, lowering my voice when I noticed the couple had followed Ash inside the room. At the sound of a loud crack, Suzanne screamed and Dick slammed the door to the lounge behind him. As if it would help, he shoved the table in front of the door.

Ash glanced at them over her shoulder before turning back to me and holding my gaze. She knew what I was thinking. There would be only one way to get them inside the Knight, and that was to get the Knight to them.

"Can we get out that way?" Suzanne said. The

fear hadn't left her voice, but she seemed to be in control of it. Dick came closer, leaning over Ash and peeking out through the door I still held at a crack.

"My God," he said in an exasperated voice. "We're trapped."

"Oh God," Suzanne added while her eyes filled with tears.

Ignoring them, I removed the shoulder bag and hung it over the back of Ash's wheelchair. Then, I pulled my spare weapon, a smaller caliber automatic and handed it to Ash. She already had her nine-millimeter automatic attached to her leg with a piece of Velcro, but I wanted her to have the a backup weapon.

"What are you planning?" Dick asked. Ash glanced at him over her shoulder. The man had turned to hold his wife.

"Mags is gettin' the truck," Ash said, sounding more confident than I felt.

"You can't go out there," Dick replied. "It's suicide."

"We can't stay here," I said. "Those zombies out there have caught your smell and they won't stop trying to get in here. Once there is nothing left to eat outside, they'll surround the building."

The man and woman looked at me as if I had something stuck up my nose. For a second I thought they had caught the stupidity of my remark about the zombies having caught their smell, but then Dick just started shaking his head.

"This is suicide," he repeated.

"Don't worry. She's good at this," Ash said as her gaze returned to me, "right." Her last word came out as a mere whisper. I leaned in to hug her and kissed the top of her head.

"Zombie-killing badasses, remember," I whispered near her ear so the others wouldn't hear. I caught the briefest of smiles on her face but knew I hadn't eased her worry.

Pulling the nine-millimeter from my holster, I readied myself at the door, taking deep breaths.

"Wait," Dick called out, "give me one of those guns."

"I don't think so," I replied. I didn't have more guns on me, and I wanted Ash to have every advantage she could get if she needed to defend herself against the zombies. I didn't mean any harm to these people, but if forced to choose, one person would come out of this building, and she wouldn't be walking.

"You gave the kid a gun," Dick said, annoyed.

I glared at him. Dick shifted uncomfortably. His wife mimicked his movement.

"Her name is Ash," I said authoritatively, "and if you call her kid again, I'll leave you and your wife behind." The man noticeably swallowed, and his eyes widened. A look at Ash told me she had trouble restraining a grin.

"Be safe, okay," I said as I took the sunglasses from her hand and placed them on her nose, and then I turned to the door and slid out.

"Don't get shot," I heard her say before I closed the door behind me.

What was I thinking? The words kept rolling inside in my head as I crept to a pallet stocked with barbecue coals. A serious amount of bullets hammered down on the zombies assaulting the truck carrying the three officers. From this vantage point, I had a clear view of them fighting for their lives. Bodies unmoving or just unable to stand covered the ground around the truck.

The shooter up on the roof kept his aim low, mainly crippling the zombies, probably so he wouldn't hit anyone inside the truck. The pile of bodies helped to keep the still-standing zombies from reaching the men through the windows of the truck. The men inside the truck emptying their weapons into the shriveled-up faces of the undead also helped.

I glanced around. Most of the cars that had been waiting for their turn at the gas pump had taken off. Whoever had survived was long gone except for the person on the roof and the officers inside the truck. A handful of zombies stood clawing at the door of the restroom, so I assumed someone was in there. Others feasted on their prizes, slumped over bodies, tearing or chewing on flesh and insides.

In the blazing heat, the mix of smells wafting on

the wind became nauseating. A bead of sweat trickled down my back as I gathered up the nerve to make a run for the Knight. In a similar situation, I would usually just stroll at a leisurely pace and take my time. The goal would be to mimic the zombies so they would leave me alone. The shooter on the roof deprived me of that option. I was afraid the person up there would shoot me, thinking I was a zombie.

I decided to take a little detour. My best bet would be to run up to the restrooms, go around the small building, and from there cross the lot to where the Knight stood parked.

It seemed like a good idea as I started my sprint. Except a few steps into my run, dirt sprang up as the bullets hit the ground near my feet. Another shot pinged off an abandoned vehicle while I fell to my knees and ducked behind the car. My heart hammered inside my chest, and my breathing came so fast it hurt to force air inside my lungs.

"Hold your fire, you dumb f—" Ash's last word drowned under a barrage of bullets, but soon after, the gunfire stopped. I stuck my head around the edge of the car for the briefest of moments. When it no longer seemed anyone would take a shot at me, I peeked out again and searched the roof of the gas station for the shooter.

Ash's head poked out through the half-opened door where I had left her. She had followed my progress. I waved and shouted, "Thanks," as she waved back.

"No problem," she shouted.

Up on the roof, I could see two figures—one in plain clothes, jeans, and a T-shirt, and a young police officer. The guy in the T-shirt seemed unaware of what had just happened as he fired his rifle at the zombies trying to get at the truck. The young officer stood frozen on the edge of the roof, his rifle pointed at the sky.

"Not a zombie," I shouted and waved at him so he could see I wasn't one of the undead. He lifted a hesitant hand. It wasn't the reassurance I had hoped for, but it would have to do. I got to my feet. I glanced around to check my surroundings, but none of the zombies seemed to have taken an interest in me. With the gas station on my right and the little restroom building on my left, the truck carrying the officers stood dead center in the middle of the lot. Just within my sight of vision, I could see parts of the Knight's massive grill as it peaked out from behind the restroom building. I figured my best bet would be to go around the building and make a run for the parking area.

The young officers still stood frozen on the edge as I left my hiding spot. My heart still raced, and the thought of getting shot by a nerve-racked police officer who literally stood on the edge didn't help. Finally, the man in the T-shirt called out to him. This drew his attention, and I used the opportunity to sprint for the restroom building.

7

Sweat trickled down my face as I climbed behind the wheel of the Knight and slammed the door shut. The noise made a couple of the zombies attacking the truck look up, sending their noses up in the air. Nostrils flared, but I knew they wouldn't find the scent zombies craved. Noise would have to do.

After I started the truck, I rolled down the windows on both sides and cranked up the stereo. Ash had my phone hooked up to the system, and I pressed play without even checking the playlist. A heavy bass line almost blew out the speakers immediately after I hit the button. I jumped but kept Jay Z's fast-paced rhymes, heavy beats, and guitar riff playing at high volume.

The zombies went berserk. Jaws stretched and snapped shut. Heads bobbed from left to right as they searched for their new snack. I stuck my head out the window and waved at them.

A bunch of them snarled, leaving the truck and its occupants behind to find a new and bigger truck with me behind the wheel. As fast as they could with their decrepit bodies, feet shuffled across the dirt. A few of the zombies dropped before they made it halfway to me. The men on the roof and from inside the other truck still fired their guns, taking out as many as they could.

I waited patiently until I had a nice lineup. They all followed each other like a bunch of lemmings—one shuffling after the other. Once they'd cleared the other truck, I pressed my foot down on the gas pedal.

The Knight's engine roared. Dirt sprayed up from the ground, leaving a cloud of dust behind me. The powerful truck quickly gained momentum, and the first zombie didn't know what had hit it. Bones cracked and pulverized under the Knight's massive wheels. Blood splashed on the windshield, and a body even managed to land on the hood before it fell to the ground.

Five zombies lay dead in my tracks. I slammed the truck in reverse and ran over two that had managed to dodge much of the first blow. Then I aimed for the remaining horde still plaguing the other truck.

I could see the three men inside clearly as I drove the Knight parallel to theirs. The truck shook as I ran over another body. Driving up to the gas station, I could see the two men on the roof, guns in hands, although the young officer had forgotten to fire it as his gaze followed the Knight. The other man showed no love for the zombies and kept firing his rifle as I made another pass running over bodies.

Two zombies still stood at the main doors of the station's shop. They had stopped banging their fists on the glass doors. Instead, they just stood there watching me as if I would bring them salvation. I didn't stop as I steered the Knight in their direction and rammed the vehicle through the front door of the shop. Glass shattered as the Knight ran easily over the two zombies and they disappeared from view.

Ash had found her way into the shop along with the husband-and-wife tracksuit team as I jumped out of the Knight, leaving the engine running. From the smirk on her face, I could tell she was pleased.

"Took you long enough," she said. I would have hugged her, but I knew she wouldn't appreciate it while surrounded by strangers. Instead, I ran a hand over her head.

"Get in," I yelled at the couple.

Ash climbed inside on the driver side of the truck, and I shoved her chair along with the shoulder bag in after Dick and Suzanne, who had climbed into the back.

Sitting behind the wheel, I slammed the door shut and hit reverse. In the rearview mirror, I barely saw the legs dangling from the roof and in a reflex jerked the wheel.

The metal strips that had held the glass door before I rammed it, cracked and buckled as the Knight's body partly crashed through the side paneling of the shop. The truck shook, and I lost my footing, pressing down on the gas a lot harder than I wanted. From the back, I heard Suzanne scream while the truck jerked backward. Frantically, I hit the break, but wasn't in time to stop the Knight's rear wheels lift of the ground as it rammed one of the gas-pumps.

Checking the mirror, I couldn't see much except for the pump now standing at an angle.

"Son of a bitch," I heard a man's voice yell. My eyes switched to the front where I saw the two men had lowered themselves from the roof and were now squatting on the ground in front of the shop. The man in the T-shirt got to his feet and grabbed the young officer by his collar. Half-running, half-stumbling, they made their way to us.

"Get your ass in there, Timmy," the man in the T-shirt shouted at the officer before he stopped at my window. "Nice driving," he said. The man looked to be in his midthirties. His black wavy hair dripped wet from sweat, and his white T-shirt had stains around his neck and under his arms. The unshaven face added to his scruffy appearance, but his gray eyes peered at me with delight and softened his features.

"Get in," I said, still a bit shaken by the off-kilter exit from the shop. The man's eyes glanced over the damage at the back of the truck along and the tilted gas pump, and I could see them change. Eyes wide, he raised his arm and waved at the other truck.

"Gas leak, Go! Go! Go!" he shouted. He climbed inside behind me and again yelled, "Go! Go! Go!"

As he said it, I remembered how Dick had dropped the hose while the highly flammable liquid still poured from its nozzle. I took the hint and stepped on the gas. Metal screeched as the bottom of the Knight broke away from the wrecked pump. Something snapped, and I could feel the air displacement around me.

Everything seemed to happen in a fraction of a second. As we bolted forward, the other truck plunged forward as well, and we came up by their side. Then, all I could sense was the enormous heat that engulfed us from the rear.

Within seconds, my eyes went from the road to the rearview mirror and then to Ash. Her eyes went wide as they met mine. I wrapped an arm around her and pulled her close as I tried to keep the Knight steady.

An explosion that reminded me of Dr. David's lab blowing up rocked the Knight. Holding on to the steering wheel, Ash and the searing heat were about the only things I registered as we drove off.

Sometime after the gas station blowing up and following the other truck, I parked the Knight on a shoulder. I stared out over the open road and watched the cloud of black smoke darken the blue sky in the distance. Except for the heavy breathing inside the vehicle, it felt as if we had gotten ourselves stuck in a vacuum of silence.

A door slammed shut in the near distance. It

tussled me out of my stupor.

"Dad, you made it!" a voice came from the backseat. At my side, Ash had turned to face our new company, and as I glanced in the rearview mirror, I witnessed how the young officer named Timmy scrambled to get out.

As the backdoor swung open, I noticed the three police officers making their way from their truck to ours. The elderly officer who had welcomed us before was among them.

"Sergeant," another voice spoke. Ignoring the voice, I turned to Ash.

"You okay?" I asked as a hand tapped me on the shoulder.

"Sergeant," the voice spoke again. I glanced up to stare into the gray eyes of T-shirt man. Impatiently he crossed his arms over his chest. I narrowed my eyes at the man whom I thought could be a bit more grateful since we'd rescued him from that roof, although the reason he needed rescuing could have been my fault. As I glanced back at Ash, who seemed equally baffled, my gaze fell on the patch on her shoulder. A single, inverted V decorated her uniform. With a quick glance on my own shoulder, I noticed there were three of those inverted Vs. It dawned on me that T-shirt man was talking to me.

I cleared my voice before I replied with, "Can I help you?" The man eyed me with a strange curiosity, and I felt sure that he could see straight through my poor attempt at pretending to be military.

"Sergeant, my name is Michael Carver. I'm with the CDC, and I need you to get me to Jackson," he said. The man must have noticed me scan his dirty T-shirt and unkempt appearance. Without a word, he pulled a wallet from the back of his pants and took out a card. My eyes went from inspecting the card to Ash, who shrugged. The man looked nothing like the picture.

"That's supposed to be you," Ash said.

The man glared at her before he flipped the card around. Then, he glanced into the rearview mirror and grinned.

"I guess. It's been a while since my last shower," he said.

Outside, Timmy threw his arms around the elderly officer. I guessed the man had found his son. The other two men slapped Timmy on his shoulder, and it looked as if they were congratulating him for their rescue. It seemed odd, knowing how freaked out the kid had been and how he had almost shot me.

Perched between the two front seats, Michael cleared his throat as if he wanted to catch my attention. I shifted to face him.

"What do you want, Mr. Carver?" I asked. The fact he had told me he worked for the CDC, or the Centers for Disease Control, something I had learned from watching certain movies, made me a bit wary of him. Ash and I didn't have the best track record when it came to similar government organizations.

"I would like you to take me to Jackson. I assume you're heading there anyway," he said. I looked him over as I considered my reply. Having someone else tagging along with us wasn't something I preferred, but considering he worked for the CDC, this might work to our advantage. I hadn't considered containment procedures before we'd left on this journey, but since then, I had realized we could run into trouble trying to enter the city. The security measures in Terry seemed easy enough to evade, but I imagined it wouldn't be that simple in a large town like Jackson. Still, I couldn't just say yes. In my role as a sergeant in the US military, I didn't think it would be very realistic if I didn't act a little cautious.

"Do you have business in Jackson?" I asked in my best formal voice.

"You can say that," Michael replied. I waited for an added explanation, but it didn't come.

"And you're not goin' to tell us," Ash said. Michael shifted his gaze to her, and although he didn't voice it, I could see him wonder about this fragile little soldier sitting in the front seat of this tank-like vehicle.

"Nope," he answered.

Ash shrugged as she replied, "Fair enough, I guess."

Michael opened his mouth to speak, but commotion from the back made him close it again, and he turned his head.

Suzanne had exited the Knight and stomped toward the officers. Dick shuffled after her. Both of them engaged in an animated discussion with the four officers. Michael pulled a hand through his hair and followed.

I watched them for a moment before I turned to Ash. "Wanna come?" I asked. She glanced past my shoulder and frowned.

"I think I'll pass."

I didn't buy the pitiful little pout on her face; she was happy leaving me to deal with our new company.

"Besides someone needs to look after our stuff," Ash added. She had a point, and I nodded before stepping out of the truck to join the conversation.

Fortunately for me, Michael did most of the talking, together with the elderly officer, who turned out to be Chief of Police Dudley. The four officers were all that remained of the Terry Police Department.

Dick and Suzanne demanded an escort to Jackson. From the chief and his son Timmy, I got the impression that all they wanted to do was to head back into Terry to get their wife and mom, although the chief morphed the argument into something more responsible, like checking if the rest of the town had gotten out all right. The two other officers seemed to agree, although I think they did it to back their chief. They didn't look eager to get back into the by-now-infected town.

"All right, then it's settled," Michael said. "We split up. You and your men head back into town in your truck, and the sergeant will take the Shaffers and me to Jackson."

"We shouldn't split up," Suzanne argued. "I say we all return to Jackson."

"Honey, these men have a duty to perform. You can't ask this of them," Dick chimed in, but the woman ignored him.

The chief shook his head, "I'm not leaving my citizens—that is not an option."

I just stood back as I watched the men and woman argue, although I started to get eager to get on the road again. We had wasted enough time, and I wanted to find out if my dad had been successful in procuring a plane for us. The adrenaline shock of the sudden zombie attacks and getting shot at had subsided—the thought of going home took over.

"Listen," a voice near my ear said. Timmy had left the conversation and stood by my side.

"I'm really sorry for shooting at you ... I ... uh ..." he said.

His face turned a shade of crimson, and his eyes kept shifting between his father and me.

"Don't worry about it," I said. "You missed."

His eyes shifted back to his dad for a moment

before he spoke again. "Please don't tell my dad."

The young man barely looked eighteen, and the shame that his action had triggered was endearing. There was also something disconcerting about it. I didn't want him to doubt himself in another one of these situations, not at times like these.

"You were protecting your dad and those men," I said. "I knew someone was up there shooting. I should have announced myself." With a smile, I extended my hand. "Maybe we can both learn from it."

He gave me a meek smile in return before he took my hand. In the same moment, Michael entered our conversation.

"Sergeant," he said.

I released Timmy's hand and turned to the man from the CDC.

"Mr. Carver."

"The officers won't be joining us, and we should leave," Michael said. I nodded in reply, but he had already turned on his heel and made his way to the Knight. I had a feeling we were in for an interesting ride.

Chief Dudley came over to me and shook my hand. "Thank you for helping us out back there," he said.

I took it and, as I shook, blurted out, "Sorry for blowing up your gas station."

Although his face didn't look annoyed, he didn't seem overjoyed either.

"I hope you find your wife," I said. The worry that flashed across his face made his forehead wrinkle.

"As do I," he answered. Before I could say anything else, he nodded and joined the other officers at their truck.

As the men drove off, I noticed an argument escalating at the passenger side of the Knight. The Shaffers had found their places in the back of the vehicle, but Michael waved a finger at Ash as he stood at the front passenger door. The man had no idea what he had gotten himself into. With a smirk on my face, I stepped closer, and heard the tail end of Ash's argument.

"You do not get to tell me where I sit," she said in loud voice. Michael drew in a breath of frustration and then spotted my approach.

"Sergeant," he said, elated, "please tell your subordinate to sit in the back."

"Why would I?" I asked. A glance at Ash told me she was royally pissed. Her eyes were wide, and her cheeks were flushed with anger. Michael glared at me in disbelief.

"Well, for one, you don't have any seats in the back," he said. I raised an eyebrow and glanced over Ash's shoulder into the back of the truck.

"There actually is a seat, and if you ask nicely, Suzanne might give it to you," I said calmly, "or else I suggest you sit on the floor—it beats walking."

Ash looked pleased with my reply and crossed

her arms over her chest, glaring at Michael.

Unfazed, the man stepped in closer. He drew in a breath, straightening his shoulders and raising his chest as if he wanted to make himself taller. That seemed to be the intention of men shorter than me and at a solid six feet tall, I got that a lot.

"Listen to me, Sergeant, or whatever it is you pretend to be," he said in a hushed tone. With that he caught my attention and even Ash leaned in to listen.

"If you want to get your ass inside Jackson borders, you better do as I say," he said. "I don't know what your goal is, but considering the gear you've acquired, I'm guessing it's on official business, and frankly, I don't care. But don't think this soldier routine of yours is fooling me one bit, especially not with that kid."

From the corner of my eye, I could see Ash shift and knew she was ready to retort on the kid remark. Before she could, I gave her a hard stare. She caught it and closed her mouth, but from her facial expression, it was clear she disapproved. Without changing my own expression, I turned my gaze back to Michael.

"What do you want?" I asked. His posture relaxed, and he pointed a thumb at Ash.

"I need the front seat and not just out of comfort. You need to get the kid into the back," he said. "Those hick cops might have been fooled, but you won't be able to fool Jackson security—I can get you in."

"What makes you think we need your help to get in?" Ash said. As she spoke, I glanced at the couple in the back. The husband and wife seemed oblivious to our conversation as they kept bickering among themselves.

"There is enough unrest between the official branches to create problems for you two, and soldiers might even take offense in your roleplaying game. I'm with the CDC, and they asked me to come," Michael said with a smirk.

Not sure of what he meant, I considered asking him what his deal was but decided against it. As long as he'd be able to get us closer to the airport in Jackson, I didn't care what he did, and without breaking eye contact with Michael, I said, "Ash, please join the others in the back so Mr. Carver can ride in the front."

I could imagine Ash's scowl, but I kept my eyes on Michael. His smirk remained until he noticed how Ash squirmed past the front seat. He didn't say it, but I could see the questions in his eyes about this kid not using her legs. He must have seen the chair in the back while we drove here, but maybe he hadn't made the connection to Ash. After a moment, he returned his eyes to me. As our gazes reconnected, I narrowed my eyes, ready to hit him with a comeback if he decided on a smart-ass remark.

Fortunately, he kept his mouth shut about Ash

and said, "We should get going."

As he stepped inside the car, I drew in a breath. The warm, dry air did nothing to loosen the tightness in my chest. The CDC man didn't seem interested in us and might be our ticket past a possible quarantine situation in Jackson, but I couldn't help feeling anxious about the whole situation. For lack of a better word, Ash and I were fugitives. Dr. Warren was still out there, and I knew for sure he wasn't happy about losing his favorite subjects. Hanging out with a CDC guy seemed a connection too close for comfort to another certain government agency. But then the thought of going home overruled my fears.

Warren

William lifted a finger in the air and swirled it around. Warren approached the desk filled with radio equipment where his aide had claimed a seat.

A few months ago, he wouldn't have had this much trouble making an international phone call. The communications room at this healthcare and research center in Minnesota looked pitiful to him compared to the recourses provided by the military installation he used to occupy in Florida. Still, he had a feeling things were about to change. If only he could find his favorite subjects, then he could use them to regain his credibility.

A light blinked on the computer screen, and William reached up to hand him a headset. As he placed it on his head, he heard the crackle of static before it changed into a dial tone. William nodded, peering at the screen.

Warren pulled out a chair and sat down. He had never been a man to choke on nerves—it wasn't his style—but he could feel his heartbeat pick up a little traction. He drew in a breath as he heard a click on the line.

"Vissers," the voice on the other end said.

"Mr. Vissers, how delightful to finally be able to speak with you," Warren said in a cheerful voice. William glanced up, raising an eyebrow at Warren. Warren couldn't help a cold, calculated smirk from morphing on his face. "My name is Dr. David Warren, head of the FMDT, and it has come to my attention that you have a predicament concerning your daughter."

9

As predicted, several roadblocks kept us from venturing off the main road. The military had turned the city of Jackson into a fortress. We had to wait in line behind other cars. I didn't recognize the vehicles but guessed some of them must have come from the gas station in Terry. Burned-out cars stood along the side of the road and created a funnel for us to drive through. Anyone who wanted to enter the city needed to pass these funnels—at least that's what Michael said. The cars had been placed there on purpose, so the checkpoints at the end of the funnels had a narrow line of fire, in case someone had brought along an infected individual or something.

I had no idea how the military would be able to contain the rest of the city. A wall of burned-out cars just seemed plain stupid.

"The idea of the funnel is also to slow the vehicles approaching," Michael said, answering the question I hadn't asked. I glanced at him sideways.

"You know, to see if you turn crazy waiting in traffic," he said.

As we waited for the car in front of us to move another few yards, the putrid smell of decay wafted inside the car through the open window. I closed it. Until then, I hadn't seen or maybe didn't want to see the bodies that had been dumped at the side of the road. People worth no more than the carcass of a burned-out car filled the ditches parallel to the road or still sat behind the wheel, black and charred as if a flamethrower had been unleashed upon them. I wouldn't put it past the military—I had seen their methods of cleanup. On I-678, they had also used flamethrowers to rid themselves of the remaining zombies, and they had used some type of firebomb dropped from an airplane to take out the lab in Florida.

"Keep your distance," Michael said as we neared the final checkpoint.

As I took my foot from the gas pedal I glanced into the rearview mirror. In the back, the Shaffers had fallen silent. They had been bickering about everything and nothing for most of the trip to Jackson, but their mouths locked up immediately after we entered the funnel. Dead bodies would do that to you.

On the mattress that served as our bed, I could just see Ash staring out the window with a thousand-mile gaze on her face, while a white cord ran up to the plugs in her ears. Those big blue eyes stuck in that endless haze always twisted my stomach into knots. It reminded me that a kid shouldn't have to go through stuff like this, especially not a kid whose previous life had been just as shitty. But then, *how many kids like her were out there right now?* I couldn't bear thinking about it, but it also strengthened my resolve and my desire to get her out of here.

I shifted in my seat to sit up straighter and put on my sunglasses.

"What do I say?" I asked Michael as we drove up to the soldier waving us down and stopped.

"Just let me do the talking," he said with an underlying tone of sarcasm. I glanced at him sideways, my jaw clenched.

"No offense, but the accent," he said as he shook his head and made a little tsk sound. "Don't get me wrong. It's not bad, but I'm not getting arrested over it."

"Why would they arrest you if I have an accent?" I said and scowled at him.

There was a knock on my window before he could answer. I turned to the man standing outside with an impatient look on his face and pressed the button to lower the window. The air filtering inside felt hot enough to burn my lungs, but luckily the smell of death had subsided.

"Your business," the soldier stated as if he were addressing a rookie. I might not have served or undergone any type of training, and maybe a year ago, I would have felt intimidated, but these days, I couldn't care less of the "I'm-the-authority-here" mentality.

Unflinching, I glared at him. Admittedly, it helped knowing he wouldn't be able to study my eyes because of the sunglasses. The soldier looked as most soldiers I had encountered—full body armor, flashy shades, and a helmet—although this one hadn't shaven in a while.

I noticed two inverted Vs on his shoulder, and although I had no idea what rank that would be, I knew with the three on my shoulder, I outranked the little shit.

The soldier cocked his head at me, probably expecting me to speak, when Michael reached over and extended a card. The soldier took it and instructed us to wait.

In the back the Shaffers had woken from their silent state.

"What's going on?" Dick asked and poked his head between the front seats.

"Just sit back and be quiet," Michael answered. "Once we're cleared here, we will get you sorted with the rest of the refugees heading across the Mississippi."

"Refugees," Suzanne exclaimed, "but we haven't brought anything. We have no clothes, nothing."

"I'm sure you'll be provided with the essentials," Michael said.

Suzanne started to cry, and Dick retreated into the back to console his wife. In the rearview mirror, I could see Ash staring at me. The sunglasses on her nose hid most of her face, but I could tell she worried—the same as me.

The soldier returned with Michael's card and handed it to him.

"Sir, you're wanted at the airport ASAP," he said. "Civilians are not allowed—they'll have to exit the vehicle over there." The soldier pointed at what looked like the parking lot of a dinner.

"Fine by me," Michael replied and waved at the man.

I glanced at the Shaffers for a final time in their colorful tracksuits, sneakers, and flip-flops. Their faces had turned grim as they waved their final good-bye.

Michael seemed to understand Ash and I belonged together. He didn't ask whether she should stay with the Shaffers and didn't mention her to the inspecting soldiers; the fact that the private sitting in the back was probably closer to the age of ten than the eighteen years required to enlist didn't seem to be a problem. He didn't even let them enter the truck, and it made me wonder what type of clearance this guy had. He must be pretty important if he could give orders to the military.

We had no trouble locating the airport, but that probably had something to do with the fact that it was well marked, and similar funnels constructed of cars and busses lead straight to it.

The city as we passed it looked deserted—not in a destroyed or wrecked kind of way, but just deserted as if life had decided to step out. I figured most of the population had left. It's what I would have done if I had found out that crossing the

Mississippi might save my life.

Of course, we came across the occasional checkpoint where soldiers bustled about. Military vehicles in all shapes and sizes appeared everywhere I looked, along with the soldiers who kept a sharp eye on us as we passed.

In a street that looked as though it used to be a fun place to shop, I noticed activity at a Pizza Hut. The place looked packed with men and women dressed in green. On the sidewalk, groups of soldiers stood in easy conversation, and there was an actual waiting line that led inside the restaurant.

The smell of baked dough, meats, and vegetables filled the truck through the open window and made my mouth water. With regards to supplies, Ash and I have had nothing to complain about on our travels, but it mostly came out of cans and cardboard boxes. It had been a while since we had some real food.

A glance at Ash through the rearview mirror told me she had a similar thought. As if she sensed me watching her, she looked up. A smile almost lit up her face. I couldn't read her mind, but I could guess what she was thinking. Our first shared dinner after we had met at the hospital back in Brooklyn had been pizza.

"I wouldn't mind a slice of that," Michael said, eyeing the place with the same longing as me. "Tell you what: after I've concluded my business at the airport, I'm buying."

Ash snorted a laugh from the back, and Michael turned to face her.

"I'm sure it's free for military personnel," she said.

Michael shifted in his seat to face the front before he answered her. "And you aren't part of that military."

An uncomfortable silence fell inside the truck. At another checkpoint, Michael presented his card, and the soldier waved us by. Michael's words echoed in my head as I cornered another street. The silence remained for the entire ride along the MS18 until we took a left turn, and I saw the *Intl Airport Old Brandon Rd* sign.

I had to figure out what Michael's deal was. He knew we weren't military, and it wouldn't be any use to try to convince him otherwise, but he hadn't shown a bit of interest in what we were doing here, and that made me suspicious of him. I wasn't fond of the idea of driving into a highly secured airport, and yet apparently that was exactly what we were doing. It made me feel like an idiot, and I decided to speak up.

"How come you're not more curious about what we're doing here?" I asked. Michael's head snapped sideways as if he were surprised to hear my voice. He recovered quickly and relaxed into his seat.

"Why aren't you more curious about what I'm doing?" he said. "It's not as if I haven't dragged you across town away from your mission."

Our mission, I thought, knowing it wouldn't be wise to tell him he had us going exactly where we wanted to go.

"It's none of our business," I replied.

"Exactly," he said, "the government is all splintered these days. No one knows what anyone's up to. You have the equipment, the IDs—I've checked them myself before all hell broke loose in Terry."

I glanced at him sideways, and he smiled at me. It looked sincere.

"It's all fun and games these days, isn't it," he said.

"I guess," I replied under my breath. Then he shifted in his seat, glancing over his shoulder for a moment and whispered near my ear.

"I am curious about the kid, though," he said so Ash couldn't overhear us. "Is she one of those FMDT projects? You know that new agency led by ... what's his name ... Warren?"

A cold shiver ran down my body at his mention of Dr. David Warren. My jaw locked in place, and I felt grateful I had placed those sunglasses on my nose. A guy like Michael would have spotted my eyes tearing up in an instance.

"What was it that stood for?" he said in low voice as if speaking to himself. "That's right, the Federal Mortem Defense Team." Michael seemed pleased with himself to have come up with the answer on his own. Fortunately, he hadn't dragged me into his guessing game, because I don't think I would have been able to say a word. "I hear things, you know—about research on cancer kids that seem impervious to the virus."

As he shifted back into his seat, I felt his eyes on me, waiting for a reply. Nausea settled in my stomach, and I felt like throwing up. I had tried very hard to forget what had happened to us at that lab in Florida, but somehow Dr. David kept haunting us. I had to clear my throat before I could speak.

"Different project," I said in a low voice. I turned to face him. He had narrowed his eyes and even with the shades, I couldn't hold his gaze.

"It's gone global," I said. Hoping he would think I meant my mission, as he had called it before, was a lot bigger than the FMDT and might explain my accent.

"I see," he said.

A moment later, Michael pointed at a turnoff, and I followed his direction to the airport checkpoint.

10

Michael managed to guide us past security easily. Soldiers nearly bowed at his credentials. We were directed past a couple of low buildings, a parking lot, and those tube things that let you board a plane, until we got to the other side of the main building. There, Michael made me stop the vehicle. Without saying a word, he opened the door and stepped out.

"Hey," I said before he could close the door. Michael stuck his head back inside the opening.

"Are we just supposed to wait here?"

He glanced around across the tarmac and the open fields beyond. The field ended at a fence that surrounded us. Every hundred feet or so a soldier was positioned to keep an eye on the fence, and several jeeps were driving around the tarmac in large circles.

"Right," he said. "Sorry, you won't be able to leave without me, but I'll make it up to you if you drop me off in town later tonight—I'm buying the pizza."

"Later tonight," I said exaggerated, "and why won't we be able to leave without you?"

"I bought you inside, so I'm responsible for you."

"So we're stuck here?" I remarked.

"Pizza," he said again in a bright tone, followed by a smile.

"I don't mind the wait," Ash spoke from the back of the truck. I glanced over my shoulder. Her lower lip stuck out, and she had removed the sunglasses to emphasize her big-eyed puppy dog expression. I shook my head in defeat.

"Excellent," Michael said, reading my expression. "I'll inform the guys guarding that building, so you can use the restrooms." He slammed the door shut and sauntered to the building at our side. For a moment, he spoke with the two soldiers sitting outside the building in garden chairs and pointed in our direction. Then, he entered the building. I still didn't know what to think of this guy.

"This feels like a mistake," I said more to myself than to Ash.

"Why's that?" she asked as she crawled her way into the front seat. "We're exactly where we're supposed to be."

"I don't know," I replied with a mere whisper.

A moment later the phone in my pocked dinged, and I plucked it out. It actually had a solid signal according to the four dots displayed in the top corner of the screen, and Mom had left two voicemail messages since we'd last spoken. They originated from that afternoon. She must have tried right after we'd left and had lost reception.

Another message had come from my dad's cell,

and we listened to that first. In the message, he explained that he had made progress in procuring a plane and that we should wait for his next call.

Listening to my mom's messages brought tears to my eyes. She talked about how glad she had been to hear my voice and how Dad was working on getting me home. Before she got cut off the first time, she riffed about the things that had happened that day, and I wondered if she had filled the other two hundred and forty-nine voicemail messages like that. While I still had refused to play them, I knew I should.

A glance at the clock on the dash told me it was ten minutes past six, and although the sun had started to make its descent, the heat outside made the landing strip shimmer with imaginary pools of water. In the distance stood an airliner, but besides it, the airport seemed deprived of planes. I hoped that wouldn't be a bad sign that this place wasn't even in operation and glanced up at the control tower. Lights gleaming from the tower and the movement at its base fueled that hope.

It could still be a while before Michael returned, and Dad wanted us to wait for his call. I decided today was as good as any and scrolled through the messages. At random I picked one.

Ash greeted the sound of my mom's voice with approval. She had been nagging me to listen to the messages all the way up to Terry. It made me feel a little anxious listening to the messages along with

Ash because I had no idea if I'd be able to contain the emotions it could bring forth, but I wanted to include her, and it would help us pass the time. Every time my mom's voice started over the speaker, her face would twitch up in various ways. Apparently, Dutch is a funny language. I wanted Ash to hear the messages even if she didn't understand them. That way I hoped she wouldn't feel left out and might even get to know my family a bit.

"From what I can tell, the Dutch have made a pact with some of West European countries and closed their borders, including Germany and France," I explained. "An article from a newspaper described how several of those countries had only opened their borders to each other for trade purposes, but travel amongst those countries would be restricted and nearly impossible."

"So it's not that bad over there?" Ash asked. I shrugged and looked at my phone.

"Can't tell. The message is a couple of months old, and there is probable a reason for it to be such a small number of countries." She eyed me with a contemplative expression. I could see those wheels turning behind her eyes.

"But if the borders are closed ..." she said in small voice. She let her remark hang between us.

"I know. I guess that's just another problem we have to face," I said and added in a lighter tone, "once we tackled the other fifty or so problems."

Ash frowned, not appreciating my comment, and I guessed neither did I.

When, hours later, Michael still hadn't shown up, I stepped out for a sanitary stop and to stretch my legs. I breathed in the summer's smell, although the sun going down did little to drop the temperature.

As I stepped out of the tiny building that housed the restrooms, I noticed the two soldiers guarding the entrance had left. I glanced over the empty airstrip. Lights in the distance reminded me of the army jeeps patrolling the fences and the posted guards.

A loud rumble overhead drew my gaze toward blinking lights in the middle of a star-riddled sky. A plane that appeared to be in the middle of its approach awoke the remnants of what used to be a busy airport to life.

Drawn to the noise, I walked to the edge of the building and glanced around the corner. A pair of eighteen-wheelers and a pickup flashing orange lights sped across the field and along an airstrip we hadn't been able to see from inside the Knight.

In the dark, I couldn't make out the approaching plane's colors, but the sheer size of it suggested some type of transport carrier. The plane's wings tilted slightly to level its approach before it touched the ground. Smoke rose up from its massive tires as the pilot hit the brakes. Roaring down the strip, I had to protect my ears as it passed by.

The massive troop carrier—at least, that's what I thought it to be—screeched to a halt while I noticed another plane's approach. This one had a high-pitched engine sound and for the longest time remained a mere blip in the darkened sky. As I watched it circle, it occurred to me this was a much smaller plane than the other one. My heart stopped as the growing hope caused friction in my chest.

As the plane descended toward the airstrip, I stepped around the corner and moved closer but kept myself concealed in the shadows of the building. I stopped behind a stack of crates and rose to my tiptoes to get a better view—only to slip and land on the concrete. Hoping no one had seen me land on my butt, I scrambled to my feet just in time to watch a jet-sized plane speed by. With one look at the colors of the smaller plane, I sprinted for the Knight.

I bolted around the corner and couldn't care less if those soldiers guarding the doors to the restroom had returned and had thought I'd gone insane. Although in the back of my mind, I hoped they wouldn't shoot me or something.

At the Knight, I threw open the door and found a wide-eyed Ash staring at me. In her hands, she held a gun pointed at the floor. She must have seen me come running like a hunted deer.

"What's goin' on?" she asked, her voice close to frantic. I bent over to catch my breath.

"I need the bino——" I started to say in an attempt to ask for the binoculars, but I couldn't get the damn word past my throat. I gestured with both thumb and index fingers in front of my eyes and then threw a thumb over my shoulder.

"I need to see something," I added. Ash reached beneath her chair and took out a pair of binoculars. I sighed in relief. She scooted over to the driver seat where I stood at the door, but didn't release the binoculars.

"I'm coming with you," she said. I raised my eyebrows and then looked over to the building where I had come from. There was still no sign of the guards, and I didn't think it would be that big a deal, but I felt unwilling to get her chair out.

"Ash …" I started to say. She shook her head in defiance.

"Just turnaround and scoot down, you amazon," she said. I always hated that comparison. I could never tell whether she was mocking me. At least she didn't call me a skinny molink anymore—whatever that meant. Just the same, I bent over and let her climb on my back, the binoculars firm in her hand.

"Let's go," she said. I huffed in reply.

I sat Ash down next to the crates I had been standing behind earlier and snatched the binoculars from her hand before she could protest. I scanned the tarmac for a moment, then found what I was looking for, and raised the binoculars.

The small jet plane had taxied to an area separated from the other larger plane. It seemed I had been partly right in assuming the lager plane's purpose. Uniformed men hustled to release the plane of its cargo and were loading up the trucks I had seen before.

At the jet, men in coveralls approached the plane with airplane steps-on-wheels followed by two men in uniform and a man in plain clothes. Even from this distance, I could make out some of their features, and I recognized one of them—Michael. Parked cars lit up the plane and gave me an excellent view of its hull.

The soldiers were expected, and I wasn't interested in them at this point. I thought it kind of weird Michael was with them, but what interested me were the familiar colors on the tip of the plane's tail. A large orange V with underneath in black and bold the letters TEC. I lowered the binoculars at the sight of my family's company logo and let out a sigh of relief. He had done it—Dad had actually done it. A burden lifted from my shoulders. When I got sick for the third time and the doctors had told me my time was limited, I turned my back on my family. I told myself it wasn't for selfish reasons, that I did it for them, but in retrospect, it might as well have been for selfish reasons, although it had never deterred my family. They never stopped trying to make me reconsider, and this plane proved that they still hadn't given up on me.

I let out a long breath while Ash took hold of the binoculars. As she peered out, I watched the men connect the steps to the plane's door. I figured it had to be one of the planes belonging to our US office. How else would Dad have gotten it here so fast when the Dutch borders seemed to be closed? Maybe he had arranged for us to travel further west to sit out the apocalypse until the borders reopened. They were all guesses, but I wouldn't mind if any of them were true.

Two of the soldiers went up the steps and stopped to wait for the door to open. When it did open, they sprang to attention and saluted the person standing at the door. Somehow, my brain registered it as strange but didn't act on it. Maybe Dad had had to cut a deal to carry additional passengers for the plane to be allowed to land. It wasn't until I heard Ash gasp and looked down at her that I realized something was wrong.

The binoculars had dropped onto her lap. She sat with that thousand-mile stare that I hadn't seen so dire since the beginning of the outbreak, while her body shook all over. I kneeled down and wrapped an arm around her shoulders.

"What?" I asked. She started to shake her head and maneuvered backward, dragging her butt over the concrete. Unable to understand, I grabbed the binoculars and stood up to look through them. It didn't take me long to find what had her so spooked.

Instinctively, I dropped into a crouch, although I

knew they wouldn't be able to see or recognize us at this distance. My body had a similar reaction to the magnified view of the people near the plane as Ash. A shudder ran through me, as if the temperature had dropped below freezing.

It was him. The man who stepped out of the plane was him. The man who had followed us since the beginning of the outbreak, the man who had captured us, had tortured us, just stood there disembarking one of my dad's planes—Dr. David Warren; *but how could this be?* Unable to connect the dots, I turned to face Ash. She was still scrambling to get away, and the color of her skin did her name proud. Forcing myself to snap out of it, I scooped her off the floor.

It wasn't hard to understand her fear. Hell, Dr. David scared the shit out of me too. The man was on some sort of personal quest to perfect his Divus serum. Something that would make inoculated soldiers immune to the effects of the Mortem virus with some added bonus effects like fast healing. I might have understood those intentions if he hadn't gone on about it as some twenty-first-century Dr. Frankenstein, using any means necessary to reach his goal, including sacrificing the hundreds of cancer patients he had abducted. That and the fact the FBI were investigating him as the possible reason behind the Mortem outbreak.

Inside the Knight, I locked us in and

electronically tinted the windows. Some of the color had returned to Ash's face, but she still looked stricken. She kept staring at me from the corner of the Knight she'd crawled into—her eyes glassy, her lips in a thin line. I couldn't help feel responsible for handing her that sliver of hope that had now crashed our resolve. I couldn't hold that stare. My eyes kept darting around the Knight's interior as if I might find a rabbit hole to crawl in and disappear.

I wasn't sure what to do. Should we take off with the chance of running into a roadblock or sit here and wait? If for some reason Dr. David was the reason Dad's plane could land at all, then he would know we'd be in the area. But maybe this was all just some sort of stupid coincidence. Although that tiny pestering voice in the back of my head had already convinced me such coincidences didn't exist. Uneasiness started to creep up my limbs. We had to do something. I almost jumped out of my skin at the sound of my phone ringing.

I fumbled for the thing and relaxed a bit when I saw Dad's number in the display.

"Dad, you're on speaker," I said before he could even say hello. I wanted Ash to understand what he had to say.

"We did it, Margje. The plane landed," Dad said with enthusiasm in abundance. Mom squealed something in the background that I couldn't understand.

"I know, Dad. I saw it land." I knew he could

hear the disappointment in my voice—I could never hide my emotions from him and stopped trying long ago.

"You saw it? You're there?" he said in an instance and then hesitated. "What's wrong?"

"There was this man on the flight—" I started to say, but Dad interjected.

"Yes, Dr. David Warren. I had to pull quite a few strings to get him in on this. It's not easy getting someone—"

"Dad," I said interrupting him. I had no idea how to explain to my dad with my mom sitting in the background what had happened to us.

"That man is up to no good," I said.

"What are you talking about? He's the head of the FMDT, the Federal Mortem Defense Team. He's in charge of everything Mortem related, including the US borders."

I slumped back. A glance at Ash told me she looked as ill as I felt.

"Listen, I've talked to him personally, and he promised you safe passage. I'm afraid he won't allow your friend Ash to leave, but he ensured me she would be taken care of." I must have lost the ability to speak because I just sat there staring at Ash.

"Did you hear what I said?" I heard through a haze of static in my head before I glanced at the phone. The time for the conversation jumped to three minutes. That was quite a connection we had there. I sat up straighter.

"Dad, listen to me: this Dr. Warren is no good. He's the one who created this virus and set it loose on the population for Christ sakes. *You can't trust him*," I said emphasizing the last words.

"Margje," he said in a voice that told me I was exaggerating.

"Dad, I'm sorry," I interjected. "You don't understand. You don't know what he did to us, and there is no chance I'm leaving Ash behind. He … hurt us." My voice broke at the memory of lying on that table inside the lab. The remembered sound of Dr. David's chuckles, knowing fully well the pain he would cause made my stomach turn. Knowing he had done the same thing to Ash was too hard to think about. Dad must have sensed my distress because the line stayed silent. After a moment, he cleared his voice.

"Margje," Dad said in a low voice, "I think I've done something stupid."

"What?" I asked. My voice felt so small as I dreaded my dad's next words.

"He knows I'm calling you," Dad said in a weak tone. I swallowed hard and glanced at Ash before I replied.

"What?" was all I could manage.

"Dr. Warren knows I'm on the phone with you now," he repeated. "He can trace this call."

Shock ran through me like high voltage. I glanced out the window as if any second an army of Dr. David's men would come crashing around the corner, which wasn't that preposterous because we happened to be surrounded by an army. The conversation time indicated four minutes and fifty-two seconds.

"Dad, we have to go. I love you … all of you." I didn't wait for him to answer and disconnected the call before I switched the phone off entirely. The phone thumped on the dash as I drew in a breath and glanced at Ash.

"Ash," I said, but she barley looked up. "Ash, snap out of it. Dammit, we've got to go." She gave me a questioning look when I moved to the back of the Knight to rummage through our stuff.

Mars had stocked the vehicle well before he had given it to us. He hadn't even bothered to remove the armament. We had four M4 carbine assault rifles, one even had the M203 grenade launcher, a SIG 50, a Remington R12 tactical shotgun, and five SIG-Sauer P228s along with a couple of cases of ammunition. It had taken a while to learn their names and read all the manuals.

"Do you have a plan?" Ash asked tentatively. I yanked an M4 assault rifle from the gun rack and then turned to face her.

"Not exactly."

| 11

I was about to climb into the front seat when I noticed the proximity alert blinking red on the console. The windows to the Knight were set for tinted so any intruder wouldn't be able to peek inside the vehicle, but that also meant we wouldn't be able to see out except for what we saw on the monitors.

Before I slid into my seat, I turned to Ash and placed a finger on my lips. She got the gesture and nodded. She checked the monitors on the dash while I readied the M4. On the screen, we could see two soldiers maneuver around the Knight.

"Now what?" Ash asked in a whisper, which could have been my question. I peered at the screen. The two men looked to be in casual conversation and didn't seem put off by the massive vehicle. Although I hadn't seen the men before, it might be they had received the same message from Michael as the two guards in the garden chairs.

Several different scenarios ran through my head —driving off, hiding in the truck in the hope that they would leave, talking to them. In my head they all ended with us being dead or in a research lab. I glanced at the M4. Shooting would draw attention. As quietly as possible, I climbed into the back and reached into a box next to the gun rack. Ash's eyes widened as she watched me screw a silencer on to the rifle.

"You can't just shoot them," she said in a whisper. My gut clenched, and I felt unwilling to face her. Killing two soldiers who might not even be looking for us felt wrong, but what was I supposed to do?

"They already know we're here," Ash said in a whispered high-pitched voice. "We have to get out." Fear accompanied her words, but she was right. If Dr. David had traced the call, he would know where we were, and maybe these two soldiers might not have been made aware of it, but others would follow soon. I glanced at the rifle—we didn't have time for the diligent approach. I let out a breath and nodded. Then placed the silencer back into the box and climbed into the driver seat—leaving the M4 in the back.

A knock on the window startled me, although I had seen the soldier's approach on the monitor. His words sounded muffled when he called out to ask whether anyone was inside. I glanced at Ash and saw relief that I wouldn't do something entirely stupid, although my next action would probably be categorized into the same file.

"You ready?" I said and reached for the ignition key.

"No," Ash said, "but do it anyway." For some reason, my lips quirked into a faint smile, and I glanced at her. The relief had vanished from her face and worry had replaced it. I nodded and flipped the key.

The engine sprang to life, and on the monitor, I could see the two soldiers jump in surprise. They raised their weapons but didn't fire. I guessed they knew this type of vehicle and figured their rifles would not be a match for the Knight's armor. I hit the button so the windows would return to normal and we could see through them again. One of them shouted something and waved a hand along his throat as a sign for me to cut the engine, but as I pressed the accelerator and the Knight set in motion, they merely stepped aside. The other soldier lifted a device to his mouth, and I guessed he'd be calling us in. It didn't matter if Dr. David had figured out where we were.

Leaving the lights off, I eased the Knight forward. As we turned around the corner, the plane came into view. Dr. David and Michael hadn't left the plane's side and seemed to be in deep conversation. One of the soldiers held what looked like a phone to his ear and gestured something at Dr. David. Even from this distance, it wasn't hard to tell something had ticked him off. Dr. David waved his arms in a questioning manner before he tapped a finger to his head. Michael merely shrugged and then pointed in our direction. He froze in place when he noticed the Knight.

Dr. David poked the soldier holding the phone in the shoulder and started pointing animatedly in our direction. I took this as our cue to leave and stepped on the gas, pointing the Knight in the direction of the fence.

Vehicles sped across the runway to intercept us. Three jeeps headed our way, and there wasn't any doubt in my head what their intentions were. As I scanned the fence, I couldn't immediately see an opening or gate. I turned left, pressed my foot down on the pedal, and the Knight picked up speed. "Put your seat belt on," I said.

"Way ahead of you," Ash said with a nervous smirk on her face.

Before any of the jeeps managed to reach us, we came up on the fence. I knew the fence would be no match for the Knight—we had done this before—and I didn't even flinch as we cut through the metal mash like a knife through butter.

The engine roared as we hit the road surrounding the airport and, within seconds, became engulfed by darkness. Either there weren't any lights, or they didn't work, but the road became too dark to see. At this speed, I had no choice but to turn on the headlights. In the rearview mirror, I couldn't see the jeeps in our pursuit. I knew turning on the lights would lead them straight to us, but I guessed crashing wouldn't be a good option either.

Ash remained silent at my side as we tore across the asphalt. At this point, north seemed as good a direction as any. Zombies were coming in from the east, and west was where we needed to go, but that was also where soldiers would be. The new border made up by the Mississippi would be west, and I didn't think the military would leave it unguarded. We couldn't use the phone, although I had no idea if turning it off would be enough. I should probably throw it out the window, but I just couldn't do it. There were too many memories on there—photos of my family, my friend Emily, Ash, and all those voicemail messages my mom had left me. Besides, I couldn't remember where I had left the thing and stopping wasn't an option. Speeding down the road, I vowed to myself I would listen to all of mom's messages if we got out of this.

"Do you see them?" I asked, peering through the rearview mirror. Ash craned her neck to look out the back. She shook her head.

"Nothing yet."

Around us, the airport ground made way for trees, and the buildings had long since disappeared from view behind a wall of green. Ahead the road seemed to split into a left or right option. Without checking for traffic, I made a hard left turn. Ash slammed into her door even with the seatbelt snug around her body. This vehicle wasn't made for a person the size of Ash. Her frail body almost disappeared in the enormous seats. She grunted some curse words and grabbed the oh-shit handle over the door.

"Where are we goin'?" she asked.

"No idea," was the only thing I could say. Focused on the road I saw some lights coming from a building as it rose beyond the trees. We were entering the outskirts of town. It wouldn't be long before we'd encounter the first soldiers. I didn't know how far the extent of Dr. David's power went. I had learned he led the Federal Mortem Defense Team.

The name was clearly new and so would be the agency or team backing it. I wasn't entirely sure how these kinds of operations worked inside the US, or anywhere else for that matter, but I knew some agencies exceeded authority over the military in crisis situations. Given the agency's name, I presumed this would be one of these cases. Dr. David would only need to claim we were escaped infection carriers, which basically we were. Not a general or other figure of authority within the military would deny him the opportunity to catch us. Anyhow, I expected the soldiers we encountered would have instructions to take us in.

The familiar sound of a jet-like engine and rotors cutting through the air reached me over the noise of the Knight's engine. A glance at Ash told me she heard it too. She slid into the back without a word and started peering out the window.

"Do you see it?" I asked.

"Hang on."

She maneuvered further down to the back window and popped up in my rearview mirror. "It's a big one comin' up behind us," she yelled.

"Crap, crap, crap," I muttered to myself. For once I would just have liked to catch a break. I hit the gas pedal harder and gripped the steering wheel so tightly that my knuckles turned white. I was pretty sure this road would lead straight to the river, and we would have to find a way to cross it. As we sped along, the eerie feeling that soldiers would be waiting for us crept up on me.

First I heard Ash yelp, and then there was a thud as I hit the brakes.

"What the hell," she bit out.

"Look," I replied. She crawled to the front of the Knight and pushed herself up on the back of my driver seat.

"Oh, shit," was all she managed to say.

As I had thought, the road had led to the river and a bridge crossing, but as I had feared, it turned out to be a dead end. There was an extensive roadblock on the bridge, and, because of the river, there wasn't a way around it. Engulfed by massive floodlights, the entire bridge seemed green with uniforms. Trucks, jeeps, and even a tank blocked our way.

I turned to Ash, who had gone bone-white while staring at the uniformed men. The soldiers at the roadblock in front of us didn't seem to have an interest in coming up to us. Either they didn't know about us, or they didn't care. For all I knew a bunch of them were boxing us in from behind, and then there was that helicopter.

Ash slid into the seat next to me and buckled in.

"The chopper hovers behind us at some distant," she said, "as if it's waiting for us." I took in a deep breath. The pounding of my heart felt relentless inside my chest. The bridge wasn't an option; being captured by Dr. David's men wasn't an option. I didn't know the area, so taking a side street didn't seem like a good idea. My hand slid to the gear shifter while my gaze fell on Ash.

"What do you think?" I asked. She lifted her shoulders in a shrug, trying to channel that indifferent teenager she pretended to be most of the time, but I could read the fear in her eyes. She turned her head so she could glance out the rear window in search of that helicopter. My eyes returned to the bridge where someone who must have been in charge started to wave his arms. It didn't take long for their vehicles to be set in motion. Through the rearview mirror, several dots of light in the dark grew in size as they approached. Without waiting for an actual reply from Ash, I set the Knight in reverse and floored it.

12

I watched the monitor, so I didn't even need to look out the back to drive the Knight in reverse. Ash gripped her seatbelt for added support.

"Is it even possible to make a U-turn with this thing?" she said. Her voice came out high pitched, which didn't add to my confidence. I decided not to reply until I could answer her question. In front of me two jeeps closed in fast, and if we wanted any chance at all to evade them and the vehicles approaching from behind, I needed to turn the Knight around. Grass and bushes passed us in reverse as the Knight plowed on. None of the plants would have caused a problem for the enormous vehicle, but I couldn't tell whether a ditch might hide in the brush cover.

The jeeps where nearly on top of us, while a truck full of soldiers followed them. A man dressed in green with a helmet on his head hung out of the window of one of the jeeps and waved at us to slow down. It occurred to me what we were driving. I wasn't used to driving armor-plated vehicles like the Knight, and sometimes I needed a reminder of what this baby could withstand. Shooting at us wouldn't do them any good. The bullets would bounce right off. I wasn't even sure if that tank could make a dent in the Knight's armor, but I wasn't willing to find out.

When I noticed a parking lot coming up on our left, I didn't hesitate. Without slowing down, I pulled the wheel and steered us in backward. Dust clouded around us as the wheels tackled the gravel littered on the ground. It wasn't a perfect U-turn— in fact, it didn't even come close as the vehicle came to a full stop.

Unfortunately, one of the jeeps crossed our path and tried to block our exit. It was the jeep with the man hanging out the window. He opened the door as the jeep came to a stop. I didn't wait to find out what he wanted, but shifted gears and floored it. I headed straight for the jeep. The man pulled his leg inside with a pale complexion on his face right before the Knight slammed its bumper into the side of the jeep.

The smaller vehicle wasn't a match as the Knight grazed its side. Ash gave another yelp when the Knight shuddered from the impact. I gripped the steering wheel even harder and then pulled it to the right. As I hit the road, the lights of the approaching vehicles nearly blinded me. It seemed that their drivers were as impressed with the Knight's size as I was because they instantly dispersed to the sides of the road. Increasing speed, we headed down the road back the way we'd come.

Dumbfounded, I glanced at the rearview mirror to check if that had actually happened the way I thought it had. Red brake lights blinked in the night, followed by the white ones that indicated reverse. I blew out a breath, relieved we had made it this far, but my shoulders couldn't relax—we still had a helicopter on our tail.

"Where's that chopper?" I called out to Ash. She immediately went to find it as her gaze shifted through the different windows.

"Never mind," I said as I spotted the thing hovering ahead, lights blinking in the dark. It was quite a distance out, and Ash hadn't exaggerated when she said it looked as if it were waiting for us.

By this time, the Knight had reached about eighty miles an hour, and we were closing in on it fast. Behind us, some of the jeeps appeared in the rearview mirror, but they seemed to keep their distance. They kept in line with us but didn't seem to be in a hurry to catch us. It could be they figured the helicopter would keep a visual on us anyway. They could easily follow us until we ran out of gas.

Ash glanced behind us, and it seemed she'd come to the same conclusion.

"Now what?" she said. I ran a hand through my hair. I had no idea what to do. In front of us, the helicopter tipped its nose. For a second I feared heavy machine-gun fire might rain down on us, or even a rocket, but when I looked closer, the machine looked more like a transport helicopter than the assault kind.

The helicopter tilted to its side as a door slid open. Ash pointed a finger at it, and I peered into the darkness. A soft green light highlighted the inside of the cabin.

"What are they doin'?" she asked.

"I don't know," was all I could reply. A person dressed in an Air Force flight suit—helmet and all—stood in the opening and waved at us. *What were they doing indeed?*

I glanced at Ash, but she had a similar confused expression as I must have had. The person in the opening kept waving and pointing at the car. I just kept pushing the car along the road. There wasn't any way of evading the chopper, and I didn't know what to do. The person waved again, and this time held a hand signaling a phone to his or her helmet.

"Eh, what is he doin'," Ash asked. I glanced in the rearview mirror and saw the vehicles that had been following us had backed off. Was the person signaling to them? But if he or she were why wouldn't they just communicate via radio or something? My eyes fell on the dash where a red light blinked on the middle console, and I flicked the switch underneath it. There weren't trying to communicate with our pursuers—they were trying to talk to us.

"Ash," I said, "I think they want us to talk to them." She looked at me curiously and then at the console.

"You want me to pick it up," she asked. I checked our mirrors and then focused on the road ahead. It looked clear, but it didn't seem smart to distract myself by talking on the phone with the same people who wanted to capture us. I nodded to Ash.

"Be careful of what you say," I said.

She grunted a nervous laugh. "Wouldn't want to give away our position." She grabbed the mic and pushed the button.

"Hello."

"Jeez, not-a-kid," an exaggerated voice exclaimed, "took you long enough." It took me a second to place the distorted voice over the microphone, but Ash didn't even hesitate.

"Angie!" she exclaimed in reply. I looked up at the helicopter and, in the soft green light that came from inside the cabin, saw the person in the open door waving at us. At the realization it might be friendlies in that chopper, my heart lifted slightly, still perfectly aware of the small army of military vehicles following us.

"Listen," Angie said without giving Ash any chance to interrupt. "We have come up with yet another plan to get your asses out of this mess you've gotten yourself into."

"Hey," Ash retorted, but I held up a hand to make her shut up. She gave me a disgruntled look but held her mouth. A muffled chuckle reached us over the mic before Angie came back on.

"Follow us. We'll guide you into zombie-land," she said. "And when the soldiers back off, we'll pick you up."

"Follow you where?" Ash said and then grunted as I grabbed the mic from her hand.

"Please explain that, and who's 'we'," I said in a firm tone.

"Magsss," Angie said, drawling out my name, "I have a very lonely FBI agent with me who is dying for some company." As she said it, a head poked out the door and waved. Because of the helmet, I couldn't tell whether it was actually him, but I felt a blush creep up my neck anyway.

Angie continued to explain that zombies had overrun a town not far from here. The zombies might keep the military from following and would give the helicopter a chance to pick us up. The mic stayed silent after that, which made me feel disappointed. This seemed stupid because jeeps were chasing us, along with a truck filled with soldiers who were looking to capture us, not to mention we were about to drive into an infected town overrun with zombies.

I glanced at Ash and could tell fear battled with relief inside her.

For some reason, the thought crept in my mind that stepping on to that helicopter would mean leaving the Knight behind. Again stupid, but this vehicle had been our home for the past several months.

Still, we had to get organized before we hit the town and that could mean a distraction for Ash.

"Why don't you get back there and pack the stuff that we need?" I said. She gave me a wary look before she managed a reply.

"You think this'll work?"

I glanced in the rearview mirror. It had better work because I wouldn't give myself up to Dr. David. I'd rather have a zombie eat me, I think.

"It'll work," I said determined. Ash managed a half smile and then made her way into the back. I heard her shuffle around as I followed the chopper onto a side road.

13

It wasn't long until the town came into view. We knew the zombies followed their meals, tracking long distances across the country in pursuit of the uninfected. We had passed them, and they had overtaken us several times these past few months, but it hadn't made me ready for what I was about to see.

Like most, this town had prepared for the zombies' arrival. They thought they could ride it out. They had seen the news stories and the footage of New York or other areas but never thought it would get that bad in their neighborhood. They were always wrong.

The main road into town sat clogged with the moaning infected. They shambled across the road in their own private parade. You could see people watching from their boarded-up houses as zombies clawed at their front doors. Some houses stood better against the infected onslaught than others. However, deadbolts and a few boarded-up windows weren't enough to keep the enormous number of zombies out of the family homes and shops. Glass shattered, cars crashed, and people screamed. You could see the uninfected running frantically to get to safety, but there wouldn't be any to find. An old man tried to fend off a couple of zombies with a cane. A woman ran across the street, carrying a baby in her arms.

I rammed the pair of zombies following her. The Knight shook with the effort, but I knew it wouldn't do her any good. Ash yelped from the back, and I saw her intention to get to the front.

"Don't come out here," I said in an urgent tone. "Just get our stuff ready, okay."

She looked at me and then at the side windows. On the floor of the truck, her view was limited. She glanced back at me through the rearview mirror.

"Okay?" I repeated at a softer tone this time. She nodded and whispered a barely audible okay.

The chopper guided us deeper into the center of town. Behind us, I couldn't see the military vehicles anymore. The plan seemed to work. I started to get my hopes up but hadn't forgotten how much of a killer hope could be.

I maneuvered the Knight down a one-way street that, instead of cars, sat infested with the infected. These zombies had been wandering around for a while, and their bodies hadn't held well against the forces of nature. Mere flesh over bone shambled across the road, but the Knight had no trouble plowing a hole through the mass of bodies. The ones we passed barely reacted. Usually, they threw themselves at anything that moved, but these zombies seemed to be to worn out, or their brains had turned even further into mush.

The chopper hovered ahead of us when I

turned into what seemed like a marketplace. The open area sat surrounded with what used to be groceries, flower shops, and what not. In the middle of the square stood an old fountain that appeared to have seen better days. A zombie had fallen into it, and its arms and legs splashed in the water.

The mic crackled and I picked it up. Angie's voice came back on.

"This is it," she said. "We need to hurry."

After I stopped the Knight underneath the helicopter, I turned to check on Ash's progress when I heard shots being fired in the near distance. The rapid report of automatic gunfire pierced the night sky.

"Ash, you ready?" I asked as I maneuvered between the front seats. She gave me a sad look when I faced her.

"What?" I asked.

"We'll have to leave everything we have," she said as her eyes examined the stuff we had accumulated over the past months, including her trusted wheelchair.

"It's just stuff," I said but felt a similar regret. Her hand brushed the frame of her chair. That chair I had brought back from a scavenger run in Bergen Beach, which had almost cost me my life all that time ago. Even so, I had a hard time saying good-bye to that thing; it had brought Ash as well as me a sense of freedom along with hope.

I grabbed my old backpack. It had been with

me even longer, and I felt glad that I could at least bring that.

"Come on. Let's get the hell out of here," I said as a metallic voice screeched outside.

"Ash, Mags, get a move on," Angie's voice boomed over a loudspeaker. Combined with the automatic gunfire, I didn't need any more incentive to move. I swung my old backpack over my shoulders and ushered Ash to the front of the Knight.

Hunkered down in the driver seat, I grabbed the mic, telling Angie we were on our way, and slammed my fist on the button to lower the window.

The closeness of the zombies milling at my window spooked me for a moment, until I realized they wouldn't have to be a threat. Our genetic makeup would allow us to step outside without being attacked, as long as we didn't arouse them too much. Still, there were a lot of them crammed against the car.

On her side, Ash had lowered her window and pulled her nose up at the smell of decay wafting in through the opening.

"We'll never be able to get the door open," she said in a concerned voice.

Another report of gunfire startled us both. The zombies, enticed by the noise, started to move in the direction of the sounds. They came from all directions and had to pass the Knight to get to the soldiers firing their weapons. Body after body slid by our windows. One or two poked their heads up, sniffed the air, and moved on.

"Let's go," Angie's mechanical voice boomed over our heads. "We'll have company any minute."

Ash shrugged and pointed a finger at the ceiling.

"Wanna try the roof," she said as if it didn't make any difference to her. I couldn't contain a smile at that.

"I'll go first," I said and eased the backpack off my shoulders again. I pushed it through the window, careful not to disturb the zombies clambering by. Without too much trouble, I placed it overhead onto the roof and started to lift my body after it. The hefty wind coming from the rotors nearly took me off balance, but I managed to climb out. Zombies brushed my leg as I lifted myself onto the roof. I waved a quick hand at Angie before I made my way to the other side of the car.

Standing on the roof, the zombie parade seemed even more massive than from the inside. The entire square had filled with shuffling bodies. Zombies in all shapes and sizes roamed the marketplace. I could tell they weren't from around here by the state of their rotten flesh. A few new ones roamed the crowd, but most seemed to have been infected for a while and had traveled quite a distance. Even their clothes hadn't fared well.

Ash had managed to lift her butt onto the open windowsill, and although she had gained strength in her arms, I could tell she had trouble lifting her weight onto the roof. I grabbed her arm and guided it around my neck. She gave me a halfhearted smile. I knew she appreciated the help but didn't appreciate the fact she needed it. She was still a stubborn kid, although I would never call her that.

Gunfire drew my attention to the street we had come from. A truck moved in slow motion through the crowd of zombies. Soldiers on the roof of the truck fired their weapons at the infected trying to claw their way up the truck. A few of them had clambered onto the hood, but bullets forced their bodies off balance before they disappeared into a wave of zombies. Angie was right; we didn't have much time. The soldiers would soon reach the Knight, and if they didn't, they might change their minds about capturing us alive. It could mean they'd start shooting at us or even at the chopper.

I lifted Ash up onto the roof and helped her shoulder her backpack. Not long after, the chopper maneuvered over us and lowered, before a rope landed with a thud on the roof of the Knight. I looked up and saw Angie's gesture to climb. The sight of the rope made my throat tighten. Climbing had never been one of my virtues. I was never one to carry my own weight, let alone with a paralyzed kid hanging off my back.

Shots were fired, and I ducked in a reflex. I could feel the air displacement made by the bullets. Over my shoulder, I saw my assumption had turned to reality. Some of the soldiers had aimed their weapons at us. They finally figured out the chopper wasn't on their side.

I slid my backpack over my chest and turned my back to Ash so she could wrap her arms around my neck.

"Don't you dare let go," I shouted over the noise of the engine roaring over my head. Ash didn't answer, but I felt her arms tighten her grip.

I took hold of the rope and managed to lift myself up, tangling my legs so the rope gave me some leverage to distribute my weight, but it didn't take long for my arms to start burning.

Again, shots were fired, but this time I couldn't hide. We hung on that rope like a sack of potatoes ready to be used as target practice. Dangling back and forth, I climbed a few more feet and looked up to see what I presumed to be Angie keeping an eye on us while Mars returned fire.

Angie lifted the mic to her mouth and said, "We're moving. Just hang on."

And that's what I did—I stopped climbing and hung on.

The chopper lifted us high above the town where it turned and started to move away. I glanced down to see the Knight engulfed by the mass of zombies, its headlights still on. My heart ached a little to know the machine that had kept us safe sat there discarded like a piece of junk.

Ash clung to me as if her life depended on it. I

wished I could have held on to her, but I had enough trouble maintaining my grip. She had to do it on her own.

"You okay," I shouted over the sound of the rotors.

"Ask me when we land," she shouted back. As she said it, I felt a tug on the rope. I looked up and saw a winch pull us up.

"I don't think we'll be landing soon," I said as the countryside flashed by me in a haze of dark shapes.

I strained my muscles, putting everything into holding on to that rope. The rush of unidentifiable images passing in front of my eyes started to make me sick to my stomach, and I closed my eyes. Fortunately, it didn't take long for the winch to pull us up. Close to the ledge, I felt strong arms lift and drag us inside the cabin.

Part Two

Cheyenne

14

The door of the chopper slammed shut as I lay panting inside the cabin, waiting for the feeling to return to my arms and legs. The effort of hanging on to the rope had drained my energy, and I felt numb. Ash still clung on to my back and hadn't moved, while my backpack uncomfortably pressed against my chest. When I managed to lift my head, I saw three sets of helmets ogle me through tinted visors. With my thumb, I motioned to Ash.

"Can someone ... release ... my load," I asked in a raspy voice. It didn't take the helmets long to start moving. I couldn't tell who was who, but someone lifted Ash from my back and sat her in a seat. Strong arms helped me off the ground and guided me to one of the other seats. I wasn't surprise when the visor lifted, and a set of jade green eyes peered into mine. His beautiful smile set off a row of white teeth against his dark skin. I had almost forgotten what a great smile Mars had.

"Hi," he said in a casual tone, "long time no see." My emotions running wild were ready for my mouth to break out into wide grin and throw my arms around him, but my Dutch "just-act-normal, that's-crazy-enough" habit kicked in. That gave my mind a mental kick, and I settled for a nervous, but tentative smile. It didn't stop Mars's smile from growing brighter as he leaned in, placing his lips on mine. It turned out Angie's statement on the mic had not been overstated.

In the back of my mind, it was exactly what I had hoped for, but his sudden gesture of affection shocked me, and I froze. As he pulled back, I could feel the heat rise up my neck and settle in my cheeks.

"Hi," I said and sensed the tiny quiver in my voice. For a moment, he watched me thoughtfully through narrowed eyes and then grinned.

"Hi," he replied as he buckled my seatbelt without taking his eyes off mine.

This pitiful exchange of words made my heart pound, and I felt sure my face was the color of a tomato. I tried to find something other than his smile to focus on as he took a seat across from me.

Angie had Ash strapped in after they'd hugged and settled into a seat. The third person still had his visor on as he spoke into a mic.

"All settled, get us home."

I reached out to Ash who sat next to me, to check if she were okay, and she gave me her usual shrug. Then I turned to our rescuers.

"Thanks for getting us out," I shouted and added, "again." Angie waved me off as if it were all part of the job, and maybe for them it was. "What's going on, and where are you taking us?" I asked.

The rotor noise inside the chopper was pretty loud, and Mars handed Ash and me a couple of headsets. I repeated my question after I put them on, and Mars answered.

"We're heading for Cheyenne Mountain complex," he said. "I'll explain once we're on the ground." He pointed a finger into the air and waved it around. The headset made it easier to talk than without it, but Mars was right: the static in my ears and the noise level was enough to make a conversation hard to follow. Still, I found it hard to just sit there and watch. Besides, the nerves that ran through my body made it impossible to keep my mouth shut.

"How've you been?" I asked. Three heads perked up to look at me. Mars, Angie, and Ash all gazed at me, and even the guy with the visor still down shifted his head.

"Open coms," Mars said with a smirk. "You have to mention a name if you want to talk to someone specific." With that, I felt the heat in my cheeks resurface and smiled nervously.

"It won't be long before we get there," Mars added.

I stared out the window, trying to make out some of the landscape. The darkness outside made this almost impossible. By the helicopter lights reflecting back to me, I could tell we passed over a body of water, but most of the time I stared at my own reflection in the window.

A surreal feeling washed over me. This morning I was more than excited about going home, exited to see my family again, eager to introduce Ash, and now we were on the run again. It made this reunion with Mars feel somewhat like a disappointment, and although I didn't want it to be, I couldn't help feeling this way. Staring at my own reflection in the window didn't help much either.

My hair had grown a couple of inches but looked like a dark-blond mess. The gaunter features of my face had disappeared since we'd last met, but it was hard to see anything Mars would like. He had kissed me twice now, and although that should make me feel better about myself, why did it feel like such a hard sell?

I leaned back in my seat and let the thoughts settle in my head. I had a feeling things were about to get hectic, and I needed a clear head. It wasn't long after I closed my eyes that the monotone sound of the rotors helped me doze off.

The descent of the helicopter woke me up. Outside, darkness still ruled, and I could see nothing of the mountain complex Mars had mentioned. I knew of it and had seen it plenty of times on TV shows. The mountain that I knew held a vast network of tunnels and whatnot to accommodate, among other things, NORAD. I couldn't remember what the letters meant, but I knew they monitored the skies in and around the United States. Built some fifty years ago, it could withstand the threat of nuclear devastation.

The chopper landed on what looked like an airstrip. The lights lining the tarmac and illuminating a couple of buildings reminded me of the airport in Jackson we had escaped from. The thought of Dr. David and what he would be up to made me shiver, and I pushed him from my mind.

After Mars helped me get out, I waited at the door of the chopper for Ash. She took her time sitting in the open door, gazing up at the sky.

"Come on already," I said impatiently, but had to smile at the big blue eyes taking in the beauty of the vast range of stars. It was probably because Ash was raised in the city and hadn't been out much in open areas deprived of city lights that she was so fascinated by the sight. It seemed she could never get enough of a starlit sky.

"Chill out, will ya," she said with a sneer. "I'm comin'." She wrapped her arms around my neck, and I lifted her out of the chopper. I drew in a deep breath of fresh air and looked around the airstrip. In the distance I could see lights coming from several guard posts and a fence surrounding the property.

Mars and Angie stood waiting for us at a blue transfer bus with dark-tinted windows, along with the man who had spoken with the pilot earlier. They had all taken off their helmets. The third man was middle-aged, and he stood with that military posture that for all I knew could have been another FBI agent. With all the cloak-and-dagger shit I had witnessed the past year, I wasn't happy to trust my first instincts on meeting people anymore.

Angie had her dark hair braided from the top of her head down to her shoulders, molded into what I assumed to be her signature-style Mohawk. She looked short standing next to Mars. His height made him seem lanky, but from my own limited experience I had gathered he was anything but lanky. The thought of Mars's strong arms wrapped around me after he had saved us in Florida made me grin.

The rotors of the helicopter started to spin again as I walked to the bus. They increased speed with every one of my steps until the machine lifted into the air and took off.

Mars seemed in an animated conversation with the middle-aged man who now looked angry. Only when the sound of the chopper had decreased, I picked up on what they were saying.

"You shouldn't have let them on board," the man said in a venomous tone. "If they had been infected, they could have brought the chopper down."

"But they aren't infected," Mars said.

It didn't take a genius to understand they were talking about us. The man's words made sense; it would have been irresponsible to lift us onto the chopper if it weren't for the fact Ash and I couldn't turn, but it seemed as if the man didn't know that.

"I think we have a fan," Ash whispered near my

ear. I nodded and shifted her higher up my back as I stepped closer.

"Mags, Ash," Angie started to say, "this is Sergeant Francis Tyler of the United States Air Force—he is stationed here at Cheyenne Mountain complex."

My assumption he was military turned out to be correct, and I felt glad that I hadn't lost my entire sense of intuition. Sergeant Tyler stuck out his hand to shake, and I managed to take it without letting go of Ash's leg.

"Pleased to meet you," Sergeant Tyler said while he switched hands to Ash. "Before we can enter the base, I need you to know a couple of things."

"Go inside where?" Ash asked before the man could say anything else. She shifted, and I knew she was looking around for a building large enough to be called a base. Tyler glared at us and then turned to Mars.

"You said they had been briefed," he said. Mars cleared his throat and placed an arm around the man's shoulder to pull him aside.

"Hey," Ash exclaimed as Angie poked her in the side, "don't do that."

"Shut up, kid, and listen," Angie said.

"I'm not a ki—" Ash broke off her sentence at the look Angie gave her. It amazed me that Angie could do that and made a mental note to ask her how that worked.

"They think you're working with us to get

Warren," Angie said in a hushed tone. "For now, just keep your mouth shut—both of you—and we'll explain later."

"Who's 'they'—" I started to say but shut my mouth as her eyes caught mine. She really had to tell me how to do that.

A moment later Mars returned with Tyler, and it seemed as if he'd been able to reassure the man.

"Right," Tyler said as if nothing had happened. "Rule number one, listen and do everything you are told. Rule number two, don't wander off—stick with the group. Everything else will be explained as we go."

Hesitant to answer, I glanced at Angie while Tyler looked at us expectantly.

"Affirmative, sir," Ash said, throwing a hand to her head in a salute. Tyler grunted something and turned to enter the bus.

I chanced a glance at Mars. He shrugged and smiled with that calmness that seemed to cling to him. Angie motioned us to follow her into the bus, and we did.

After I dropped Ash into a seat next to Angie, I found a seat at the back of the bus. I should probably have been more joyous for making it out of Jackson, but the disappointment of not being able to go home hurt. Before all this zombie crap happened, I wasn't too eager to go home. It would have meant I'd be dead by now, and back then I couldn't face the fact of my family watching me wither away.

A zombie sinking its teeth in me had changed all that. The virus it carried had some strange reaction on the cancer that had been eating me alive. Getting infected along with meeting Ash were probably the best things that had ever happened to me, and I wanted to share them with my family, people I loved and loved me back. That wasn't going to happen now, but even so, I felt jitters reeling inside my belly as I noticed Mars talking to the driver.

I slumped in my seat and closed my eyes as the engine of the bus rumbled to life. It wasn't long until we stopped, and I heard Mars's voice talk to what I presumed to be a guard at a guard post. I didn't bother to open my eyes. Ash's excited voice filtered in next, alternating with Angie's. They were exchanging stories about what had happened after we'd all escaped from Dr. David's lab in Florida before it had exploded and we'd parted ways.

Despite the sleep I caught on the chopper, I still felt exhausted. My head pounded, and I wasn't in the mood to enter the banter, so I shut them out.

I jerked up as I sensed someone at my side—my heart hammered in my throat, and I reflexively flung out my arm. It hit something other than the back of a seat.

"Easy," a familiar, calming voice said. In the dark, I found Mars sitting next to me. His presence didn't settle the pounding of my heart, but I felt my body relax some and shafted in my seat to face him.

"Sorry, didn't mean to startle you," he said.

"I'm not ... you didn't ..." I said. I fumbled the words and apparently, that amused him.

He chuckled as he replied, "So you punch everyone in the face after waking up."

I blinked and felt a blush creep up my face.

"Sorry," I said, and I folded my hands on my lap. He lifted his hand to my face, and I managed not to pull away when he traced the burn-like scar that ran from my left temple down to my jaw. It was actually more of a faint line, and I didn't think he'd be able to see in the dim lights of the bus, so he must have remembered. For me the memories of crashing that truck on I-678 were still very vivid.

"I had kind of hoped you'd be happier to see me," he said. His bluntness surprised, me and although bluntness was something the Dutch seemed notorious for, it caught me off guard.

"I am," I said in a nervous reply. Then I let out a breath of air, "I just hoped ..."

"You wanted to go home."

I raise my eyebrows at him. *How had he known about that?* But then, *how had he known where to find us?*

"We knew about your dad's plane," he said. "It'll be explained later. I just ..." Mars huffed out a breath. The gesture made me smile. This was a side of him I hadn't seen before.

"And you were such a smooth talker when we met," I said playfully.

"That was just the redirecting of nerves in the face of certain death by zombie," he said and grinned. "In normal life I'm just like the average male and have no idea what to say."

"Well, that makes two of us then ..." I said and paused to figure out if I had just said I resembled the average male. "I mean, know what to say ... I mean not know." I huffed in frustration, and as I fumbled, the words made me feel like the tourist I probably still was.

Mars offered me his hand along with that disarming smile. His hand felt so warm in contrast to mine. My heart hammered at a frantic pace as I gathered the courage to face him. As I looked up, I found a twinkle in his eyes that would have turned my legs to jelly if I hadn't been sitting already.

"I don't know why I'm so nervous," I said.

"Well, you should be," he said in a serious-sounding voice. I narrowed my eyes at him, curious to see whether he was serious or not.

"I want to know everything," he said.

"You ... w-w-what?" I said with a stutter.

"Everything about you—now!"

I chuckled. The words, combined with his sheepish expression, disarmed me.

"I don't want to talk about me," I said, turning my eyes away from him.

"Why not?" he asked with genuine surprise in his voice, "I wanna know about you, prezombie invasion."

Unsure what to say, I glanced out the window, but darkness prevented me to see the passing landscape as the bus drove by.

"I never really liked that person ... I mean, this is who we are now, right?" I said and forced a smile as I turned to him. "Maybe you should talk about you."

His face scrunched up, and he narrowed his eyes at me; then he cleared his throat.

"Maybe we shouldn't talk then," he said at a whisper and leaned in.

Thousands of internal conversations with myself rushed through my head for the seconds it took for his lips to reach mine. They ranged from good for me, bad for me, I don't know this guy, to future long-distance relationships, which seemed ludicrous, but they all grinded to a stop as I realized that in a different life I should have been dead. This could be a second chance, and maybe I should take it. After that, all I could feel and taste was Mars, and it tasted better than the candy his nickname suggested.

"Mags, you comin'," Ash yelled, louder than necessary. Startled, Mars and I pulled apart and peeked over the seat.

Through the window, I could see the bus had parked on what looked like a road inside a building. Dim lights illuminated concrete walls and a couple of soldiers standing in front of a massive entranceway.

At the front of the bus, I could see Angie carry Ash on her back, and they were about to step out of the vehicle. That image looked somewhat odd to me, because although I knew Angie to be a strong, capable woman, she was on the short side and the proportions with Ash on her back seemed all wrong, so I chuckled.

Mars extended his hand to help me up. The grin on his face was unmistakable. As I stood, I stopped for a moment to gaze into his eyes and could not help smile at the cheekiness they revealed. Knowing the bus had emptied, I allowed myself that chance to kiss him again before I let him guide me down the aisle and out of the bus. His hand on the small on my back felt strangely reassuring.

"Check it out," Ash exclaimed as we lined up outside the bus. "That's the actual door they used in *Stargate*."

Tyler beamed with pride as he glanced at Ash hanging off Angie's back.

"I thought you didn't know anything about Cheyenne," I said.

"Well, I don't, but Tyler explained, and I've seen the show once or twice."

Sergeant Tyler's smile reached a point where I was afraid it might get stuck.

"That is a three-feet solid-steel door that weighs about 25 tons," Sergeant Tyler started to explain, "and we have three of them." I didn't share his or Ash's enthusiasm. The thought of being inside a mountain didn't excite me as much as it did Ash, but I gave the sergeant appreciative nods as he spoke.

We followed him past one of the massive doors into a large cavernous space that partly looked like an actual cave with ragged rocks, but in other parts had pristine white walls along with windows that made up several buildings. Vehicles passed us as we walked in a line behind Tyler. Around us, men and women dressed different military gear moved with purpose, either performing some job like driving around forklifts or working mechanics on engines or running around with a clipboard. It was a lot to take in.

Sergeant Tyler led us up a few steps and then had us weaving through several hallways. I had also seen some of that TV show Ash had mentioned before, but besides the doors and probably the entrance to the tunnel, which I had missed because I was otherwise engaged, it didn't look anything like it. To me, it all looked like a giant office building with barren hallways and lots of doors. The only thing missing was light filtering in through windows, which added to my claustrophobic feeling. The fact I hadn't seen anyone since we made the last couple of turns felt a little off as well.

Sergeant Tyler stopped at a T-junction in the hallway. He pointed down one end of the hall where two soldiers stood on both sides of a door.

"Your accommodations. I suggest you freshen

up, and Agent Meadow can show you around," he said. "Guards will be assigned to you twenty-four-seven. If you need anything, you can ask them."

"Wait a minute. Around the clock guards?" I said agitatedly. "Are we prisoners?"

Tyler turned to face me as he spoke. "You are our guests, but we cannot have you wandering around this place. You'll have free access to certain facilities like our mess hall, but only if you have an escort."

I frowned at the man to show my disapproval, but he had already turned his attention elsewhere.

"Agent," he said to Mars, "if you follow me, the general would like to speak with you."

Mars nodded at the man before he turned to me.

"Wait up for me?" he asked in a whisper. I nodded and watched him follow Tyler. Before he cornered the hall, he glanced back at me with a grin. My heart lifted as if I were a schoolgirl with a crush.

When my focus returned to Ash and Angie, I noticed them staring at me with sheepish expressions.

"Come on, Juliet. Romeo shall return soon," Angie said.

Ash burst out laughing, and it returned my feet firmly to the ground. As my face went crimson, I pulled a hand through my messy hair and followed.

Warren

"Are you telling me, you drove in with these two?" Warren yelled as he pointed at a couple of pictures stuck to a whiteboard. "These two, right here." He slammed his fist against the board next to one of the pictures whose serial number ended with 102. Warren's inner fury threatened to overtake him, and he knew he needed to reel it in. Besides, the man sitting at the table across from him didn't seem the least bit impressed.

Warren eyed the man for a moment. He had carried an ID that made him out to be Michael Carver, employed by the Centers for Disease Control, but from his appearance the man could have been a bum. His face was unshaven, his clothes were dirty, and frankly, he reeked.

"How could I have known these two were fugitives?" Carver said in his defense. "It's not as if I would expect escaped science projects to drive around in a highly equipped military vehicle, carrying a decent set of IDs."

Ignoring the man from the CDC, Warren stood, walked to the window of the airport lounge, and stared out into the darkness. They had been right out there beyond this glass, so close but out of reach.

"Why is it exactly the CDC wasn't made aware of the existence of these two?" the man behind him added. "If these two women can add in any way to finding a solution to the Mortem virus, then the CDC needs to know about them."

Warren turned and looked at the man sharply. The last thing he needed was another agency interfering with his work.

"What exactly is your business here, Mr. Carver?" Warren asked. Carver straightened in his seat and folded his hands on the table.

"I was supposed to arrive this afternoon to help with the evac but came across a little trouble in a town not far from here," Carver said. "Meeting those two probably saved my life." Carver pointed at the pictures hanging on the whiteboard.

"I see," Warren replied. "And?"

"I was late meeting Captain Brocket. Someone pointed him out to me on the tarmac. I followed him there, and that's where I overheard your conversation about them and pointed them out to you," Carver said and pointed another finger at the board.

The men locked eyes, and neither seemingly wanted to be the first to look away. Warren lost this game by glancing at the door at the sound of a knock. William entered and closed the door behind him. The sour expression on the big man's face told Warren it wasn't good news.

"What?" Warren said exasperated.

"They got away," William replied in a way that could have been mistaken for a growl.

"How?"

"A helicopter pulled them out," William added.

Warren drew in a sharp breath to force his anger down.

"Do we know who?" Warren asked.

"The chopper appears to be air force."

Warren's eyes widened. He knew of one person of importance with interest in his work that had wriggled her way up the ranks within the air force, Dr. Kelly Matley. He had worked with her for a long time before she too ridiculed his endeavors.

Warren shook his head. *How had she made the connection?* While working together, Warren had made certain that Matley never knew his subjects' names. Somehow she had learned of their escape and the significance they meant to his research or else she would have never sent a helicopter after them. His head shot up to face the pictures on the board before he turned to William.

"The FBI," he said under his breath. The words were meant more for himself than for William, but the big man nodded in understanding.

The fractions in the different government agencies had been severe. Working together to solve the problem wasn't always a viable option anymore. Organizations like the CDC proved to be a liability while others like the CIA had their perks. To have highly trained men at his disposal was something Warren could appreciate, especially when a man like William had his much needed connections within the agency. Perhaps the FBI had sought support from the air force and that's how Matley would have gotten herself involved.

Warren snorted a laugh. That bitch would do anything to steal his work.

"Excuse me," Carver said as he stood, "but I have a lot of work to do and I still need to meet with Captain Brocket."

Warren looked at Carver and then glanced over the room. The lounge, in better days used by pilots and other airport personnel to get a bite to eat or just relax, looked eerily quiet. He had requested it like this.

"It is time to leave," Warren said as he turned on his heels to exit the room. "Please take care of Mr. Carver."

He barely heard the light pop of the silencer as he casually walked down the hall. He had one concern on his mind. He had to find Matley if he wanted his subjects back.

16

"Welcome to my humble abode," Angie said as she guided us past the guards and a solid-steel door. First, I thought it strange that the sergeant had left us standing there on our own after he had specifically told us not to venture out on our own, but I guessed the guards down the hall meant we weren't alone.

"So do you get to walk around without the babysitters?" I asked Angie and pointed at thumb at the door after I closed it. Without turning around, she replied,

"I didn't at first, but it's more of a precaution, so you won't get lost or enter areas you're not supposed to. Don't worry about them; they're only temporary."

"If you say so," I said.

The two airmen outside would spend the night there until they were relieved of their duty. Maybe the military wasn't as adventurous as the ads wanted us to believe.

The room itself was a letdown. While I didn't expect hotel accommodations, a six-by-eight concrete box with two sets of twin beds stacked on top of each other felt a bit of a letdown. I stepped into the row that separated the two bunks.

Ash, hanging off Angie's back, gripped the rail

of the top bunk and used her arms to climb on the top half of the bed. Angie's shoulders sagged when Ash's weight eased off her, and she plunked down on the lower half of the other bunk bed. I stepped in line with the bed to face Ash. She looked so tired. I tussled a hand through her hair and she swatted it away.

"Sleep," she said, drawing out the word. My pack sat on the lower bunk. It occurred to me that I had forgotten all about it and hadn't seen the thing after departing from the helicopter. I glanced at it for a moment and then shrugged. What did I care how it had gotten here? Angie must have noticed and spoke.

"Mars."

I glanced at her for a moment, unable to stifle a smile and reached for it. What was left of my stuff was all squeezed inside this backpack. I rummaged through it and found my phone along with the earplugs. I handed them to Ash. She took them greedily.

"Thanks," she said and wedged the earphones in her ears. I regarded her for moment, wondering if I should say something. She had been this tough kid ever since I met her and probably before, but I felt the urge to protect her. As she settled in her bunk, I placed my hand on her shoulder. She looked up and nodded with a faint smile. It was her way of telling me she was okay, but I wondered if it was true. Prodding her to talk had proven useless in the past and I wouldn't push her now.

I sat down on the bunk. Angie had already hunkered down. She was fighting with a pillow, trying to settle it under her head when she looked up at me.

"You okay," she asked. I managed a shrug but didn't feel much like talking. Something did bother me though.

"They don't know about us, do they?" I said in a low voice. Angie perched on an elbow.

"We didn't think it be in your best interest," she said. "They think you're part of our investigation into Dr. Warren, and that isn't a lie—exactly."

I managed a half-smile; with all the conflicting emotions and thoughts running around in my head, it was all I had to give, but unfeigned. Ever since I had met her in that town with Father Deacon's church and flock, she'd had our best interest at heart —especially Ash's.

At the time, Angie worked undercover for the FBI to keep an eye on Father Deacon. While I hadn't known her then, I had helped her when a zombie had tackled her and brought her to the ground. She had fought it to keep it from sinking its teeth in her until I kicked it in the head.

Coincidentally, Angie and Ash had met before, and Angie had provoked a similar distaste in zombies. Angie had cancer like Ash and me, except hers hadn't been canceled out yet by the Mortem virus. That's why the zombie that had tried to bite her hesitated. The fact she looked like shit told me she was still battling it. She hadn't been bitten like Ash and me. The zombie virus, or Mortem as the doctors tended to call it, had mutated our cells, and they had stopped growing out of control. The fact we hadn't turned into zombies probably came down to sheer luck, but the answers behind it was what Dr. David was looking for.

"How's that going," I asked, "investigating Dr. David?"

"Ugh," she replied and waved a hand to dismiss it. "Save the shoptalk for tomorrow—but let's just say that you shouldn't get your hopes up."

There was a knock on the door. It opened before any of us managed to lift their butts off our bunks. The door clicked open, and Mars stuck his head inside the room. He glanced at me for a second, which was enough for my heart to skip a beat, but then he turned to Angie.

"Can I talk to you for a second?" he said and motioned to her to get out into the hall. Angie groaned as she slid off the bunk. She half rolled her eyes at me and then stepped outside. I let out a long breath while my eyes stayed locked on the door. As if affected by an electrical current, my heart picked up speed. Although it had been a while since I had felt this way, and the heat flushing my cheeks told me that this was more than just a crush, which seemed odd because of the brief moments Mars and I had actually met.

The door clicked open again, and this time it opened all the way. Angie stepped in with a lightweight-model wheelchair that looked close to the model I had picked up for Ash on that scavenger run. Instead of the bright yellow of the wheelchair that probably still sat in the back of the Knight in a town filled with zombies, this one had a fluorescent green color. The black leather seat appeared unused.

"Hey, not-a-kid," she said in a loud voice to attract the attention of Ash over the music that was pounding her ears. I couldn't see Ash's reaction from my lower bunk, but the expression on Angie's face told me it was the good kind. While Angie helped Ash down the bunk and sat her in her new chair, I watched Mars hover at the door. His eyes darted from me to the floor, to the chair, back to me, and around again. He looked anxious.

"What do you say we take this thing for a spin and some food?" Angie said.

"Excellent," Ash said with a grin, the need for sleep long forgotten. Although I felt exhausted from everything that had happened the past hours, the smile on Ash's face was infectious.

"Check it out," Ash added while she balanced on the back wheels. I got up from my bed and tussled her hair.

"Back in action," I said.

Mars stepped out of the way as Ash rolled past him and through the door.

"Thanks, Mars," she said on her way out.

"You're welcome," he said.

Angie followed Ash, but before I could, Mars stepped into my path.

"Can we talk?" he said. Those tense eyes took hold of me, but the sudden stomach twisting sensation made me look away while my cheeks lit up. I glanced down the hall where Ash and Angie had decided not to wait for me.

One of the soldiers who remained posted outside our door gave me a curious glance when Mars stepped past me into the room.

My heart started to pound in overdrive. I closed the door behind me. My hands felt cold as I pressed them against my hot face and turned my back to Mars. I was so not used to these kinds of situations. For a long time, my life had all been about avoiding people. With the knowledge you're about to die, it didn't seem fair to let people in, especially not in a way I wanted to let Mars in—and I would let him in. I had already somewhat made the decision on the bus, but I expected it wouldn't come naturally to me.

Warm waves of his breath tickled my neck as he stood behind me. At the sound of a click, I flinched and turned around. He just stood there flashing that great smile.

"What?" I said. His hand lifted to my side, and I heard another click.

"You're still wearing your load-carrying system," he said as he continued to open the vest, and he lifted it from my shoulders. With a thud, the vest dropped into a corner and the he went to sit down on the lower half of my bunk.

Nervously, I glanced around the room for somewhere to sit, wondering if I should sit across from him on Angie's bunk. He made the decision for me when he grabbed my hand and pulled me down to sit next to him.

"I have a confession to make," he said as he wrapped both his hands around mine.

"Oh?" I said.

"Yeah, I kind of already know everything there is to know about you," he said casually.

My eyes grew wide at his admission. He perked out his lower lip and nodded.

"Clothes, shoe size, family, schools, number of boyfriends—" he said before I interrupted him.

"What!" I said in a raised voice.

"Well, not exactly about the boyfriends," he said, "but in my defense, I work for an agency that deals with information, and I had a lot of time on my hands."

I didn't know what to say and just glared at him for a moment. Was he serious?

"Why? And didn't you have anything better to do?" I asked a bit dazed.

"Well, not on my downtime, and you got stuck in my head," he said, "and I wanted to know."

My mouth dropped slightly open, but before I could speak, he placed a finger on my lips.

"But to level it out," he said as he reached into a pocket to remove a piece of paper, "I've done the same search on me … for you."

I narrowed my eyes on the piece of paper as he handed it to me. Mars shifted on the bed and suddenly seemed nervous. His eyes flickered from the piece of paper to me and back. Seeing him nervous made such a difference from the cool, collected man that could face anything in the field— it made him look adorable like a little puppy.

"This isn't exactly the best way to get to know each other," I said softly.

"I know, and I know I promised you that date, but the zombies kind of screwed up the dating scene, so I improvised," he replied.

For a fraction of a second, my mind transported me back to that darkened hallway somewhere on the grounds of JFK where he had first promised me that date and felt it brighten my spirit.

He returned my smile with one of his own as I fiddled with the piece of paper between my fingers. I didn't need a piece of paper to tell me who this guy was. I could see it in his eyes, and I could tell how he had fought to rescue us from that lab. The resolution I had made on that bus came back to me, and while Mars's calm demeanor seemed to disintegrate, I knew what to do.

"You want me to read it to you?" he asked.

I shook my head.

"I could just tell you."

I shook my head again. He opened his mouth to speak again and this time I pressed my finger to his lips.

"Shh," I said at a whisper, "we need to do this first." With that, I leaned into him and pressed my lips to his.

My hands slid up his arms and shoulders until they wrapped around the back of his neck. I pulled him closer. I wanted to feel him.

Mars deepened the kiss, and with the gentlest force, he eased me backward until my head hit the pillow. He released me for a moment to catch his breath.

"About that date," he said in a breathy voice.

"Shut up and kiss me." It was the last thing I said for quite a while.

17

I wondered if Mars had informed Angie of his intentions, because she took her time before she returned with Ash. She didn't say anything when she found Mars and me sitting next to each other on my bunk. Although I could see her gaze drift over the disheveled blankets and sheets on the bed. She merely smiled and helped Ash onto the top bunk.

I followed Mars outside into the hall but could count on about the same measure of privacy there with the two airmen placed at our door as inside the room. The look on those men's faces made me blush in an instance. Mars didn't seem to be bothered with it, but then I think I might have been the louder one. In my defense, it had been some time.

After an awkward good-bye, he crossed the hall and entered his own room. I closed the door behind me and then had to face another pair of curious eyes. Ignoring both Ash and Angie, I crawled under the blankets of my bunk.

Although I had hoped to get some rest, I couldn't sleep, but it wasn't for a lack of trying. Ash and Angie were on a roll. After they had informed me of their sightseeing tour of the base, which included a trip to the mess hall and to one of the bigger control rooms, they started to exchange stories. They just couldn't shut up and had to drag me into their conversation. I was grateful, though, that they had thought to bring me some sandwiches from the mess. My little exercise routine with Mars had left me hungry. I was even more grateful that they didn't mention the fact I had spent over an hour alone with him.

"So then you stayed at the beach," Angie said.

"Yeah," Ash replied, "it was great, the weather was great, and I even learned how to swim." Angie shot me a friendly smile before she turned on her side to look up at Ash.

"That must have been some sight," she said, "flapping around in the water like a puppy."

"Hey," Ash replied before she chugged a pillow down from her bunk. It hit Angie square in the face, and I couldn't help but snort a chuckle. That awarded me with the same pillow in my face. The room filled with laughter.

After a moment, I glanced at the clock and noticed it was almost twelve.

"So what did you do all summer," Ash asked Angie. Before she answered, she perched her head up on a hand and shifted glances between the two of us.

"Not that much," she said. "My leg had to heal, which ran into trouble infection-wise. Mars had to do all the hard work, like avoiding being discovered by Dr. Warren. That didn't work out that well."

"He found you out?" I asked.

"Yeah, his watchdog had sought us out." I

remembered her mention of the word *watchdog* before I figured it out.

"You mean William, beefy guy with the head the size of a cantaloupe," I said. Angie nodded with a smile.

"Yeah, seemed nice at first, but turned out to be a mean motherf…" she said but swallowed her last word with a glance at the upper bunk.

"Fucker," Ash chimed in. I knew Ash wouldn't shy away from completing the word. From the moment we met, she'd had a very uncensored vocabulary. Still, I couldn't give up on a chance to shuck the pillow at her. Of course, it was followed by a grunted "Hey."

My eyes fell on Angie's pale face as I leaned back. She smiled up at Ash, but dark circles underlined her eyes. She didn't look well.

"How are you feeling?" I asked in a soft voice. The curses coming from the upper bunk died down.

"Okay, I guess," she said as her head lowered to the pillow. "Still here." Silence filled the room for a moment until Ash spoke up.

"You could get yourself get bitten by a zombie," she said. Her words tightened my throat. Angie knew what had happened to us, but she also knew the risk. She had seen the victims of Dr. David's trials in Florida. Most of the cancer patients he had infected with Mortem had turned into a newer version of zombies. They seemed similar to the brain dead, but at a closer look you could see them thinking behind those white, fogged-up eyes. They still craved living flesh but knew what they were doing, unable to stop themselves. I couldn't imagine a worse fate, along with withering away until death found you, which was something I had feared for most of my adult life. They had to face what their bodies did to other human beings. Even the slimmest chance of becoming that would stop me from trying. I wasn't hard to imagine Angie would feel the same way.

"It doesn't work that way, kid," Angie said and turned to her other side to show us her back.

"Don't call me kid," Ash said annoyed.

"Then don't say stupid shit," Angie retorted. "You know you were lucky for Mags to be around or else you'd be crawling around on your stomach like a freaking zombie."

"That doesn't mean it wouldn't work for you," Ash fired back. I poked my head out and looked up at Ash.

"Does it," she said as she looked down. A glassy sheen filled her eyes. I shook my head. We didn't know why we hadn't turned. Dr. David had done some extensive research on it, and he still hadn't figured it out. With a hurt look on her face, Ash's head disappeared from my sight. I reached for the lamp standing on a side table and switched it off.

The silence felt uncomfortable as I lay in the dark, unable to fall asleep. Too much had happened in not enough time, and it crowded my head. In the bunk above me, Ash's breathing had evened out, but in the other bed, Angie grunted and kicked the sheets of her legs to sit up. Her elbows perched on her knees, she hid her face in her hands.

"What is it?" I whispered. Her head perked up, looking surprised at the sound of my voice.

"You're supposed to be asleep." Without a word, I shifted to lean on an elbow and waited for her reply.

"I promised myself I wouldn't tell you ... but I'm scared, you know ..." she said.

I considered turning the light on but didn't want to wake Ash.

"Tell me what?"

"There is a doctor here, and she thinks she knows what's needed to make it work," she whispered. The concerned look on her face told me there was something else to it.

"But," I replied.

"She needs more data."

"Angie," Ash said in a tiny voice and poked her head over the side of the bed.

At the sound of Ash's voice and the knowledge that she was awake, Angie kicked her foot out, and her boots placed next to the bed scattered across the floor.

"That's a good thing, right?" Ash said.

I flipped the switch to turn on the lamp and glanced at Angie. A single tear ran down her cheek. She gripped the side of her bed and gave me a hard look before her eyes flicked up at Ash.

Then she refocused on me, and it wasn't easy to hold her stare. Her words hadn't been meant for Ash's ears; they were meant for me.

"She hasn't been able to test her theory, this Dr. ..." I asked.

"Matley," she said and shook her head. It wasn't a hard thing to figure out what Angie was asking. She was looking for a way to survive, and this Dr. Matley had handed her an option. Considering the fact Ash and I had been Dr. David's favorite research subjects, I figured this Dr. Matley would welcome us with open arms.

"Wait, what tests," Ash asked.

Angie sprang to her feet and reached a hand out to Ash.

"This is not for you to worry about," she said in low voice.

"But do you think we can help?" Ash replied.

"No, I'm sorry, kid. I shouldn't have mentioned it."

I blocked out the rest of the conversation and turned to face the wall.

Angie would never ask Ash. She would never put Ash through more anguish, and I appreciated that, but she hadn't asked Ash. If this Dr. Matley were to come up with something to help Angie, then she would need ways to test it. And I would need to step up.

When I woke the next morning, Ash had found her way into my bunk. In the Knight, we had slept next to each other for quite some time, and I felt grateful for the familiar wake up, although the Knight was a bit more spacious.

I had heard Ash toss and turn for most of the night. Sleep hadn't come easy for me either. The conversation with Angie had reawaken the gloom I'd been trying to fight off, and although my time spent with Mars was anything but gloom—and it was probably the one thing I did want to think about—my mind kept shifting to Angie's unspoken request. She had barely said anything, and I probably should have asked more questions, but I couldn't bring myself to do it—especially not with Ash inside the room. Even the thought of drawing blood made my stomach lurch, and the word *test* made a shiver run up and down my spine. Our time spent with Dr. David had turned me into a testophobic or something.

Ash turned, and her elbow hit me in the face. I groaned and prodded my jaw as Angie turned on the light.

"Rise and shine," she said. My eyes snapped shut at the bright light that filled the room. I pried an eye open to look at her. She seemed perky enough for as far as Angie could ever be perky.

We got ourselves ready, and along with our two chaperones, who had changed during the night, we made our way to the mess hall. Ash, having learned the route yesterday, took the lead. The fact she had her own transportation today made me feel grateful. Although Ash wasn't the greatest burden to carry around on one's back, my shoulders felt tight enough without carrying her around all day. Our trusted guards walked behind us with enough space to have a conversation without needing to fear they would catch every word.

"Are you okay?" Angie asked while we trotted along a corridor. I glanced at her sideways and shrugged.

"I'm sorry. I shouldn't have dropped this on you like that," she added.

I couldn't reply. Anything I'd say would be the wrong thing, and I didn't even know what that thing she dropped exactly meant. All I could think of was what Dr. David had done to us—the needles, the cutting into my body, the pain. I shuddered at the memory.

Angie grabbed my arm and pulled me to a stop. The two soldiers walking behind us closed in, and Angie shot them a glare.

"Do you mind?" she said in a hard tone. One of the men lifted his hands in surrender, and they both took a couple of steps back. Her hardened look softened as she glanced up at me.

"Would you please talk to me?" she said more tentatively.

I stared at her—unable to think—what should I say. I'm sorry, you're my friend and I like you, but I have to think about it. Could I say that to someone who had risked her life to save me?

After a moment, her gaze dropped to the floor, and her shoulders slumped.

"Please, I don't want you to consider talking to Matley," she said at a whisper. "It was stupid of me to mention it. They don't know who you are, and they will never find out from me. I was just ..."

"Scared," I said filling in the blank with a half-hearted smile. "I know that feeling."

She glanced down the hall. Ash hadn't noticed our sudden stop. Angie's gaze darkened as she stepped in closer so her words would stay between us.

"I hadn't thought it through," she said as she glanced over her shoulder to where Ash disappeared around a corner, "not until this morning when I saw how she crawled down that bunk—that kid needs you to be okay."

Facing me she added, "She likes me, but she doesn't need me. I can't give her what she needs, so whatever you do, don't make it about me. Make it about her."

Some of that darkness lifted, and although her words were amiable, they felt a little threatening. Still I nodded in agreement. Angie had a point: I wasn't on my own anymore. Whether I liked it or not, I had a kid to take care of even if she wasn't my own. Angie started to walk, and I watched her for a moment. Just what I needed, another conflict in my life. With a shrug, I started to follow with the two airmen in tow.

The mess hall seemed quiet when we entered. It turned out most of the men and women working here had already been in and out. Some of them worked in shifts, but for most, nine o'clock in the morning was a late start. While we sat down and ate, I kept an eye out for Mars. A bagel and some fruit later, he still hadn't shown up. Although the food was great and the abundance of it blew my mind, I felt like some stupid schoolgirl waiting for her prince to arrive. I didn't know whether Ash noticed, but I think Angie caught on after about a minute of sitting down.

I returned from a restroom break and noticed Ash had left the table.

"She wanted hot chocolate," Angie said when I asked her about it. I scanned the room and saw her sitting several tables down in conversation with a messy head of red hair that obscured, presumably, the woman's face. As I plopped down in my seat across from Angie, my eyes automatically scanned the mess entrance. Angie rolled her eyes at me and then shook her head.

"What?" I asked as I refilled my coffee.

"Romeo is working," she replied. "Probably in cahoots with the top brass around here."

I scowled at her for the Romeo remark and then sagged in my seat. I glanced around my new surroundings and didn't know what to make off it. Although the mess hall didn't show it, the knowledge I was on a military base, combined with the fact I sat inside a mountain, gave me the creeps. It all added to the claustrophobic feeling that threatened to crash down on me. Even the blue air force flight suit they had me wear reminded me of being stuck in that cell all those months ago—although that suit had been orange then.

"What's going to happen to us?" I asked.

"I don't know. Our plan hadn't developed into that stage yet," she said as she leaned in. I sat up to follow her example and edged closer.

"How were you able to find us anyway?" I asked.

"You dad's plane raised some flags around here, and we kind of had to act in a hurry," she said, her voice barley a whisper. "Mars had an inkling you might show up."

"How they'd find out about the plane?"

Angie raised her eyebrows. "You do know where you are, right?" she said incredulously. "It's kind of what they do around here—you know, watch the sky. Besides, Warren was on that plane. It said so on the registered flight plan."

She paused as if to gauge my reaction to the information.

"Yeah, we saw him exit the plane," I said with a groan and then hid my face in my hands. "I just wanted to go home."

"I know," Angie said. The sympathy I heard in her voice seemed uncharacteristic, and I dropped the hands from my face. She stared at me with those dark eyes that seemed to be filled with anger most of the time, but now I couldn't read them. "Borders are closed," she said as a matter of fact. "It'll be a while until international travel is permitted, and even then I doubt it'll be public or even private transport. They might permit nationals to come home, but ..." Her voice trailed off, but she didn't have to say the words for me to know their meaning —Dad had already said as much: Ash would never be allowed to come with me.

I leaned back and let my shoulders sag as my hands dropped along my sides.

"I already overstayed my visa," I said in all seriousness. "Think you can help me out with the paperwork."

Angie kept a straight face for the longest time, and it started to make me feel uncomfortable, until one side of her mouth curved into a smile and laughed. Glad the agent had a sense of humor, I smiled back. It seemed my trip had extended indefinitely, and I could use all the friends I could get.

Around us, the mess hall had emptied out, and the food counters closed. It unnerved me when I couldn't see Ash and turned to check the room behind me.

"Have you seen Ash?" I asked Angie. She looked

at me in surprise and then around the room. Besides the two airmen who had escorted us here, the place looked deserted.

I stood to look around.

"She couldn't have passed the guards," Angie said. "Maybe she found her way into the kitchen."

I raised my eyebrows: that could be something Ash would do. It seemed that the kid had a thing for kitchens. Grabbing my tray from the table, I noticed sergeant Tyler enter the mess hall heading straight to us.

The expression on the man's face was beyond serious, and this strange foreboding feeling washed over me.

"Agent Meadow," Tyler said as he stopped at our table. Angie stood to face the man.

"I would like you and … your guest to follow me, please," he said. Angie shot me a look I couldn't read, which didn't make me feel better.

"Let me find Ash, and we'll be right—" I started to say, but Tyler cut me off.

"You will meet the child there."

"Meet where?" Angie asked.

"You'll see soon enough," he replied. She shot the man a hard stare and didn't seem amused by Tyler's vagueness. Tyler however remained unfazed.

18

Tyler took the lead as we walked down an unfamiliar hall. In a single file, we were led deeper inside the facility. Angie walked ahead of me, and our two escorts from before took up the rear as we passed military personnel in all sorts of getups. People of all types of ethnicities and genders went by in efficient workers' clothes similar to the flight suits we wore, but there were also some in full dress uniform of different colors. I wasn't familiar with the United States military and didn't know all the designations, but they seemed to resonate from all the different parts of the armed forces. I even spotted several Canadian officers. The tiny flags on their shoulder made them easy to identify.

We passed rooms that looked like overequipped offices. Huge monitors hung on the walls, displaying all kinds of interesting data. Some had maps of the world, others the top half of North America and Canada.

Without success Angie had tried to gain some answers from Tyler, but the man kept his mouth shut. Every step, not knowing where we were going, added to the tightness in my chest. The fact that Ash—who hadn't left my side for over a year— wasn't around didn't help, and neither did the concerned look Angie shot me over her shoulder.

Tyler stopped at a white door and opened it for us. He stood by it as he ushered us inside a tiny room. Glass surrounded us on every side, and a sharp fluorescent light hung overhead. It reminded me of the boxlike rooms I had seen in Dr. David's lab, and I felt my throat tighten.

"Standard decontamination process," he said. "You know the drill."

"Wait … What?" Angie said, turning to face Tyler. Without explanation, he closed the door and left us standing alone.

"You little shit!" Angie exclaimed and stormed at the door. There weren't any door handles on the inside, so she wouldn't have any chance of opening it. Instead, she kicked it and cursed some more.

My eyes darted around the room. Beyond the glass, I saw people working at different workstations. Each station carried a computer screen, but the rest varied per workstation. Some had small devices hooked to the computers; others were loaded with glass bottles and test tubes. My eyes roamed past the desks where an examination table stood. I swallowed hard and balled my hands into fists so my shaking hands wouldn't be too obvious.

As if she could sense my discomfort, Angie started to explain.

"Standard decontamination," she said in a low voice. I nodded as if I had any idea what that meant.

A faint smile curved on Angie's face and she

said, "Don't worry. It's just a shower, but we have to take our clothes off."

I felt my eyes grow wide and stared at her. Then I shifted my view to the glass wall overseeing the lab on the other side. When I turned back to her, Angie grinned and shook her head before she slammed a button mounted on the wall. Within the same second, the glass seemed to turn into a wall, although I knew it was tinted glass, just as the windows of the Knight had been.

After we stripped our clothes, a panel in the glass wall opened, and that tightening feeling in my chest grew again at an alarming rate. Angie guided me through every step of the process and explained it as if I was a child, and I gladly let her. She wasn't disrespecting my intellect, and I knew that. It was her way of giving me a handhold, something to focus on. It actually worked, and I felt the urge to freak out and slam my fists against the glass fade. She warned me when to close my eyes as a cold substance that bit my skin poured over us, and when to hold my breath as a white fog released from something that looked like a showerhead sprouting from the ceiling.

When the white fog had dissipated, another panel opened, and we stepped through. I felt relieved to see the windows inside this room had been tinted as well. Angie pointed at two piles of white fabric displayed on a stainless steel cart. After we had changed into not-so-charming hospital gowns, Angie pressed a similar button to the one she had pushed in the first room.

A geeky beanstalk of a man with black, wide-rimmed glasses and wearing a surgical mask opened the door to let us out and guided us to a section of the lab separated by white plastic sheets.

"The doctor will be right with you," he said from behind his mask in a high-pitched voice before his gloved hands closed the sheets of plastic that almost looked like a see-through wall and left us to our own device.

I looked at Angie, in search of answers, but she shook her head.

"I don't know," she said, "but if I don't get any answers soon, I will punch someone."

I raised an eyebrow at her, and she smirked.

"Don't worry. It won't be you," she said.

As I opened my mouth to reply, someone else spoke.

"I hope it won't be me either," a kind, but a raspy voice said. I turned to the sound of a woman in a dark-blue skirt and suit jacket standing on the other side of the plastic wall. The middle-aged woman, with wild red hair that she had tried to tame in a ponytail along with a bunch of hairpins, approached us with a warm smile.

"I apologize. I won't be able to shake your hands," she said. "I'm not wearing the proper attire."

My mouth fell open, and it wasn't because of

the obvious plenitude of pounds the woman carried that made her clothes seem too tight and uncomfortable.

"Welcome to Cheyenne Mountain. You can't imagine how glad I am to finally meet you. My name is Dr. Kelly Matley," said the woman who I had last seen talking to Ash.

"Where is she?" I said through clenched teeth. Even Angie glared up at me in surprise at my tone of voice. Matley seemed startled, but I could tell she knew exactly whom I was talking about.

"Now calm down," she said raising her hands. "The girl is fine."

"What!" Angie piped in.

I pointed a finger at Matley and said, "I saw her talking to Ash in the mess."

Angie stepped in line beside me and crossed her arms. Her dark eyes looked as if a shadow had fallen over them as she gazed at Matley.

"You better start talking right now," she said.

Matley took a step back, her hands still in the air. "The girl came to me," she said in her raspy voice. "She wanted to help."

Blood started to boil as my hammering heart pumped it through my veins. I wanted to calm down. We were in a good place. Angie and Mars would have never taken us here if we'd have been at risk. I glanced sideways at Angie, who seemed as pissed off as I was.

"The kid is here?" she asked.

"Well—" Matley started to say, but I didn't let her finish. I pushed past the sheet of plastic.

"No, stop, wait, you can't ..." she said and tried to step into my path. "You can't leave this area." Then she must have thought the better of it and stepped aside. If she hadn't, I would have probably shouldered her out of my way. I stepped past her and into the lab. Keeping my cool would probably have been the wiser thing to do, but labs, doctors, and Ash missing weren't a good combination for me.

"Please, if you just let me explain." Matley's voice echoed behind me.

"Oh, shut it," Angie said as she followed me.

On bare feet, I stomped through the lab to the area where I had seen the desks before. Around me lab technicians glanced up from their work, and I felt their eyes bore into me. Angie came up from behind me.

"It's like they've never seen a skinny ass before," she said in a loud voice as she met a couple of the ogling eyes with an angry look of her own.

"I was kind of trying not to think of that," I said to her in a low voice, fully aware that the flimsy gown wouldn't cover my butt. A few of the technicians shifted uncomfortably as they returned their attention to their work.

"Yeah, pretend you're working," she said in that same loud voice.

Ignoring the lab techs, my eyes scanned the beds lining the wall beyond the desks.

"There," I said as I recognized Mars sitting on one of the beds.

Angie followed as I moved past the row of beds to where he sat with Ash.

"Mars," Angie said as we closed in.

He turned to face us, a grim expression on his face, and got to his feet. I stared at the scrawny form that lay lifeless on the bed.

"Ash," I said under my breath.

"What the hell, Mars!" Angie exclaimed.

In unison, we moved closer to the bed. Mars shot me a pained expression as he stepped back. Anger threatened to overtake me, but my concern for Ash pulled me to her, and I ignored Mars. At the side of the bed, he touched my arm, and my head shot up. His eyes widened, clearly taken aback at what would have been a venomous glare.

"I didn't know. Matley called me, and I found her like that," he said as fast as he could, while his hands shot up in defense. His words registered somewhere in my brain, but the emotions coursing through me were overwhelming. I bit my tongue and decided to focus on Ash.

Her eyes were closed, and the color of her skin had reduced to the reason she was called Ash in the first place. I stroked her head as my eyes slid down her neckline past the white hospital gown and along her thin arms that had been strapped to the bed.

My head snapped up, and facing Angie's darkened expression, I knew she had noticed the same thing. I started to undo the straps as I registered Dr. Matley's raspy voice.

"Please, don't be alarmed."

"Are you fucking kidding me," Angie said.

"Agent Meadow," Mars said aloud.

"What!" From the tone of her voice, I could tell Angie fumed with anger.

"Please ..." he said and paused as if to compose himself, "just let the doctor explain."

The room around us must have gone silent, because I couldn't hear a thing. Not that I cared. My focus lay with Ash. I scooted onto the bed next to her head and pulled her onto my lap. With the edge of her sheet, I wiped some saliva from the corner of her mouth and heard Matley suck in a breath.

"The child came to me," she said. "She volunteered."

I glared at her, hoping, waiting for a better explanation.

"She thought her blood might be able to help Agent Meadow over here," Matley added and paused to glance at Angie. In turn, Angie's face went crimson, and she shot me an apologetic look. I shook my head. This wasn't Angie's fault.

"Anyway," Matley continued, "the child freaked out as we attempted to draw blood, and we had to sedate her."

I didn't know whether it was the red hair, her tone of voice, or the why are you all so upset expression on her face, but it worked on me like a red rag on a bull.

"And you think it's normal to act on a child's offer like that." My words rushed out in rage. I felt like punching the woman.

"Now, now, it's not like there are any parents to consider, but I must admit I overestimated her courage. She freaked out and nearly stabbed one of my men's eye out with a syringe. We needed to sedate her before she could hurt anyone."

That was it—this was all I could take from this woman. I slid off the bed, replacing Ash's head on the pillow within the same motion and charged at Dr. Matley.

"You bitch," I said and balled my fists. "Consider this for a parent." Ready to punch her I stepped forward. Before I could get anywhere close to her, Mars wrapped his arms around my waist and held me in place. It didn't keep me from swinging at her, but I hit the air. Matley stepped back as shock spread across her face.

"Mags, stop," Mars said near my ear as I kept trying to get at the doctor. "The kid is okay. Matley didn't mean any harm."

Anger peaking and my heart pounding, I whirled in his arms.

"Don't call her kid," I said and shoved him in

the shoulders so his arms would release me. "She doesn't like it."

Mars stared at me with those pale jade eyes that would have made me melt at any given time, but the anger inside me made me pick up on the sympathy behind them, which added fuel to the fire. I hated it when people gave me that sympathetic look as if I was something fragile—about to break. I opened my mouth to spit out something I knew I would later regret, but fortunately, a loud voice interrupted me.

"Would someone explain to me what is going on?"

I turned to see two men in full dress uniform standing behind Matley. Their presence suddenly gave me the urge to stand at attention.

Before I had gotten stuck here in this country, I had never even been in contact with the military, let alone knew how to stand at attention, but these two men demanded it with their presence. One of the men stood tall, with a bald head and what seemed like a permanent frown on his face. The other one was significantly shorter, with a round face and gray hair, but what he lacked in height he made up for in presence.

I sucked in a breath to compose myself and saw Angie glaring at me. Unlike Matley, it wasn't shock, at least not in the negative sense of the word. Her face seemed filled with pride. She nodded, her way of telling me it was okay, when a tiny voice made our heads swing in the direction of the bed.

"Mags." Ash had pushed herself up on her elbows and watched me with a raised eyebrow. Ignoring everyone around us, I moved to the head of the bed and wrapped my arms around the scrawny kid. I pulled her close and knew she didn't mind when she hugged me back.

"You okay," I said after I kissed the top of her head. She nodded her answer, which I didn't think to be a good sign.

"Hey, kid," Angie said, standing on the other side of the bed as she rubbed a hand over Ash's back.

"Don't call me that." Ash retorted.

Angie glanced up and nodded at me with a smile.

"Where you about to punch Dr. Matley?" Ash whispered. I let out a nervous chuckle—the anger from before almost forgotten.

Angie leaned in and whispered near Ash's ear, loud enough for me to hear, "I think she would have taken her out."

Ash pulled away from me and glanced up at as her mouth curved into a smile.

Before she could say anything, a loud *"Ahem"* filled the room.

The shorter man stepped forward and extended his hand. He shook Angie's without introducing himself and then came over to our side of the bed. He shook Mars's hand and asked him how he was doing before he turned to Ash and me.

"My name is General Leon Whitfield, and I am the commander of this base," he said as he extended his hand for me to shake. Startled, I looked at my own hands that were still holding on to Ash.

Unsure of what the man had seen of my little outburst, I felt heat creep up my neck and settle in my cheeks when Ash shifted and grabbed the general's hand.

"Ash," she said in a firm voice, "pleased to meet you." The general politely switched his gaze to Ash, but I wasn't sure he was too interested in her. He turned back to me and once again offered his hand. This time I took it.

"I am very glad to finally meet you, Ms. Vissers," he said. Shocked to hear my last name, I fumbled the words into a "Nice to meet you too," and shot Mars a look. His eyes had gone wide, and he shook his head in an almost imperceptible no.

The general smirked as he shifted his gaze from me to Mars.

"Did you really think you'd be able to smuggle someone inside my facility without me knowing who they were?" General Whitfield said. "The doctor here recognized our young friend Ash from her stay in Florida."

"Sir …" Mars started to say, "I never—"

The general cut him off with a wave of his hand.

"Later," he said with a firm voice. Then he turned to the man who was now standing behind him. "This is my second in command, Colonel Nathan Cornwell."

Colonel Cornwell stepped closer and shook both our hands.

"We have a lot to talk about," he said and then turned to Matley. "Doctor, why don't you provide our guests with some proper clothing so they'll be more comfortable as we speak."

19

They'd put the three of us in those blue air force flight suits and whisked us off to some kind of meeting room. Reluctantly I had agreed to this meeting and only after General Whitfield had personally guaranteed that nothing would happen against our free will. It wasn't as if that made me flourish with trust in these people, but what choice did we have? We sat inside a heavily guarded mountain, and it wasn't as if we'd be able to stroll out.

With Ash once again latched on to my back, I surveyed the room that seemed as if it could hold the assembled board of a large company. A dark-blue carpet covered the floor, with warm, sand-colored walls and an impressive collection of pictures. An enormous conference table stood in the middle of the room surrounded by ten seats. A soldier sat at a desk in the far corner and nodded at us in greeting. In the other corner I spotted something that caught my attention, and mindlessly drawn to it, I headed in that direction.

"Oh God, here we go," Ash said as she spotted where I was heading.

"What?" I asked in an innocent tone. I stopped at a table that had on it the most beautiful coffee machine. The machine itself wasn't that impressive, but the difference with a lot of the others that I had seen over the past year was that this one worked and had actual beans. A pot stood ready, filled to the brim with the beautiful dark brew.

Brought up by a mother who valued her kids to have manners, I would usually have sought out the soldier sitting at the desk and asked whether I could pour myself a cup, but after the stunt that had just been pulled on us, I threw etiquette out the window and fumbled for a mug.

"Here, let me help you," Mars said and took the mug from my hand.

Too embarrassed to look up at him, I kept my eyes locked on the table and shifted Ash so she sat higher on my back. Mars poured a second cup as I readied myself to speak. I cleared my throat and found the courage to face him.

"I'm really sorry about before," I said. The words came out a mere whisper but knew he had heard as he angled his face to look at me sideways. A crooked smile lighted up his face.

"Sorry for what?" Ash said. Of course she had heard.

I closed my eyes and blew out the breath I had been holding. For as much as I enjoyed Ash's company, it killed any privacy I had.

"Exactly," Mars said. He set the pot of coffee down and took hold of my lower arm. "I should have come to find you the moment I found Ash in the lab, so no apologies."

"Well, then you'd have probably still been looking for me in the mess and I would have punched Matley," I said elated.

"I would have paid to see that," Ash said with a chuckle.

"This was probably the better way," Mars said as he looked over his shoulder. "Angie, want some coffee?" Angie grunted a yes and joined our little group around the table.

It wasn't long after that a door opened and Matley, joined by General Whitfield and Colonel Cornwell, stepped inside the room. Their presence, especially Matley's, made me uncomfortable, and I diverted my attention to the coffee.

"See if they have a soda in that fridge, will ya?" Ash asked over my shoulder. I looked down at the small fridge that stood about knee high and groaned. Ash was enough of a weight without having to kneel down.

"I'll get it," Mars said. He kneeled down before I could step back and felt him brush past my leg. The touch was innocent enough, but I could feel my head turn bright red.

"You two should get a room," Ash said.

"If only," Angie said under her breath and then quickly hid her smirk behind the steaming mug of coffee. I glared at her—pretty sure my face couldn't turn any redder. Mars got up, shooting Angie a glare of his own and then handed Ash a can of soda. His action coincided with a loud but by now familiar "Ahem."

"Take a seat. We have a lot to discuss," Colonel Cornwell said and gestured at the seats around the table.

"Come on, Ash," Mars said. "Let's get you seated." He took Ash in his strong arms, and I watched him carry her to one of the seats. I was still staring when he turned over his shoulder and said, "Bring the coffee." I forced myself to wake up out of this idiotic state. This wasn't the time. I grabbed the two mugs and set one down in front of Mars. Instead of taking the seat next to him, I moved around the table and took the one next to Ash, which seemed like an even dumber idea because now I had to look straight at him.

The general seated himself at the head of the table and the colonel slid in next to him. Dr. Matley sat on the right side of General Whitfield, next to Angie, Ash, and then me, but she didn't stay seated for long. She motioned at the soldier sitting behind the desk to dim the lights.

"Maybe we should start by informing our guests a little about what's happening, before you begin," Whitfield said as the lights dimmed. Dr. Matley motioned again at the soldier at the desk, and the lights went up again.

"My apologies," she said with a red-tinged face. It pleased me I wasn't the only person able to embarrass myself. The doctor cleared her throat and sat down.

"Yes, and perhaps you should also apologize for what transpired in the lab," Whitfield said. He looked pointedly at Dr. Matley as he waited for her to speak. The doctor seemed shocked, but quickly composed herself and nodded.

"Again, my apologies," she said.

Addressing the room Whitfield said, "It seemed Dr. Matley became a little too eager after learning Dr. David Warren's favorite test subjects have come into our midst."

The mention of Dr. David's name felt as if someone punched me in the gut. Next to me, Ash shifted uncomfortably in her seat and across from me Mars' face hardened.

Whitfield leaned forward, folding his hands on top of the table. "I'm sorry," he said, "I know the remark is inappropriate, but that is how we have come to know you."

A similar feeling that had risen up during my confrontation with Matley stirred inside me, but I kept my mouth shut. It didn't seem like good idea to chastise the general of a military base.

"Colonel Cornwell will explain," Whitfield said.

From that point, the colonel took over. The bald man with the permanent frown started with a little backstory on how Cheyenne Mountain had survived the initial outbreak, which didn't seem like much of an achievement because the place was built for situations like these. He explained their standing orders that were also what they always did: observe the homeland and abroad skies for any threats. It got more interesting when he started to mention the discord creating a rift within the government.

"They've split right down the middle—one side, including the president, had originally decided to place their faith in a multimillion-dollar pharmaceutical company called Pharma-Militum, who at the time happened to employ a man named Dr. David Warren, who on his turn also collected a government check," Cornwell said. "The other half, that can count on the support of most of the military branches, believed Warren and Pharma-Militum to be responsible for the outbreak in the first place."

Cornwell paused as he glanced around the table to see whether anyone had a question. "The allegations helped destroy the company's reputation, and while their stocks plummeted, Pharma-Militum pulled out altogether."

"This has placed the president, who up to this point refuses to concede his faulty judgment, and his supporters in a precarious place—as you can imagine," Whitfield added. "This is why the FMTD was created in the first place—to act as a subterfuge so they could claim that the current administration was doing everything in its power to stop the spread of the virus."

I didn't know whether I could imagine. It occurred to me he meant the rift between the president and the opposing part of the government. I was guessing it was that, because the president was often seen as the most powerful person in the world, in control of his military, and opposing him seemed unimaginable.

Back home, we didn't do political extremes. We didn't see our prime minister as a high and mighty entity. He'd just be the guy who showed up riding his bicycle to work and part of his job just happened to be running the country. He actually taught sociology as a guest teacher at a secondary school.

"Placing Dr. Warren in charge reinforced the growing rift between the fractions, especially when the FBI proved his involvement in the outbreak, but it seems the president has no intention of acting on those allegations," he said in a voice that sounded regrettable, "and on both sides we know forcing the situation will divide our country's leadership further, which, considering the outbreak, is something we can't afford."

He turned to face Angie, and then he nodded at Mars. "We have learned a lot about Warren's research thanks to the FBI and Dr. Matley, who has worked with Dr. Warren for years. We strongly believe finding a solution to the Mortem virus has to be our first step in rebuilding this country and eventually its government." Whitfield's face hardened as he narrowed his eyes, expressing his evident disapproval as he addressed Mars. "That said, I should also add our disappointment to learn you have tried to keep certain information from us," he said as his eyes shifted to Ash and me. "Fortunately, Ms. Vissers's name turned up in the recovered information from the Florida lab, so when we discovered that a plane linked to your father's company was flying to Jackson, along with Agent Marsden's added interest—we decided to act."

It didn't surprise me that they ultimately found us because of my dad trying to redirect his planes. Obviously, these guys would know about it. Tracking planes was one of the things they did here. Whitfield's admission of how he had found out about us filled me with insecurities. On some level it was something to be grateful for, because if they hadn't, I wouldn't want to think of where Ash and I would have ended up—probably on Dr. David's dissecting table—but it also meant he wanted something from us. The fact Mars had tried to hide our identities added to my appreciation of him and Angie.

Finding out that Dr. Matley had worked with Dr. David disturbed me, though. I glanced at Mars in search of comfort, but his eyes had turned stone cold. Fortunately, they weren't directed at me. He eyed Dr. Matley with a clenched jaw. Next to me, Ash had zoned out, fidgeting with the fabric of her flight suit. Automatically my eyes went to Angie, but the wariness in her face added to my discomfort.

Whitfield eyed me expectantly as if he wanted me to say something. I drew in a breath, held it for a moment and then let it out, before I asked, "What is it that you want?"

"Perhaps Dr. Matley can answer that question," Whitfield said. He glanced at the redhead, and she got out of her seat. Again, the lights in the room dimmed. Dr. Matley moved to the end of the table where Ash and I were sitting while a large white screen descended from the ceiling. An image that looked like a backlit gray mass appeared on the screen.

"Meet Mortem Ostium Inanimatum," Dr. Matley said as she pointed a red laser light at the image. "This is the nuisance that has placed this world in utter turmoil, and these are the facts."

She pressed a button and the imaged changed into a slideshow. Several bullet points appeared with text added as she spoke. "One, we know the virus was developed in a government lab in DC. Two, we know the developer's name is Dr. David Warren." She glanced at all of us one by one as if we needed to let this information sink in, but I think everyone was well aware of the fact. When no one reacted, she continued. "The fundamental reason for developing this virus was the initial indications that it had the potential to increase healing powers within a human body. This would give a significant advantage to the likes of the military forces, but would also help to reduce healthcare costs, etc."

"Yes, yes, yes, I think we know all this," the voice

of Colonel Cornwell, on the borderline of annoyance, pierced the dimmed room. He was probably unhappy with the fact his own government had something to do with the creation of zombies, but I wasn't going to point that out.

Dr. Matley cleared her throat. Although she didn't say anything to the colonel's comment, her face expressed how she felt about the military's intentions for the virus. She continued.

"There is enough evidence to support the claim that Dr. David Warren is responsible for releasing the virus into the general population. His actions since then support existing theories that he is focused on finding a way to incorporate these added healing properties into the human body. From the early stages of his research, it had been evident that this solution would be found in neoplasma malignum carriers—also known as the abnormal growth of tissue, or cancer in laymen's terms. The virus showed an adverse reaction to the accelerated growth of cells."

I let out a long breath as Dr. Matley continued her tale. I'd heard it all before, sitting on the floor of a jail cell. The memory of Mars sitting on the other side of those bars drew my eyes to his seat. He too wasn't paying much attention to the doctor's explanations. He was watching me, and even in this dimmed room, I caught the twinkle in his eyes. Despite the seriousness of the conversation, my mouth curved into a smile.

"The information we have gathered on the doctor's research has let me to believe that the so-called Divus serum or DS occurs in twenty percent of female neoplasma malignum carriers, due to the fluctuation in hormones ..." Matley said and paused for effect. She glanced around the room as if to see whether her words would trigger a combined aha or eureka moment. Glances crossed over the table, but no one seemed to get what Matley meant, and she continued. "This means women at the time of ovulation when their hormone levels peak are impervious to the virus." She went on to explain her theory that it had something to do with the rise and fall of hormone levels in our bodies.

"This is where Ash's results have clouded the research," Matley said.

For the first time during the presentation, Ash's head perked up.

"I did what?" she asked.

Matley turned from her sheet presented on the screen and faced Ash.

"Your hormone levels were never high enough to fight the Mortem virus alongside your cancer. That's what put Dr. Warren on the wrong track," Matley said.

"So," Ash inserted.

Matley sighed at the interruption before she answered, "He kept digging deeper while the solution for his problem lay on the surface." Once again, Matley glanced around the room expectantly.

"A monthly menstruation cycle," she simply said. "Ash hasn't had one yet and still she hasn't turned."

Ash scrunched up her face in disgust at the thought of the monthly discomfort that would fall upon her in the near future.

"So why hasn't she turned?" I asked. All eyes in the room glanced my way.

"That is where you came in," Matley answered. "At this point it is a guess, but as I see it, there must have been a breach where your altered virus has invaded Ash's body."

"So why didn't it work in Warren's lab?" Angie said. "He had tons of test cases and access to Mags's blood."

"Because during her stay at the lab, Ms. Vissers's hormone level, specifically her luteinizing hormone level, was low some time before her ovulatory phase. That's when levels peak and because Warren primarily tested on men ..." Matley replied.

"Huh?" Ash said.

"She was bleeding at the time," Matley rephrased, sounding annoyed.

I sank deeper into my seat, hiding my face behind a hand. The fact we sat in a high-security facility, in a meeting with the general himself, talking about my monthly cycle made me feel uncomfortable as hell, and it projected on my face as it turned red.

"I didn't turn into a zombie because you were

ovulating when your blood mixed with mine," Ash said pulling up her nose. "I don't know what's more gross."

I peeked at her through parted fingers and caught her smirking at me. She patted my shoulder and said, "It's okay. I still love you."

With a finger, I poked her shoulder and sat up. At the same time General Whitfield cleared his throat.

"What does this mean?" he asked.

Matley waved at the soldier sitting at the desk to turn on the lights. She returned to her seat at the table as the screen lifted up into the ceiling. As she sat down, she was careful not to look at Ash or me. Instead, she focused on Angie.

"It means we can move to the next stage," she said. The unsatisfying answer annoyed Colonel Cornwell as much as me.

"What does that mean, Doctor?" he said in a hard voice.

In a clinical voice Matley started to explain how they had been studying trials on animals for some time and had some positive results in creating DS. They all had the same thing in common: all test subjects had progressed stages of cancer and were all female with a high hormone count.

"If we are ever to find a defense against Mortem, we need to be able to make our military defenses impervious against the virus, meaning mostly men. That means creating a way to inoculate them," Matley said. She glanced around the table in search of approval.

"Go on, Doctor," Whitfield said.

"We would like to start a human trial, and we need to do it fast before there isn't anything left to save on the eastern side of the Mississippi," she said. "We need to see whether we can—"

"You want to use us as guinea pigs," I said, cutting her off. It came out more as statement than a question.

I glanced at Ash who seemed to have almost disappeared in her chair. "Not a chance in hell," I added in a firm voice. We didn't run from one mad scientist to be poked and prodded by another. Ash looked up and seemed appreciative of my answer.

Matley immediately started to explain, but I wasn't listening. I got up out of my seat and turned to Ash. She pushed her seat from the table and let herself be picked up.

With Ash in my arms, I strutted to the door. The fact we were in a high-security military facility kind of sank in when the soldier who had been making notes at his desk stood and blocked our way. Anger started to surge through my veins. *Who the hell did these people think they were?* Did they think they could just do as they pleased as long as their reasons were just? Well, fuck them. I turned on my heel ready to spew my guts as Angie spoke up.

"Mags, please listen for a moment."

I glared at her. She helped us get out of that

place in Florida, why? So we could trade it for this?

Angie stood at the table—they all stood—their eyes fixed on Ash and me.

"They don't want to test you," she said in a strained voice. "That would kind of defeat the purpose. You're already impervious to the virus."

I glanced around the room, running Matley's words over in my mind as I ran through the different phases in my mind. One, hormones, cancer, Mortem—subject, i.e. me, survived, check. Two, cancer, Mortem and some added hormones—subject named Ash survived, check. Three, add a combination of hormones and cancer—I had no idea how that would work, but it seemed the logical step. Angie was right—it would be a waste of time to test on us.

The concerned faces across the room suggested that it wouldn't be as easy as it sounded inside my head. I walked toward the table. Ash was getting heavy in my arms and sat her down on the tabletop.

"I'm listening," I said.

Except for the soldier who had returned to sit at his desk, everyone stood. Matley leaned forward, placing her knuckles on the table as she spoke.

"Agent Meadow is our best candidate for initiating phase two."

Angie didn't flinch at Matley's words, although her complexion had turned paler. It seemed we had done a similar math, but mine didn't add up. Hadn't we passed that stage?

"I don't get it," I said. "You already know that phase works—we've seen it with Ash."

"Actually we don't," Matley replied. "We need the solution to work as a vaccine, which means we have to synthesize it using your blood, and then there is the matter of the evolved state of the virus."

I shuddered at the memory of the zombies I had seen that seemed as if they'd been aware of what they'd become but couldn't do a damn thing about it. Dr. David had done something to them to make it worse—that's what Angie had said back at the lab in Florida.

"We need a viable test case to monitor the results before we can continue with the next phase," Matley continued. "And at this point, we have no guarantees."

"So how dangerous is it then?" Ash asked.

"It's dangerous, but I'm afraid we are not asking for permission to perform those tests," Matley said. "Nor are we asking you two—at least not in a way you might think." Her words came out calculated and cold and sounded similar to Dr. David's. A chill ran down my spine at the thought of the two of them working together. Before I could respond, Mars slammed his fist on the table.

"What are her chances?" Mars said. He had been silent for so long, but I think he had enough of Dr. Matley—as had I.

"About fifty-fifty," Matley said without an ounce of second-guessing.

"Wait, what are you sayin'?" Ash interjected. "There is a fifty-fifty chance Angie is goin' to turn into a zombie, and you want us to be okay with that." I locked with her wide-eyed gaze. There was fear in those eyes, something I had wished I wouldn't face again. She shifted her butt over the table to get a better view of everyone. "Does anyone else think that's wrong?"

"Sir," Mars said straitening his back, "this is unacceptable, I will not have you force one of my agents—"

Whitfield cut him off and said, "Agent Marsden, at this point I am hoping that the ladies decided that we need their help, and they'd be willing to give it. We are not in the habit of forcing things."

He directed his gaze at Dr. Matley. "Is that understood?" he said. Matley didn't answer but nodded.

This statement from the general didn't settle my nerves—the bigger the stakes, the easier it became to run morals out the door. Ash knew this as well and even voiced it by yelling at Dr. Matley, "I never should have come to you in the first place, you bitch."

Unable to face Ash, I closed my eyes and took in a deep breath. I couldn't let myself panic; I needed to be calm if only for Ash.

"I think we need a break," I said. Without waiting for Whitfield's reaction, I lifted Ash up from the table. This time the soldier at the desk didn't try to stop me, so I opened the door and stepped inside the hall.

"We'll be back in ten," Angie said behind me, but I didn't wait for her and stomped off to the bathroom down the hall.

Inside the bathroom, I checked if the stalls were empty before I sat Ash down on one of the toilets. I knew our guards—who hadn't left our side since we'd arrived—would be standing outside by the door, but I didn't care.

As I kneeled in front of her, wide eyes stared back at me, and her expression seemed locked in place. Her gaze went straight through me.

"Hey," I said, "remember to breathe." She blinked and refocused.

"It's not fair," she said. Her words echoed in the tiled space. "Why does this happen to u—" she started to say and I broke her off.

"Don't think of it that way," I said, pushing a strand of hair from her face. "A lot of bad things happen to all kinds of people. I don't think fairness has anything to do with it. Besides, we're still here while we shouldn't have been." She let out a breath and opened her mouth to speak when there was a knock on the stall door and Angie's face peeked inside. She glanced over her shoulder before she snuck in. Amusement graced her face.

"That was quite an exit you made," she said. "I thought Colonel Cornwell was having a fit when you left." Her smile widened when she stepped inside the stall and knelt on Ash's other side. "He argued with Mars about your rudeness when I followed you out," she said.

"They can shove their military protocols up where the sun don't shine," I said.

Angie chuckled a laugh. It turned out Angie had actually a great laugh, and I could see it lightened Ash's mood.

"So, what's up," she said. "You okay, kid." Without warning, Ash smacked a fist into Angie's upper arm.

"Don't call me kid."

Angie laughed harder at that. "I think she'll be okay," she said to me. It became eerily silent after that as we hunkered down in the tinny stall next to a toilet. My legs started to protest when I felt the pins and needles in my feet.

"What are you going to do?" I asked Angie.

"What can I do?" she said with a shrug. "Damned if I do and damned if I don't, but I'm not alone in the decision making here."

Our gazes locked before my head rocked back against the stall. She was right—Matley wanted all our participation.

"Whitfield said he wouldn't force you, and I surely won't, especially not this one," Angie said and rubbed a hand through Ash's hair. Ash looked up, but she still seemed dazed.

"And you think he'd keep his word?" I asked her.

Angie smirked in a what-do-you-think kind of way. "I guess not," I added.

Another awkward silence fell in our confined space. Angie shifted to her butt, and I followed her example, although her short legs fitted better inside the stall than mine did.

For a moment, I watched the scrawny kid sitting on the closed lid of a toilet in the blue flight suit that matched her eyes. The sight of her triggered a chuckle that forced its way up my throat, but I managed to bite my lip in time to stifle it. Her eyes narrowed with suspicion.

"What?" she asked. I shook my head and pulled at the fabric that had crept up her leg. I don't know why, but suddenly it became clear what I needed to do. All I wanted was to keep this kid safe, and if I volunteered, I might be able to keep Ash out of Matley's clutches.

"I hate to be the devil's advocate here, and please don't punch me," Angie said. I raised an eyebrow and glanced at her sideways. "Don't look at me like that. I've been getting a somewhat aggressive vibe from you today, and I'm sure Matley would agree."

I grinned at her, but the smile on Angie's face quickly dissipated.

"We could make a deal to keep her out of it," she said.

"I was thinking the same thing," I replied.

I still absently nodded in agreement as Ash's

head jerked up.

"Wait, what?" The expression on her face had gone from a vulnerable teenager to defiant one. "You're both goin' to do this willingly because you think it might stop them from usin' me?" She glared at us in turn. "You're crazy. These are the good guys, remember? They wouldn't do that: the general promised."

I could see the confusion in her face as she thought about it. Ash is not an idiot, and she must have noticed how Matley saw us as if we were just another science project, but in the end, she had always been a bigger sell on hope than me, and I guessed her sense of hope transcended her rational thought.

"These aren't bad people," Angie said tapping Ash's arm with a finger and, drawing her attention. "But there are bigger issues out there than us, and they need to address them. A survivor more or less isn't a concern to them."

"But ..." Ash stopped herself from finishing the sentence. "I know ... I just hoped," Ash said at a whisper.

"Hope sucks," I said, "and we have to look out for ourselves." Ash angled her head to inspect the floor.

"I don't need you to protect me," she said. "I don't want you to—" Angie didn't let her finish the sentence.

"That's where you don't have a choice, and

don't worry: it's not because you're a kid." This time I punched Angie in the arm. Both of them looked at me with raised eyebrows.

"You've carried enough weight to last a lifetime," I said as I scrambled to my feet. Ash was brought into this world by her parents with one purpose and that was to save her sister Alison. Those parents hadn't expected that sisterly love to grow so big that Alison took her own life to safe Ash from further turmoil and examinations. Although I believed Ash would have continued doing it for the rest of her life if it meant keeping Alison in it.

I leaned in to kiss the top of her head. "Now it's our turn," I said. She glanced up with a sad look on her face.

"Oh, come on, enough with the puppy dog eyes," Angie said as she got to her feet. "We have a very pissed off colonel waiting for us out there along with a general and some other folk. Let's see if we can piss them off some more."

With a grin on her face, she stepped out of the stall and trotted to the bathroom door, which she held open for us. Ash glanced from Angie to me and shrugged. I answered with a shrug of my own and bent down to pick her up.

20

It didn't turn out to be a hard negotiation. None of them seemed eager to use a kid for their research, not even Matley. Although I got a sense that it wouldn't have stopped them in the name of the greater good if we hadn't threatened to sabotage their work.

Relief hit me as Mars picked up Ash from the chair next to mine. We had come to an agreement, and Mars would look after Ash while Angie and I got to spend some time in the lab with Matley.

Before he raised himself to his full height with Ash in his arms, he paused and whispered into my ear.

"We'll see you later, okay," he said. I nodded and watched him exit the room. Ash lifted a hand in good-bye as she peered over Mars's shoulder, a grim expression on her face. It was when the door clicked shut that my relief transformed into unease. *What had I gotten myself into?* A glance at Angie told me she wasn't too happy about it either.

After Mars and Ash had left, a young woman in plain clothes entered the room. She looked like secretary and was holding a file folder. As she handed it to General Whitfield, she whispered something in his ear. Something changed in the general's posture as he nodded, and the woman quickly left the room.

"Let's wrap this up," he said in a stern voice. It seemed something more important had found the general's attention.

This didn't sit well with me—frankly, it pissed me off. These were our lives, and they were playing with them like chess pieces on a board. Although on an intellectual level I knew bigger things were at stake and the general had a whole lot more on his plate, I couldn't help feeling resentful toward him for rushing us out.

"I know this won't be easy for you, and we appreciate your taking the risks that you do, but we can't afford to leave a single stone unturned in our war against this virus," he said, rising out of his seat. "Still, we aren't in the business of treating people like lab rats, so if there is anything you need or if you have questions, please address them to Colonel Cornwell. He'll be overseeing this project."

Whitfield gestured at Cornwell, who had remained seated at the table. After that, he left the room while Angie and I were rushed into the lab.

Sitting in a corner of the lab, I looked away from the tube as it filled with my blood. Dr. Matley loosened the strap around my upper arm while her eyes never left the tube. My legs dangled over the edge of the bed I was sitting on, and I glanced around the room. Angie sat in another corner of the room, a lab technician hovering over her. They sat far enough away that I couldn't tell what the man was doing or what they were saying, but I guessed it probably involved tubes and needles.

Dr. Matley's lab was uncharacteristically empty, considering the rest of the mountain base. You couldn't go anywhere in this place without bumping into one person or another. Matley had created her own private little island buried underneath the earth.

"Have you known each other for long?" Dr. Matley said. Her voice pulled me back to our little corner of the lab.

"Who?" I asked, unsure if she meant Ash or Angie. She looked up with a kind smile.

"Special Agent in Charge Marsden," she replied with a mock grin. I wasn't expecting that, and guessed she must have seen us. It wasn't as if we'd tried to hide this newly formed relationship, although I wasn't that eager to share the details with Matley.

"A year or so," I said, which was somewhat the truth even if I had seen him only on about three of the three hundred and sixty-five days. "Why?"

"You seem close," she said. I watched as she switched a tube of blood for an empty one. I wondered what was on her mind but refused to ask.

"This is a dangerous game you play," she finally said.

I turned to her in surprise. What was did she mean?

"What's it to you," I bit out. She wiped a speck of blood from my arm with some cotton and then finished loading the filled tubes onto her tray.

"I'm not judging you," she said as she turned from the bed, "but you are a risk to people."

My mouth must have fallen open, because for a moment I couldn't form words.

"What does that mean?" I said.

I could feel the resentment that I had previously accumulated toward this woman build up further, and she must have heard it in my voice. She set the tray down and turned to face me. Her butt rested against the table as she crossed her arms.

"You might appear to be a healthy person, Ms. Vissers, but you are still infected and that means you are a threat to people."

My stomach dropped, and all of a sudden I felt sick. The metal edges of the bed cut into my fingers as I gripped it tighter. Thoughts raced inside my head. *Could I pass the infection on to others? What would it do to them? Would they turn into a zombie? Was it already too late? Oh my God, Mars.*

"I'm not trying to scare you, but you need to be careful," Matley said, breaking into my thoughts. She stepped closer and placed her hand on my shoulder. I tensed up at her touch. I didn't like this woman, and in that white lab coat of hers, she reminded me too much of Dr. David. She must have noticed because she squeezed my shoulder once and then let go.

"I know there is no reason for you to trust me, considering my behavior," she said. "Although in my defense, I am looking out for the world."

She paused as if she wanted a reaction, but continued after I ignored her.

"It's not as if you should be treated as a leper," she said, "but be careful with the extracurricular activities. I mean ... look at it as if it were HIV."

I glared at her in shock. She had this fake concern plastered on her face. It had to be fake—this woman didn't give a shit about Angie, Ash, or me for that matter.

"Is this supposed to make me feel better?" I said aloud.

On the other side of the room, I could see Angie's head poke up and turn in our direction. Our eyes met, and I shook my head.

"Everything all right?" Angie shouted from across the room.

"Fine," I replied in a strained voice. After a moment, Angie returned her attention to her own lab tech, and I took in a deep breath to calm myself. Matley shifted her feet and then moved around the bed.

"Now, I would like to start with a cervical smear, get the annoying bits out of the way first," she said in that clinical voice I'd started to hate. *How could a person hit you with news like that and then be all-businesslike a second later?* The stupidity of the thought hit a moment later. I'd come across these people most of my life. Regular doctors in a hospital acted the same way—they had to. This was a job to them. One moment they'd be telling someone she was about to die, and a moment later, they'd be asking someone out for a cappuccino.

I looked up at Matley, who stood in front of me, waiting. The sickening feeling in my stomach rose, and I felt the color drain from my face. Matley raised an eyebrow, unaware for the reasons of my discomfort and oblivious to the fact she had told me I might have infected Mars with Mortem.

"Ah, yes, the wonderful things about being a woman," she said.

Dr. Matley had kept her examinations to the strict necessities and a day later weren't even memorable. She needed some time to do her thing, and while Mars remained on active duty, Ash, Angie, and I had some time to kill. Mars had Angie almost forcibly removed from one of the control rooms. I had the privilege of being witness to that conversation, although it hadn't been pretty. She had pained Mars by not telling him about her cancer, and it told me how much he cared about his partner and friend.

Taking her off duty was probably a good thing because I didn't think her head was in it. I surely knew my head was all over the place, and I needed a distraction. It had brought us to the recreation room, which turned out to be a big gym. The guy who took care of all the equipment had told us that before the outbreak, the room had been packed with people throughout the day. Most employees belonged to the military and wanted to keep their bodies fit. But with the outbreak, priorities had shifted, and except for a couple of muscular types throwing around weights, the room was empty.

Ash had decided on honing her basketball skills. As she explained it, she needed to work on her game, although I doubted she had held a basketball before in her life. This meant I had to be the opponent or something while Angie sat on a bench with her knees pulled to her chest as she watched us.

Rap music blared over the tiny speakers of my phone, but with the constant pounding of the ball, it disappeared into nothingness. Fortunately, one of the people on staff here had a spare charger. We only owned the charger that we had used inside the Knight and it wouldn't fit into any of the outlets. Ash would have been intolerable if we hadn't found a way to charge the damn thing.

Two airmen stood in the corner to watch over us while Ash rolled around the court. She knew how to use that chair better than most people walked, and even dribbling a ball seemed to come natural to her. Scoring or even reaching the hoop turned out to be a greater challenge.

I, however, had no problem hitting the hoop or the board, but then bouncing off didn't count as a point.

"Son of a ..." Ash called out when her effort grazed the net. I caught the ball in a rebound and stopped at the line for a three-point shot. Lo and behold, it went in.

"Oh," I exclaimed, "nothing but net!" With that, I ignored the fact the ball bounced about three times before it went in.

"Are you kiddin' me," Ash said as she retrieved the ball. "You're not allowed to walk with the ball. You fouled that one."

"Don't give me semantics. I nailed it," I said. unable to mask the broad smile on my face.

"Ahh, bite me," Ash muttered. I waved her the bird while I moved to the bench to grab a towel. All this exercise had caused me to sweat, although I didn't feel the exhaustion of running around on this court for an hour and a half as much as I used to. Apart from being infected with zombie juice, I was in the best shape of my life. Still, I'd had enough for today and sat down next to Angie while I watched Ash put in some more effort.

Angie kept a stoic face as she watched the court. I wondered if she even noticed Ash's antics. A game of basketball had kept my mind off things for a while, but one look at Angie kicked my thoughts into gear. I hadn't had the chance to talk to Mars yet; Whitfield called him in last night after dinner, and I hadn't seen him since. The look he gave me, though, after he wanted to kiss good-bye as I turned my cheek from him, had kept me up during the night. Being close to him was a risk I couldn't take, and I know I should have talked to him, but that didn't come easily. I wasn't ready to let go.

"You seem like you're in a galaxy far away," Angie said as she stared out at the court.

"In a spaceship next to yours, I guess."

"Nah," Angie started. "I'm way ahead of you."

"I doubt it."

Angie glanced at me sideways, stretched her legs out, and leaned back.

"Did Matley give you the infection speech?" she asked. "The one where you shouldn't think of yourself as a leper? She told me I had that to look forward too—*if* their synthesized version of your blood works on me."

Mimicking her posture, I leaned back and stretched out my legs, although mine were a lot longer. I let out a long sigh.

"I guess she has," Angie said. "I'm telling you, that woman doesn't have a subtle bone in her body."

I didn't know how to respond to that; it didn't matter how she told us. The problem was she had told me too late—it might be too late. Angie didn't wait for my reply; it seemed she already knew what I was thinking.

"I noticed your little exchange with Mars last night, or should I say lack of," Angie said. I shot her a hard look, warning her to tread carefully—but who was I kidding? This was Agent Meadow, gun-slinging FBI agent, and it didn't stop her from continuing her sentence. "I'm sorry," she said. I looked at her in surprise. Those weren't the words I expected.

"What," she said, reacting to the expression on my face, "you thought I'd go lecture you on telling him?"

I blinked and then shook my head.

"I don't know," I said under my breath. "Maybe."

Angie sat up, resting her arms on her knees. "Maybe he won't care," she said, tilting her head sideways. I stared at her dark eyes for a moment. Angie knew Mars better than I did, although I didn't know for how long they had worked together. Maybe he wouldn't care, but that wouldn't mean it was smart to continue a relationship—especially not where certain physical contact could be lethal.

"It doesn't matter," I said, sitting up. "I won't take that risk."

We sat in silence for a moment, listening to a blues track called "So Many Roads" between the thumping of Ash's ball. The live track didn't seem to fit the rest of the playlist.

"Hey," Angie said as she nudged my shoulder. Her face held a mischievous grin, and her dark eyes gleamed. "Maybe the serum works, and they'll inoculate everyone on the planet. Then we won't have a problem."

I grinned, but it quickly faded.

About ten minutes later, Ash gave up without

having sunk one ball.

"Maybe you should try it with a tennis ball," I said. A moment later the basketball flew my way. It bounced of my fist, and Ash caught the rebound. She stopped about an inch from my feet with a cheeky grin.

"Here," I said as I threw her a towel. Along with the sweat on her brows, her grin disappeared. I ignored her thoughtful expression to loosen my shoelaces. While the loud and obnoxious Ash wasn't always easy to bear, the silent, brooding Ash was even worse. I looked up at her and raised an eyebrow. "What?" I asked.

"You two haven't said anything about your visits to the lab," she said.

"Not much to say," I replied with a shrug. "It went okay." I could almost see her ponder her next words.

"It'll work, right?" she finally asked. I tapped my foot against her chair, unsure what to answer—I didn't want to lie to her.

"It's all this complicated scientific stuff, and we don't know," Angie said when I didn't reply. "I guess we will find out soon enough."

I watched Ash fiddle with her towel, but she refused to make eye contact with me. One of the airmen who stood at the door started to approach us, and Ash's gaze shifted to him. He stopped a few feet from us and cleared his throat. I looked up to face him.

"Agent Marsden called down," he said in a formal tone. "He wanted to know whether you would join him for lunch."

Shit was the only thing I could think as I stared up at the man. He patiently watched us, waiting for an answer. Angie stepped in when it didn't come from me.

"We'll meet him in the mess in an hour," she said.

I managed to nod a *thank you* at the airman and then had to swallow hard as I turned to Ash and Angie.

"Guess it's time to hit the showers," I said.

21

Lunch came and went in the form of a coarse meal engulfed by awkward silences. I purposefully didn't sit down next to Mars, instead opting for the seat next to Ash. It felt safer to have him at a distance, but it turned out to be the same mistake I had made with the seating arrangement in the boardroom. He kept watching me with those pale jade eyes, careful at first, adding a caring smile, but as the meal progressed, I could see concern rise to the surface when I failed to respond to his gestures.

I followed Ash and Angie down the hall as we walked to our room, Mars by my side. His hands sat hidden in his pockets and his chin all but touched his chest. His head perked up a couple of times, and I thought he might say something, but then I just caught him watching me. Maybe he was waiting for me to speak. After all, I was the one acting weird and I should have been the one to speak, but I just couldn't get Matley's words out of my head. What would I say to him?

We weaved through crowds of soldiers wearing greens and blue until we cornered a hall nearing our sleeping quarters. It seemed that our rooms were chosen on purpose, separated from the rest. The hall sat abandoned as Angie opened the door to let Ash roll inside. She waited for me at the door, a sullen expression on her face. The two soldiers guarding us took up their usual post.

Angie stood her ground in the door opening and didn't move as I gestured to her to go in. She eyed me for a moment and then turned her gaze to Mars. After she cleared her throat she said, "I know I sort of said I wouldn't tell you what to do, but you're depressing me and the kid, so get a room and talk it out." With that, she stepped inside and slammed the door shut.

"I'm not a kid," Ash's muffled voice came from behind the door.

I blinked at the closed door, startled by what had happened. Next to me Mars had a similar startled expression. Our two guards, though, couldn't contain a smirk.

Mars nodded at the men as he took my arm. "She'll be back," he said.

The men didn't reply, but one of them conspicuously cleared his throat. I turned around and glared at them both. Mars guided me across the hall to his room.

Inside I found a similar space to ours, except there stood one bunk bed instead of two, with a desk shoved against the other wall. Papers covered the desk, and clothes hung over the chair beside it.

Mars closed the door behind me, and I drew in a long breath. This was it, the moment I'd been dreading ever since Matley dropped the *you're-infected* bomb on me.

"You've been avoiding me," Mars said. His warm voice fell over me, and I knew I shouldn't let it in. If I did, it might prevent me from saying what needed to be said. My arms wrapped across my waist to steady myself. Unable to turn around, I opened my mouth to speak, but froze as his arms wrapped around me. His warm breath caressed my neck before he followed it with a soft kiss.

"You're not having second thoughts, are you?" he whispered near my ear.

"I ..." I started to say, but hesitated. His arms released me, and he gently turned me around. He narrowed his eyes, gazing at me thoughtfully as if he were looking for a way to get inside my head.

"What are you afraid of?" he asked. I peered into his eyes, those beautiful pale jade eyes that usually made the reality around me fade away, but this time the added worry kept me in place. Without thinking I said, "That I turn you into a zombie."

His eyes grew wide at my admission. Internally I scolded myself for my Dutch subtlety. It lasted but a moment before that familiar twinkle in his eyes returned. His mouth drew into that brilliant smile. It wasn't the reaction I had expected.

"Matley told me ... I can't ... I don't want to ..." I said, fumbling the words in an attempt to explain. Great timing to start messing up the language again. My mouth clamped shut as Mars wrapped his arms around me and pulled me close.

"I knew that," he said, looking relieved.

I glared at him in disbelief, before he added, "I thought you'd read my note and had changed you mind."

What note? Became my final coherent thought before his lips pressed to mine.

My back leaned against the door as my hand ran though his jet-black hair. Mars had pulled the zipper of my flight suit down to my belly button and had his face buried in my neck while his hands were elsewhere. Some form of rational thinking returned to me before his hands ventured into the place that would have made that impossible.

"Stop," I whispered and repeated it a little louder when he didn't respond. "Mars … Stop."

He pulled away reluctantly, but far enough to gaze into my eyes. His heavy breathing hit my face in waves as his chest heaved.

"We can't just … ignore … this …" I said, panting as hard as he was.

"I have protection, so don't worry about it," he said as lowered his head to nuzzle my neck. I sighed, indulging him for a moment and then pushed him in the shoulder.

Surprised, he stepped back as I turned away from him. I pulled the flight suit over my shoulder and zipped it up to cover my chest. There weren't many places to sit inside the room except the bed, and that didn't seem like the best option now. I took it anyway.

I plopped down on the bed and pressed my face into my hands. I heard another zipper go up, and then a hand pressed to my back as Mars sat down next to me. He pulled my hands from my face and forced me to look at him.

"I know what this virus does," he said in a low voice. "I've known the moment that creature sank its teeth into your skin on I-678 that if you survived, Mortem would always remain in your system."

With a finger, he traced my neckline to the discolored scar tissue that peeked out from under my flight suit—an unpleasant reminder of what zombies could do to a person. Then he pulled me into his arms and kissed the top of my head. "I've been investigating this thing for a long time, even from before the outbreak," he continued. "Trust me: I know what it does."

"It scares me," I said into his shoulder. "I don't want to be the one-" I broke off. I couldn't even say it aloud because I could never forgive myself if Mars turned into a mindless rotting corpse because of me.

"Maybe if you'd learn more about it and understand it better," he said. "We could take it slow until then, so you could get more comfortable to the idea."

The doubt in his voice was palpable but combined with hope. He wanted me to give us a chance. I nodded, afraid my voice would betray my own doubt, and leaned into him.

When I returned to our room, Angie looked up expectantly from the magazine she'd been reading. I shook my head that I didn't want to talk about it.

"Not now, okay," I said at a whisper. She let out a breath, and returned to her magazine without a word.

Ash lay on the top bunk on her stomach facing the wall. Music blared from her earbuds, and her eyes were glued to the pages of a book. She hadn't even heard me come in, and I decided to leave it at that. I climbed into my bunk and turned to face the wall.

It wasn't as if my conversation with Mars had gone wrong or badly, but it hadn't exactly eased my mind. I should have broken it off with him. Instead I let him talk me into taking it slow. I knew everything I needed to know about this virus: if you caught it without the proper hormone levels or a touch of cancer, you'd turn into a mostly brain-dead, rotting, living corpse that ate human beings for breakfast, lunch, and dinner.

My hand reached under the mattress as I remembered the note Mars had mentioned. He had given it to me as a sort of peace offering. He had learned things about me during his investigation into Dr. David, and he wanted to level it out by telling me about himself. The note had kind of gone forgotten that first night. My face turned red at the memory, and I pressed it into my pillow, unable to withhold a smile.

I sucked in a breath to compose myself and then pulled the note from its hiding place. As I unfolded it, I could feel my heart pick up speed inside my chest. The paper shook in my hands as I started to read. By the time I'd finished, tears streamed down my face.

Behind me, I heard the magazine drop to the floor and Angie shift on her bed.

"Mags," she said, her voice barely a whisper.

"I'm fine," I said with more force than I wanted to.

"Okay," Angie said at an even lower whisper and shifted back onto her bunk.

I buried my head into my pillow—wanting to disappear, to hide from it all and crumpled the piece of paper in my hand.

22

An airman nodded at me before he opened the door to the small waiting area. The room linked to Dr. Matley's lab turned out to be similar to it but a different one from the room Angie and I had visited before. As in the other room, a large window gave a perfect view of the people buzzing next door, except here the glass was like those they used in interrogation scenes on television where you could see through one side of the glass and the other side acted as a mirror. I figured it to be the less expensive variant of the other window.

Angie sat on a gurney in the middle of the room, watching the activity on the other side of the glass. Except for a couple of chairs and a table with a pitcher of water, the room was bare.

It seemed early for Matley to start her tests, for it had only been four days since her initial examinations of Angie and me. However, Matley had access to Dr. David's research, including the data from the tests he had done on me for a long time before we showed up. I just hoped it would work and Angie wouldn't turn into a zombie.

"Nice dress," I said as I stepped inside and closed the door behind me. Angie inspected her white, paper-thin gown and shook her head.

"I love to dress up."

"Brings back memories of how I met Ash," I said, "rolling around the hospital in that old chair wearing that flimsy gown."

Angie looked up with a smirk.

"I've had a similar meeting," she said with a snorted laugh. "The kid kept worrying her naked butt stuck out."

I thought back to that first day I had met Ash and remembered the gown streaked with blood and gore, but hadn't notice if her naked butt stuck out. But then she had been sitting in either the car, the wheelchair, and later on that toilet after we entered that gas station.

"Did it?" I asked.

"Oh yeah, but I didn't tell the kid that."

"You shouldn't call her kid," I said when the nervous laughter died down. "She's been through more than most of us."

"That's why I think I should," Angie replied. "I think she needs to be reminded sometimes that she actually is a kid, you know." There seemed to merit what she said. Kids should be able to be kids. I let out a breath and nodded in agreement.

"Nervous?" I asked.

Angie plastered on a brave face and shook her head while she answered, "Hell, yeah." I raised an eyebrow at the confusing signal contradicting her words.

"Well, if you need to verbally abuse someone, I'll be right here behind the glass," I said and pointed at the window. Before she could answer, there was a crackle and a voice came over the intercom. On the other side of the window stood a middle-aged man with a thinning hairline who seemed to speak into the wall.

"It's time, Ms. Meadow." he said. Angie nodded and scooted of the bed. She turned to look up at me.

"I might take you up on that offer," she said.

"I'll be here." A faint smile twitched at her lips before her gaze dropped to the floor and the door to the decontamination area slid open.

I took up a seat in one of the chairs in front of the window. Inside the lab, Dr. Matley had set up a miniature containment area around a bed. Sheets of thick see-through plastic made up the little room. She had told us they needed to use this as a precaution because of the evolved state of the virus. It didn't surprise me that most of the occupants had left the room and that a few dressed in full biohazard gear remained behind, including Dr. Matley.

A person in a plastic suit guided Angie to the plastic room and asked her to lie down on the bed. She didn't argue when one of the men in a suit and mask started to restrain her arms and legs. Her eyes drifted to the glass wall I sat behind, and I held her gaze although I knew she wouldn't be able to see me.

The men and women in the biohazard suits all looked the same to me. They reminded me of the people working in Dr. Warren's lab. They too had worn similar suits. I had hated them while they held me at that lab, but the thought that most of them had perished in the blazing volcano that destroyed the lab wasn't a comfort. They had been similar to these men and women, working a job trying to save mankind from a zombie-turning virus.

Dr. Matley's bulk of a body stood out from the crowd. She seemed cramped in that suit like a whale in basin. It made her easier to bear, and the memories of my experiences in the Florida lab faded as I watched her work.

Behind me, the door opened, and Mars stepped inside. I had hoped he wouldn't come, but deep down I knew he'd be here for Angie. He cared about her probably even more than I did. It had been four days since we'd spoken, and I had decided to take it slow. And as I'd left his room that afternoon, I'd wanted to believe we could somehow make this work, to find a way to live with a disease as so many people had done before and not let it become a barrier that cut us off from the people we loved. But I couldn't do that. I had never been able to do it—not with my cancer, not with this, and certainly not after I'd found his note. That had changed everything, and so I had continued to avoid him.

I could tell it disappointed him; I could see it in

his eyes, but he honored my approach, probably thinking I was taking it at a snail's pace. As hard as I fought to smother the fire that still burned in both of us, it was also me that kept it alive, and I hated myself for it.

Wordlessly he sat down by my side and draped an arm around my shoulder. I wanted to lean in, to let him comfort me, to let him reassure me Angie would be okay, but I resisted the temptation. Instead, I stepped closer to the window and pressed my forehead against the cool glass.

"I thought Ash would be here," he said after a moment of uncomfortable silence. I shifted my head so I could see him out of the corner of my eye.

"She was angry with Angie for doing this and with me for supporting it," I said. "It's probably better this way."

Mars got up to stand at my side as Dr. Matley fumbled with the plastic sheets to create an entrance large enough for her to enter the plastic room and stood by Angie's bed with a nasty looking needle. She said something I couldn't make out, but I saw Angie's head move in a nod. I forced myself to watch as the needle came down and plunged into Angie's arm.

Dr. Matley stepped out, shifting the sheets of plastic and addressed the room.

"Now, we wait."

With that, she moved to one of the desks with a series of computers stacked on top and what I presumed was a man sitting behind them. Except for Dr. Matley, the suits made the people inside the room indistinguishable. I couldn't make out their conversation or what they pointed at on the screens, but they seemed to be in agreement.

For the better part of the morning Mars and I kept alternating between standing at the window and sitting in one of the chairs as we watched the mostly idle activity inside the lab.

The procedure took place in two steps. First, they would inoculate Angie with my version of the Divus serum, and once they felt confident it had taken, they would inject her with the latest form of Mortem. This meant the new strain conjured by Dr. David, which gave the zombies awareness. For being the test subject, Angie seemed the most comfortable of us all. After a few hours, my back started to ache from sitting on a plastic stool while she seemed to have dozed off on the bed.

I got up to stretch my legs and poured myself a glass of water from the pitcher on the table.

"You want some," I asked Mars. He shook his head, but then he stood and made his way to me. His butt leaned against the table while he took my hand in his. He leaned in to kiss me, but as I had done in the mess, I turned my head away from him. Instead of pulling back, he pressed his forehead against my temple.

"This isn't taking it slow," he said at a whisper. "This is pushing me away."

"I'm not ..." I started to say as I took a step back from him, but stopped myself.

Mars folded his arms across his chest and clenched his jaw. He waited for me to speak as his eyes bored into me. It was as if the world had disappeared from underneath my feet, and I was about to free fall into eternity. I wanted to run, but my feet and this place wouldn't let me. This wasn't fair to him, and I needed him to move on.

My hand shook as I pulled the crumpled pieces of paper from my pocket and started to unfold it.

"I read it," I said in a quivering voice. He nodded without changing the expression on his face. "You have a son."

Mars lifted his chin and narrowed his eyes as if he expected me to say that. When he didn't reply I added, "And he lives with his grandparents in California."

I still felt the anger that rushed through me after I had read that last word—California. He had lied to me. He had lied when he had left that message on my phone about his family living in Colorado. Had it been all a ploy to get us here, to help Matley with her research? He hadn't told them about us after we arrived, so the stupid girl with a crush hoped he had done it to get her here, because he wanted to be with her. Feeling stupid for hoping, I forced the thought from my mind. It didn't matter—the sooner he realized I'd be a risk to him and the rest of his family, the sooner none of this would matter any longer.

"His name is Rowdy, and he's three years old," he said. His eyes lit up for as much as he let them at the mention of his little boy. It made me relax a little.

"This boy needs you," I said, "and I can't be a part of that. I'm not going to risk you or that boy."

Mars closed his eyes and shook his head.

"That's it," he said as he opened his eyes. "You're going to use my son against me, my own son." For the first time, I could hear anger in his voice. "Your mom said you'd be creative in coming up with reasons to push people away."

"What did you say?" I asked in shock.

"Yeah, I finally managed to get a call through last night, nice lady," he said. "She told me some things that made a lot of sense about that person you didn't want me to get to know."

"You talked to my mom," I said in exasperation, "but ... how-" Mars cut me off and I couldn't get the words over his rant—he was on a roll.

"She told me how you pushed everyone out of your life, and not in the nicest way, I might add, all in the pretense that you were protecting them," he said. "Your mom, your dad, brother, and sister, even your friends. I think the last one is still sitting in an infirmary at JFK. Did you even care how it made them feel?"

Tears stung my eyes at him mentioning my family and Emily, who I had left behind at JFK after she had become infected. It didn't stop Mars from throwing words at me. I had never seen him like this. All I knew was this calm, collected warrior.

"Except it is not about protecting others, is it? You're only protecting yourself," he said in a venomous tone. The words hit me like a sledgehammer.

"It's not about people losing you. It's about you. You're so afraid of loss, you won't even let anyone in in the first place."

His gaze honed in on me, and I could see the anger burning inside his eyes. I couldn't handle the truth he revealed and took another step back.

"But what about me, huh," he said. "What about the people that need you? What about the kid?"

"Leave Ash out of it," I said in a loud voice.

"You're gonna leave her too when it gets too hard."

At that, I slapped him in the face. He had hit a nerve.

"Get the fuck out," I shouted. Inside the lab, biohazard suits shifted their heads to the mirror, and Angie's head perked up. Subtlety wasn't my strong suit, but at this point I couldn't tell what I was feeling—anger, fear, shame, or all of the above. Mars let out a breath as he watched me. Then he walked to the door. He lingered for a moment before he turned back to me.

"You're not getting rid of me that easy," he said

and stepped out.

It was as if, when that door clicked shut, gravity kicked in pulling me down. I balled my fist in an attempt to stop my hands from shaking and slummed against the wall. I sank to the ground and pulled my knees up to my chest. My mind raced, running through the conversations of my past. It wasn't long before tears streamed down my face.

Something rattled inside the lab. It sounded like a tray or something falling to the ground. A glance at the clock told me it had been five hours since they'd put Angie on that bed. I still hadn't left my corner of the room, and I gathered myself up from the floor. My muscles ached as I pulled them out of my crouched position and wiped the residual tears from my face.

At the window, I could see Angie was awake. Why wouldn't she be? She'd been sleeping for most of the day. Behind me, the door cracked open and my heart sank. I wasn't up for another visit from Mars.

"Hey," a tiny voice said. Ash's head poked through the opening.

"Ash, you okay?" I asked. She sounded nothing like the loud obnoxious teenager I knew, which had me somewhat worried.

"What's taking so long?" she asked. I looked out the window where Matley waddled to Angie's bed with another big needle.

"They're ready to start phase two."

Ash pushed the door open further and rolled her chair to the mirror, and I noticed my backpack hanging of the back of the chair. The thin white earplug cables ran out from it and rested on Ash's shoulder. I made some room and closed the door behind her.

"Are you sure you want to be here?" I asked.

She shook her head, but added, "I think I should, you know."

I claimed a seat at her side and watched Matley maneuver between the plastic sheets. The sight of that alone would have been enough to get on Comedy Central. Ash glanced at me sideways for a moment before she turned in full to face me.

"Have you been crying?" she asked with a combination of surprise and concern.

"No," I answered in a defiant tone, squinting my eyes and keeping them from Ash's field of vision.

"You have," she said, convinced. "What happened?"

I didn't really want to discuss my nonexistent love life while someone was about to infect a friend with a deadly virus, and I sure as hell didn't want to discuss it with Ash.

"It's nothing. I got something in my eye," I said. "Now shut up. They're injecting Angie." Luckily, at this point she cared more about Angie than bawling, and she shifted her attention.

| 23

Angie didn't even wince when the needle dug deep into her skin. Ash, however, sucked in a sharp breath as if the needle had broken her own skin. Her eyes followed Dr. Matley intently as the woman in the too-tight suit made her way to one of her stations. Matley checked a monitor with what I expected were Angie's vitals. Another one of the suits joined her, and they seemed content as they examined the data.

Matley stopped at another table and then made her way over to the airlock to decontaminate her suit. She had been inside the lab for as long as I had been sitting in this tiny room. I wondered if she expected the virus kicking in would take as much time as the Divus serum. If that were so, I could use a break myself. I had allowed myself to stray off to a bathroom, but that hadn't helped with the hunger that started to stir.

As if on cue a growl erupted from my midriff, and I placed a hand on my stomach as if I could soothe it.

Ash looked up with a smile. "You want me to ask one of the airmen if he can get you somethin' to eat?"

"I doubt they'll let themselves be used as our hired hands," I said.

"Then you just don't know how to ask," Ash said. "It needs a little flair." I turned to face her.

"Yeah," I said, "how would you do it?" From out of nowhere Ash's eye grew wide and her lower lip puckered. I snorted a laugh. "That'll never work." She shrugged and backed up her wheelchair.

"Watch and learn," she said as she rolled to the door and opened it.

Through the opening, I could see one of the airmen kneel in front of her. I couldn't believe my ears as I heard how she charmed the man. He gave her a kind smile and stood to leave from my sight.

Ash closed the door and faced the room with the biggest grin. "He couldn't promise he'd manage a turkey special sandwich, but said he would try." I just shook my head.

"You are amazing," I said with a mock grin. Ash bowed and then rolled her chair by my side.

My mind wandered as we waited for the food to arrive. I couldn't get my conversation with Mars out of my head, and I glanced at Ash a couple of times. *Did he really believe I'd abandon her? Would I abandon her?* I gave myself a mental shake in an attempt to avoid wallowing in self-doubt.

Inside the lab, Angie seemed to take a turn for the worse. Although she had slept through most of the Divus trial, I could tell this wouldn't be a cakewalk. Her wrist strained against the restraints, and her face contorted from what I imagined to be pain. Ash picked up on it and nudged my shoulder.

"Yeah, I see," I said at a whisper.

One of the suits sat at a table with his back turned to Angie, and the other suit stood at the far end of the lab. They both couldn't see Angie's pained expression or the way she fought her restrains. Minutes ticked away. I tapped a nervous foot on the floor until Ash placed her hand on my knee. Something was wrong—we both knew it. I banged a fist on the glass and shouted to get the attention of one of the suits inside the lab. They either ignored me or couldn't hear me inside those masks. My eyes darted from the lab to the inside of this stupid room before I saw it.

An intercom panel sat on the wall next to the window. That doctor's voice had come through that panel when he asked Angie to enter the lab. I stood to inspect it. The panel had one button and a kind of microphone. I glanced over my shoulder to look at Ash.

"Do it," she said anxiously. I pressed the button and spoke.

"Eh, doctors in suits, I think you need to check on your patient." The man at the table jerked up at the sound of my voice. His masked face swung to the window before it went to Angie. He stood abruptly, hopefully noticing something was wrong, and I saw his mouth move. A colleague of his also got to his feet before he sprinted to the exit, probably to get Dr. Matley. Then he just stood there watching Angie.

"What is that ass doin'?" Ash said.

"Come on, do something," I spoke over the intercom. The man glanced at me over his shoulder and shrugged.

"I can't believe he just shrugged," Ash said, rolling her chair closer to the glass as someone knocked on the door. I turned and saw one of the airmen enter with a tray of food. I flipped a switch on the intercom panel so we could hear more clearly to what was happening inside the lab before I turned to the airmen. The smile on his face vanished when a scream tore through the lab. I froze at the sound of my name as it ripped through my core. Pain, fear, anger, it all resonated within that single word. The words that followed made my heart stop.

"Kill me," Angie screamed at the top of her lungs. I couldn't move. It was as if my feet were nailed to the floor. Beside me, Ash and the airman stood frozen as well as my name echoed through the lab again.

"Goddammit, Mags, where are you?"

The man in the suit glanced over his shoulder before he bolted for the decontamination room on the other side of the lab. I glanced down at Ash, who looked terrified. Then my eyes fell on the airman holding the tray of food. Somehow, it woke me out of my frozen state.

I stepped around Ash and went for the man. He still stood frozen, watching Angie struggle in her bed when I reached for his gun and pulled it from the holster. He jerked and released the tray. It clattered to the ground, but it was too late—I had his gun. I clumsily pointed it at him. His hands rose up in a reflex. Without hesitation, I made my way to the door that would lead me into the lab.

I fought my way through the thick plastic sheets of the decontamination room behind the door. Something snapped and broke, but I ignored it and bolted to the bed in the center of the room. As I stepped closer, I could see Angie watching me. Her chest rose and fell in a fast-paced rhythm. She pulled at the restraints with such force that blood started to trickle down her wrists. Even through the thick plastic, I could see her skin glisten with sweat. I sucked in a breath and swallowed hard before I grabbed a sheet of the plastic and shifted it to a side.

I wasn't ready for what I saw. It was one thing to face the infected on the streets or at an airport. Even seeing Emily, the friend I left behind at that airport after she had been bitten by a customs officers, hadn't hit me this hard. Maybe because I hadn't known what the fog swimming in front of her irises meant. But seeing Angie's eyes all fogged up scared the shit out of me. I gasped and took a step back.

Angie sensed my presence, and her milky white eyes focused on me. She blinked, and I noticed her eyes weren't as bad as those of other zombies I've seen. I took in a sharp breath and stepped closer.

"Please," she said in a raspy voice. "Kill me." I glanced down at the gun in my hand. My hand was shaking like someone with Parkinson's disease. "Please," Angie repeated. My gaze shifted to her face. Her sweat-coated skin and terrified expression was hard to look at. Still, her voice held determination within.

I lifted the gun and leveled it with her head. The shaking worsened, which forced me to add the other hand. *Could I do this?* Her eyes were focused on mine, which didn't make sense. Normally the change was quick. Emily had turned within minutes, although I hadn't noticed at first. Others changed even quicker. I held her gaze, recapturing that moment on I-678 when a stowaway zombie had sunk its teeth into my shoulder. The British flight attendant named Elizabeth with whom I had fled the airport hadn't been so lucky. She turned within seconds of the bite and ended up with a bullet in her head. I remembered how Mars had guided me to that alley to keep me from falling in the hands of the military, but then had left me to my own devices.

Then the gun that Mars had left me had shaken in my hands, just like the gun I was holding now. Although then, I'd tried to come to terms with shooting myself. I can't even recall how long I had sat there on the ground hidden behind a dumpster. Sounds and smells rattled my brain—zombies roaming at the mouth of the alley. Vague, blurry images swam across my vision. Had this thing that was happening to Angie, happened to me? Had I reacted this strongly when the virus started to invade my body? At this point the memory eluded me.

"Please," Angie repeated and I snapped out of my daydreaming memory. Her eyes hadn't changed any further. *How long was I supposed to wait? Did I need to make sure she fully turned or couldn't I do that to her?* Especially with the mutated virus, parts of her brain would remain functional—she'd know what she had become. I couldn't do that to her.

I pressed the muzzle of the gun under her chin. Warm tears ran down my cheeks. All this time, running around the United States with actual zombies moaning and groaning as if they had stepped out of a movie, I hadn't once stopped to think that I might have to kill someone I knew.

Although we'd known each other for only a short time, Angie had become a friend. More than that, she was someone I trusted with not just my own, but Ash's life. I knew that if something were to happen to me, she would take care of Ash. If I pulled this trigger, that person would be gone.

"Kill me." Her voice had become a plea—a plea for death.

"Don't." Another voice registered in my brain. Breaking through my mental haze, I glanced at my side where Ash had parked her chair. "Please don't," she said. Ash's big blue eyes had filled with tears. The sight of her tightened my throat so I couldn't utter a word.

"She needs time to fight it," Ash said. Angie shook her head at Ash.

"I can't let her turn," I managed to say at a whisper.

"She won't," Ash said determined. Angie shook her head and looked up at me.

"How do you know?" I asked Ash.

"How did you know?"

I held her gaze as the memory of jogging home with Ash in my arms replayed in my head. A zombie had torn her leg to shreds. She had passed out, and I hadn't been able to tell whether she had turned or not, but it hadn't stopped me from carrying her home.

Angie fought against her restrains when she sensed my hesitation. The hissing sound of pressured air displacement shifted my gaze to the decontamination area. From her chubby form, I recognized Dr. Matley rushing through the decontamination procedures. Unlike Ash and me, I guess the doctor wasn't willing to risk stepping inside the lab without the protection of her suit.

If I were going to shoot Angie, I should probably do it before Matley stormed in with her troops and disarmed me. I couldn't think of what they would do to Angie. Even the information her turned body held might be gold to researchers. I took in a breath and tightened the grip on the gun.

My eyes went wide when Angie's body started to

convulse. Shock forced me to take a step back. Her body twitched and shook so hard I was afraid she might break her bonds. Within seconds, her body went rigid, and she let out a long breath.

I gazed down at Ash who hadn't seemed to have changed her mind. She shook her head. "Just wait."

I looked up to see Dr. Matley approach us with careful steps. Luckily she had come alone. She lifted her arms from her sides as if to look disarming, although there was nothing disarming about the bulky figure in the biohazard suit.

Ash grabbed my arm and forced me to focus on Angie. Within an instance, I lowered the gun. My lips curved into a half smile, but it was as if my brain were afraid to be relieved. Angie looked up at me with dark hazel eyes. The fog swimming in front of her irises mere seconds ago had vanished. They were clear, and I could see the relief in them. The rest of her body slumped into the bedding, and her breathing steadied.

"It worked," Dr. Matley's excited voice called out. "I would have to do some added testing to confirm the results, but I was right."

I glared at her sourly. Was that all she cared about, the fact that she was right? She needed some serious reevaluation of her social skills.

Ash rolled her chair closer to the bed and grabbed Angie's arm.

"I knew you'd be okay," she said. Angie smiled a bit absentmindedly. I reached to tug the gun into the waistband of my pants when I noticed that wouldn't work with a flight suit and stashed it in a pocket. Loud banging broke the silence.

My head snapped up to the window where Ash and I had been sitting earlier, and I discovered my own reflection. I had to remind myself that the image staring back at me was me. I had become so used to the bald head over the years fighting cancer that every time I saw the dark-blond hair on my head, it still surprised me weeks after it had started to grow back. I was also glad to see that some added weight had made my lanky form look human again.

There was another bang on the window before a screech over the intercom announced that someone inside the room behind the mirror had pressed the button.

"He's here," Mars's frantic voice came over the speakers. I exchanged glances for a moment with Matley, but she had the same blank expression as Ash and Angie. Raising my shoulders, I gestured to the glass that we had no idea what he was talking about.

"Warren," Mars said, "he's here. He's talking to Whitfield."

My mouth opened into an "Oh shit," but I doubted anyone heard it. I just stood there, essentially watching myself in a mirror. The room fell silent as we all digested the information Mars had dumped on us. It was Dr. Matley who started to act. She moved between the thick plastic sheets, walked to the intercom box on this side of the room, and pressed the button.

"Does he know what we're doing here?" she asked in a businesslike voice. The speaker cracked, and Mars's voice filled the room again.

"I think he knows Mags and Ash are here," he said. "I spoke with Colonel Cornwell on his way to meet the general and Warren, and he told me they figured out the chopper we used belonged to the base."

Matley turned to us, a grim expression on her face.

"Then we have to assume he knows," she said. Without explaining, she moved to one of the stations with a computer. Her arm lifted to wave at someone standing near the door at the other side of the decontamination area. The figure in a biohazard suit shifted into action and stepped inside the decontamination room.

Warren is here was the one thing that kept running through my mind. Warren was here for us. He would finish what he'd started if he captured us.

Angie was the one to snap me out of my haze.

"Get me some clothes," she almost shouted. I looked at her and then at Ash, who had lost all the color in her face. She watched me with those big eyes as if she had shifted into some sort of trance. She must have been thinking the same as me. I tapped her shoulder and squeezed it. Her eyes shifted into focused.

"Find clothes for Angie, okay," I said. She lingered for a moment, but then her hands went to the wheels at her side. I helped her pass the plastic sheets and then turned to Angie. Darkness had shifted over her gaze along with a focus that I found somewhat intimidating. Her hand lifted, wriggling her restrained wrist. I got the message and started to undo the straps.

With her arms and legs free, Angie sat up and almost keeled over. I grabbed her underneath a shoulder to steady her. She nodded before she slid off the bed on to unsteady feet. We exited the makeshift room, and I helped her onto a chair close to the station that Dr. Matley occupied. Matley seemed unfazed by the fact I had release Angie from her restrains. She clicked on her keyboard as if her life depended on it. And maybe it wasn't her life but ours she clicked away at. Ash returned a few moments later with a stack of clothes.

"Where'd you get these so fast?" I asked when she handed them to me.

"There are lockers in a room next to the observation room," she said. "I had noticed it a couple of days ago." I smiled at her perception. I handed the stack to Angie, and she sifted through the mostly camouflage covered pants and a couple of black T-shirts.

"Boots," she said. Ash rolled back and turned. A pair of boots hung by their laces on the handlebars of her chair, and another pair poked out of my backpack.

"You are something," Angie said, delighted at Ash's choice of footwear. The first pair were too small, but while the second pair seemed a little big, they would do fine.

I stepped in line with Dr. Matley and watched her work for a moment.

"What are you doing?" I asked. Unsure of what to do, nerves started to creep up on me. If Warren was talking with Whitfield, it would mean we had minutes at the most. We needed a plan.

"I'm copying my work to several portable drives so you can take them," she said. "We need to make sure this information gets out of this mountain before it falls into the hands of Warren."

"And take them where?" Angie asked before I could.

"Alaska," Matley merely replied. I glanced over my shoulder at Angie, but she had the same dumfounded glare I must have had.

"Alaska?" I said questioningly. Matley stopped what she was doing and turned to us.

"You need to get these to Dr. Theodore Chen at the Cancer Center in Anchorage, Alaska. He will know what to do with them." Matley's eyes examined us one by one. "There is a plan, based on my assumptions, which Angie proved to be correct," she said. "I had hoped we would have been able to implement it here, but with Warren inside the base,

I doubt we'll get a chance. Chen will know what to do."

"Why us?" I asked.

"You are still part of this research," Matley answered while she locked eyes with Angie, "especially you."

"And how do you suppose we get ourselves out of this mountain," Angie said in a cynical manner, "let alone three thousand miles across the country?"

Matley's gaze turned to the mirror.

"Agent," she shouted as she pressed a button on her keyboard, "you back there?" The speaker crackled again, and Mars replied, "Yep."

"Find Sergeant Tyler and tell him we have a code ZS4T. He'll know what to do." The speaker crackled again as if his finger hesitated on the button.

"Agent, now!" Matley yelled.

"I'm on it," he said.

Matley went back to her work at the keyboard. When her large frame shifted without any regard for me, I stepped out of her way. I pulled up a chair and sat down next to Ash. We all looked at each other for a moment, unsure what to do. We couldn't just sit here waiting for Warren to appear. I glanced outside the room where several soldiers had gathered around the door. The man who had stepped inside the contamination room still occupied the space. He seemed to be waiting for a signal from Matley. For safety reasons, the door to the contamination room could only unlock if the decontamination procedure had cycled from beginning to end. As long as the man inside didn't initiate the cycle, the door wouldn't open. The soldiers on the other side attempted to start a conversation with the guy, in what looked like an effort to persuade the man to leave the room, but he didn't budge. I understood then what he was doing. His being in the box kept the soldiers from entering the room and eventually from entering the lab. Matley and this stranger had bought us some time, but where would we go when Warren showed up? Would General Whitfield be able to keep him from us? It seemed somewhat ridiculous to think Warren would wield that kind of power that he'd be able to order a commander in his own base, but I wouldn't put it past him.

Ash placed her hand on my knee. My foot was bouncing up and down again. I could feel the nerves creep up my limbs, and my throat felt as dry as sandpaper. My hand slipped over Ash's and squeezed it. She shouldn't be the one to give support.

Dressed in her borrowed clothes, Angie stood on shaky legs, but it didn't take her long to get her bearings. She glanced at the entrance and, with her FBI mind, calculated the blue-suited man's intentions. She turned back with a tight grin on her face. It looked painfully concerned, but still it was a grin.

"What are you thinking?" I asked. Angie didn't answer. Instead she joined Matley at her table.

"How loyal are Whitfield's men?" she asked.

Matley didn't look up from her screen when she answered, "They are military. What do you think? They'd follow their commander to their deaths."

"But do you think they'd still support him if, let's say, another body of authority would come into play?" This time Matley did look up to face Angie.

"It would depend on the authority, but I think our chances are good." With that, she returned to her screen. Angie took in a deep breath and let the air slip past her lips as she glanced around the room. Her eyes didn't show any evidence of the foggy substance that clouded zombie eyes, and I was glad to see Angie back in her FBI mode. Angie seemed deep in thought before her focus fell on Ash.

"We'll have to do a little evading," she said in a tentative voice. "Just like we did in the hospital, remember." Ash nodded, but kept quiet, which felt out of character for her. But what was there to say? We all knew what was coming next. It wouldn't be long before soldiers, guns, and Warren would become a recipe for mayhem.

Angie snapped a finger at me. My eyes followed her gaze, and I saw Sergeant Tyler on the other side of the door. He seemed to be calling out orders, and the soldiers standing outside the lab listened intently, while Mars stood by Tyler's side.

Mars distanced himself from the group and

moved to the window that separated him from the lab. He waved and gestured for us to get closer.

Angie was the first to move. She went to the window. Mars, whose voice couldn't breach the glass, gestured at the decontamination room.

"He wants us to come out," Angie said over her shoulder. I raised my butt of the chair and joined her at the glass. It felt hard to look at Mars so soon after our altercation, but I had to put that aside. He seemed to have similar difficulties because his gaze kept shifting to the floor.

"What do you think?" I asked Angie.

She cocked her head sideways and shrugged. "Not much of a choice."

Ash still sat at Matley's side, watching the images on different monitors, I called her to come over, and she pushed her wheels into motion. As she rolled into earshot, I explained what Mars wanted. She glanced at the room and then at the soldiers on the other side.

"But we're not wearing protective gear," she said, pointing a thumb in the direction of Dr. Matley. "They wouldn't let us step outside." She had a point, but we couldn't stay here. As if on cue, Dr. Matley came over as well.

"Here," she said, extending three black plastic sticks as she explained. "Backup drives—you each take one, just in case." I took hold of one of the stick and inspected it. It was a basic flash drive that could contain about one hundred and twenty-eight

gigabytes of data. I wondered if she had to use all
its space with the information that might save the
world or if it was just one stupid text file. I stuck it in
a pocket of my flight suit and zipped it closed. Dr.
Matley turned and her biohazard suit squished as
she walked to the door of the decontamination
room.

"You have to go now," she said and opened the
door. "I'll follow as soon as possible. I still need to
erase the hard drives."

I sucked in a breath and stepped in line behind
Ash. With a little push, I helped her over the
threshold. Angie followed, but Dr. Matley stayed
behind.

"Good luck," she said before she closed the
door. I watched her for a moment as she returned to
her desk. She didn't even look back.

A white mist fell over us as the decontamination
room did its thing. I was a little late sucking in a full
breath of air, and my lungs started to burn when the
showerheads finally ceased spraying white mist. A
red light posted at the door blinked green. The door
clicked, and Angie grabbed the handle. As if she
couldn't see the men on the other side of the glass
door, she opened it with care.

The soldiers didn't raise their weapons, and I
considered this a good sign. Sergeant Tyler stepped
forward. The man did not look happy. The soldiers,
including Mars and the sergeant, formed a half-
circle around us. Just far enough out of reach. Ash

had been right. Although they had let us out of the room, the men didn't trust the decontamination procedure enough to come close to us.

"So now what?" Angie asked in a none-too-friendly voice.

"We are getting you out of the mountain, without Warren finding out," the sergeant said. Surprised, my mouth spoke before I had a take on it.

"He doesn't know we're here?" I asked. I noticed a touch of overexcitement in my voice. Mars shook his head.

"He knows, but the general is denying him access to buy us time," he said. "The general knows how important it is to get this information out, including the three of you." Angie glanced around at the faces of the two men, including the three soldiers. As usual in their similar getup and close-cropped hair, the men all looked alike to me. Fortunately, they wore name tags.

There was Cullen who seemed to be the highest-ranking of the three. He had a seasoned face and a touch of gray coming out from under his cap. He also stood in front of the others. Donovan was younger and the shortest, while Stevens towered over both of them, but he was shorter than I was.

"You guys all agree with your commanding officer?" Angie asked. "Even though the man that sits in his office right now has the authority of the president." Her words hit me as shock. Did she have to emphasize the power Warren wielded?

"We know who Warren is," Cullen said. "He might have the president's ear, but we know he had a finger in what caused all this. All of us have lost loved ones to what that man did."

Angie nodded in satisfaction. "Then lead the way."

Part Three
Outbreak

Warren

"So this is where you went to hide," Warren said as he stepped out of the decontamination room and into the lab. One of his men had deactivated the room's decontamination facilities and he hadn't bothered to change into one of the biohazard suits like Matley wore. Although the defined regulations served their purpose, he knew the chance of contracting the infection was slim.

Matley eyed him thoughtfully as he approached her where she stood next to her desk. She had removed her protective mask, which in itself was proof to him that the lab was safe to enter. Sweat coated Matley's face, and her usually fuzzy red hair sat matted on her head.

"Not hiding," Matley replied in a strained voice. "Just found a better work environment."

Warren grinned and let his gaze wander across the lab. This place looked fine for run-of-the-mill research but had nothing on the laboratory he used to occupy in Florida. Matley knew this from having worked there alongside him. Fortunately, she couldn't have known about the pathetic resources he had to work with now and said, "I see ... better." He pulled up his nose and followed it with a smug expression. His current lab might be inferior, but that wouldn't stop him from feeling the satisfaction of berating his former associate—even if it was based on a lie.

General Whitfield might have used every bureaucratic tool at his disposal in an attempt to delay handing over his two guests, but Warren knew it wouldn't be long before he had them again. It had taken one phone call to Trenton Doyle, the White House chief of staff who turned out to be willing to provide him with access to the facility, and his men were already roaming the insides of the mountain to find 101 and 102. Doyle would do anything to protect his president and, with him, himself. He wanted a cure, and Warren was the only one that could give it to him.

"We could have solved this problem already if you hadn't interfered," Warren said as he walked up to Matley and stopped in front of her. The bulky woman crossed her arms, unimpressed by his gleeful smirk.

"Is that the problem that turns people into mindless corpses or the one where you can't seem to figure out how to make an enhanced human being?" Matley said. "Because I solved the first one."

Warren's eyes widened at Matley's admission. *Had she actually figured it out?* He narrowed his gaze and cocked his head. She wasn't the type of person to boast. If she had solved the problem, it would significantly boost his mood.

"I'm listening," he said. Matley snorted a laugh. The sound made a chill run up Warren's spine. For as long as he had known the woman, his body had revolted against her presence.

"You expect me to tell you," she said and laughed in his face.

"I expect you to tell the president of the United States," he said.

"Oh, is that who you work for these days," Matley said amused. "I must have missed the memo."

Warren's gaze drifted to the computer on the desk, and he shrugged. "You can either tell me, or we'll just have to find it ourselves."

Matley's face hardened, and Warren noticed her nostrils twitched. The hate that radiated toward him coming from the woman's eyes was palpable.

"You couldn't find your head up your ass," she said through clenched teeth. As she said it, Matley's gaze shifted to the door that opened into the lab. Warren didn't have to look behind him to know William had just made his entrance and a smile crept on his face.

"Dr. Matley, you remember my aide William," he said. Matley's eyes widened as she watched the bulk of a man approach. She knew William all too well. The man who had no qualms doing the things others deemed inhuman. Matley had used his services. The woman might act all self-righteous, but Warren knew that she would do anything to reach her goals. That's why the two of them had worked so well together. Well, almost anything. She hadn't responded well in Florida as he ordered every cancer patient in their care to be inoculated with the concoction he'd made from 101's blood. Although he still didn't know whether Matley's discomfort had been caused by the body count or the safety issues concerning the lab.

If he had a little more time, he might have asked her, but then William stopped at his side. Matley retreated a little. Her eyes shot from left to right as if to find a way out of the lab. Warren knew William would have taken care of any prying eyes, and Doyle would have occupied the general to the point of death by boredom.

"I'll give you one last chance to work with me," Warren said. "You can help me solve this puzzle."

Matley sucked in a deep breath and swallowed hard. Then she clenched her jaw and tried to stand firm. Warren shrugged and glanced up at the big man standing next to him. "Perhaps you would like to take care of this," he said, "and then see whether you can get some men up here to help me search this dump's mainframe."

William nodded as he took a step closer to Matley.

| **25**

We moved at a rapid pace through the bowels of the mountain. Cullen and Stevens walked ahead while Donovan walked behind us. The sergeant and Mars took up the rear. I couldn't bear to look at him —afraid of what I would see in his eyes.

Although all of them seemed to have vowed to get us out and knew the vaccine flowing through Angie's veins might become the salvation of the human race, it occurred to me that they all, including Mars, kept their distance from us— probably assuming we were contagious. I didn't know whether that was true, though. I didn't feel any different, and Angie didn't act any different. Not wanting to chance it, I kept my arms close.

Ash adjusted her pace to my stride and rolled by my side. I was afraid to look at her—afraid to be the one she had turned to and not being able to meet certain expectations. Mars's words haunted my thoughts, creating doubts in the darkest corners of my mind.

The halls around us changed as we went from the darker inner workings of the main facility to the brighter, more office-like interiors from, well, offices. We heard some turmoil as we entered a narrow hallway. Voices echoed down the hall from around a corner. One of the airmen lifted an arm in a balled fist. Cullen stopped, and behind him, we all followed his example.

In silence, we listened to the commotion. The voices were distinct, although I didn't immediately recognize them, except for one. I would have recognized that booming voice anywhere.

"We are here under the authority of the president of the United States, you will let us pass," William spoke in a loud voice. The protests must have come from a couple of guards posted at the section that connected this building to the large, open cavern and the massive doors we needed to reach in order to exit the mountain.

"Shit," Angie said under her breath. I seconded that, but kept quiet. The sergeant moved past us and stopped at Cullen's side.

They exchanged a few words before Sergeant Tyler waved a flat hand toward the rear. He motioned us to go where we had come from. Ash gave me a worried look, and I imagined mine wasn't far off. She would have recognized William's voice too. The man had pretended to be our friend. We had helped him and had let him into our home, only for him to betray us by turning us over to Dr. David.

As I turned, I caught Mars's gaze as well. He too looked worried, but his worry seemed to be directed at me. He took me by the arm as I walked past him. Shocked, I looked at his hand. He was the first person to touch one of us since we'd stepped out of that decontamination box. Mars, however, seemed indifferent. He drew me in with those eyes, and though I could still feel the pain he had caused with his words, I couldn't pull away.

"Stay close, all right. This is no different from JFK," he said in a low voice. Not sure how to react, I nodded. He was probably right, although it had been zombies chasing us down the hallways of JFK and not men with guns. He flashed me a grin and for the first time in a couple of days saw that twinkle in his eye. It reminded me of that conversation we'd had on the bus where he had explained that in face of a certain death by zombie, he needed to redirect his nerves, which had turned into flirting with me.

I forced myself to restrain the smile that twitched at the corners of my mouth; for the sake of my own sanity I couldn't afford to let myself get into this again.

The others shuffled by while we stood there in that empty hallway with William's voice booming around a corner. Ash waited for me halfway down the hall—her expression curious.

Mars released my arm, and without another word, he turned to follow the others. Ash waved at me to hurry up, and I did.

The soldiers directed us the long way around. A single hall must have separated us from that open area, and now it seemed we were miles away. Hallway after hallway appeared around every corner. Steps led up and down until Cullen motioned us to stop with his fisted hand. Tyler gestured for us to lower to the ground. I held on to Ash's chair to keep my balance. This was not my thing, although, ever since JFK, running around hallways seemed to have become a theme in my life.

Behind me, Angie and Mars sat in a similar crouch. Ahead Donovan moved forward to check if the coast was clear. Ash shifted in her chair so she could glance over her shoulder.

"I think I preferred the zombies at the hospital," she said in a nervous whisper. I hadn't been at the hospital with her during the first stages of the virus outbreak, so I glanced in turn over my shoulder to check Angie's reaction. She nodded at Ash.

"No argument from me," she said with a slight grin. I hadn't been there with them, but I needed to agree. Zombies didn't frighten me as much. Nor I assumed would they Angie or Ash. We all had the same zombie repellant running through our veins. As long as we kept out of their way, they'd keep out of ours, although the thought of them being held at bay by the Mississippi River was a comforting one, if only for the people living west of the river.

At the end of a hall, Donovan came to a stop. He waited for a moment before he turned on his heels and waved at us to retreat. Someone must have been coming if he was this spooked. Sergeant Tyler sprang into action and tapped the shoulders of the two other soldiers. As if they were synchronized swimmers, they turned and ran to us.

I grabbed the handles of Ash's wheelchair and spun her around. Using the momentum, I shoved her chair so she'd pick up speed and then headed after her. Angie and Mars followed.

With that chair of hers Ash had almost reached one of the junctions that veered off to the right before any of us had managed a decent sprint. She slowed her chair and spun around to wait for us. When I caught her gaze, I waved and mouthed the words "go, go" at her. She nodded and grabbed her wheels to turn into the hall when suddenly all her movement stopped. Her eyes were fixed on something I couldn't see. I ran faster, and arms and a torso came into my vision. A black coat with hands covered in black gloves reached for Ash.

A scream tore from my throat as those hands grabbed Ash and yanked her out of the chair. The figure stepped out into our hallway, turning to face me, and recognition flared. William held Ash by her collar, raised above the ground. Her skinny legs dangled as he held her up with one hand. With a single motion, he threw Ash's limp body down the hall. She hit the ground hard, and I screamed her name as she skidded across the floor like a rag doll. It occurred to me he didn't want her to take off in her chair. I had to adjust that thought when that big man grabbed the chair to lift it over his shoulder.

My eyes grew wide at the sight of a wheelchair heading for me midflight. I ducked against the wall.

The chair grazed me but kept its momentum. I didn't stop to check where it landed, but instead continued my sprint toward William. William held his ground. Of course, he would. The man looked like an oversized football player. What the hell was I going to do?

Too late I remembered the soldiers at my back holding guns, but by then I couldn't stop. I slammed my shoulder into his waist and felt as if I had run into a wall. William wrapped his thick arms around me and pinned my arms to my side. He squeezed so hard some of my bones cracked, although I didn't think he had broken anything. Still, it hurt.

William stood several inches taller than me, and I looked up at his square jaw that had formed into a nasty grin. Behind me, I heard voices followed by footsteps further down the hall.

"Lower your weapons," voices called out in unison. I couldn't see, but I figured from the widening smile on William's face that they were his men. He squeezed harder, and I had trouble breathing. Behind him, I saw Ash pushing herself up in a sitting position. Fear radiated from her face.

Without any expectations, I tried to wriggle against William's strong arms, but it was useless—he was too powerful, I realized—until I brushed a hand along a pocket of my flight suit. I could be the biggest idiot at time. The gun I had grabbed of one of the airmen at the lab still sat in my pocket. I just needed to reach it.

Behind me, the men argued. I heard Tyler's voice disputing the authority of the men and explaining that as long as general Whitfield hadn't said otherwise, they were to escort us to the main hall. Another man, whose voice I didn't recognize, repeated his request for the soldiers to drop their weapons.

"We are here in the name of Dr. David Warren, head of the Federal Mortem Defense Team under the authority of the president of the United States," the man spoke. Apparently, the soldiers didn't comply because he repeated his words.

At that point William seemed distracted enough, and I reached into the pocket of my flight suit. I grazed my thumb along the weapon to check if the safety was off. Then I wished I hadn't because for the life of me I couldn't remember if the switch had to be up or down.

Refusing to dwell, I eased the gun from my pocket. As she noticed it, Ash's eyes widened, but in the same instance, she shook her head in disbelief. It wasn't the first time I had forgotten to pull a gun in trouble.

It had happened when we'd first met Father Deacon, one of Dr. David's lackeys who collected infected people so David could experiment on them. The poor old priest had believed there to be a cure so that his family and the members of his parish would be saved. Still, I hadn't drawn the gun while it was sitting on my lap, and if I had, it might have spared us a lot of trouble.

I hoped this time it wouldn't turn out that way. Blindly, I aimed the gun and hoped to hit William in the leg. It should be enough to bring him to his knees. I pulled the trigger. The loud blast echoed inside the closed-off space. William twitched, but only so minimally that I feared I must have grazed him. I started to pull the trigger again when his eyes fell on mine. Then he stumbled a little as if he needed to find his balance.

"You stupid bitch," he fumed. Spit from his mouth reached my face. He shoved me backward with such force that I didn't even feel the motion until I hit the wall. Pain shot through my back. My vision swayed when my head connected with the concrete. My feet miscalculated the distance to the ground, and my body slumped to the floor.

I heard Ash calling out to me, but the sound barely penetrated the haze that roared in my head. Shots were fired, and I shook my head to focus. When my vision returned, I could see one of the soldiers on the ground. He lay face down and a pool of blood spread across the floor. I couldn't tell which one of the soldiers it had been. Without being able to read the name tag, it was hard to keep them apart. It didn't matter though. They were all men performing their duty; none of them deserved to end like that.

It took me a moment to register the rest of the scene. About five men in black stood halfway down the hallway past Mars, Angie, Sergeant Tyler, and the remaining two soldiers. Behind the men in black at the beginning of the hallway stood more men in green. I couldn't make out how many, and I couldn't tell on whose side they were. Other than Mars and Angie, everyone seemed armed and had raised their weapons. The fact that Sergeant Tyler and the remaining two soldiers had kept their weapons raised made me hopeful. Maybe those men in green at the end of the hall belonged to us.

Mars had his gaze locked on me, which made me feel better. His lifted his hands at his side in a nonthreatening manner. He hadn't raised them over his head, but he might have well had. Angie had a similar posture.

It took a second for my brain to start working again, and I looked up from where I lay on the ground. The gun was gone from my hand and had found its way into the big, clumpy fingers of William. I glared into the barrel of the nine millimeter automatic.

He must have waited for me to get my shit together, because immediately after our eyes locked, he limped toward me. Mars protested, but William only had to point the gun in his direction for him to stop.

As he had done with Ash, William lifted me off the ground with one hand as if I weighed nothing. His hand gripped the fabric of the flight suit so tight that I heard it rip. He lifted me until our eyes leveled out. Nothing of his expression held the friendly, cheese-cracker-eating tree of a man that we had met in Bergen Beach. This time everything about him screamed stone-cold killer. It's somewhat frightening to know what a person would be able to hide at face value.

"If it weren't for Dr. Warren," he said through clenched teeth, "I would snap you in half." The hate in his eyes told he'd be capable of the literal act.

"Please don't hurt her, William," Ash said in a pleading voice. I didn't see the puckered lower lip, but I knew exactly how her face must have appeared. The fragile little kid with her big blue eyes. She could have been playing William just as she had the airman, but I thought that to be a stretch even for Ash. Still, her voice got to me. It reminded me of the time William wanted to take care of Ash, so to speak, after she was bitten. Anger started to build inside me and morphed fear into rage. When William snapped his head to a side to face Ash, I didn't hesitate.

My arms, first limp at my side, now reached up to grab William's head. In that unguarded moment, I pulled him close and strained to lash out. My toes barely touched the ground as I sank my teeth into his ear. I refused to think about the taste of his blood in my mouth, the growl that came from William's throat, or the crunch his ear made as it gave way.

As I spit out the chunk as he released me from his grip. My feet fumbled for balance I couldn't find, and I crumpled to the floor. I hit the ground while William stumbled backward. He grabbed the side of his head with both hands. Frantic eyes went from the piece of ear on the ground to me.

"I'm gonna fucking kill you," he roared. He stepped forward, his arm already moved back so he could hit me. My eyes widened, and I scrambled backward on hands and feet but couldn't dodge the trajectory of his fist. Blood spilled from my mouth as my jaw clamped shut, and I bit my tongue. White flashed across my eyes, and for a moment everything went silent.

As I opened my eyes, all I could see was the gray, concrete floor and the blood that had pooled there as it dripped from my mouth. My hearing returned a fraction later as the grunts and moans that accompanied a scuffle reached my ears.

"Hold your fire!" someone shouted.

I lifted my head and spit out some of the blood that didn't seem to stop accumulating in my mouth.

A body crossed my vision as it slammed into the wall, and Mars slumped to the ground.

"I'm gonna crush your head," William shouted as he raised a boot. Mars ducked, and William missed. With his attention on Mars, William missed the warnings shouted at him by his men and didn't see how Angie had come up behind him with a backspin kick to the back of his knee. His leg buckled under the impact, and he dropped to one knee.

It all happened so fast that I hadn't seen a couple of the men in black rush forward, guns raised. The men in green still occupied the hall but didn't act. Shit, had Whitfield caved under Dr. David's pressure?

Mars raised his arms to the barrel aimed at his head. Angie hadn't seen the men coming—she was too busy with William. I wanted to shout, but no sounds came from my mouth. She raised her foot, ready to kick William in the head, but he caught her boot in midflight. It took her off balance, and she fell to the ground. William seemed to have gone off the edge—he roared like a wild beast and went after Angie. He grabbed her throat and slammed her against the ground.

None of the men holding guns acted—they weren't going to stop him. I spit some more blood from my mouth and then scrambled up on unsteady feet. There was no way I'd be able to help Angie against William, but I had to do something.

Unfortunately, I wasn't the only one with that idea. My heart sank when I saw Ash clinging to William's arm. Enraged, she screamed before she sank her teeth into his black jacket, to no ill effect. William flung his arm out, and as Ash connected to the wall, she released his arm.

Even on unsteady legs and a head pounding as if it was going to explode, I could feel the rage stir in my veins. I jumped on his back and wrapped an arm around his throat. I clamped it tight with my other hand. It didn't seem to affect William; he kept his choke hold on Angie with one hand.

Underneath him, Angie sputtered and coughed as she tried to suck in air. William jerked his body like a bull, forcing me off balance before he spun me off his back, and I hit the ground next to him. I expected a backlash from the uninvited ride on his back, but he kept staring at me as I coughed up some more blood. I must have bitten off a piece of my tongue for all that blood to keep flowing.

William's eyes grew wide as he looked down on me. A shaking hand rose to where a chunk of his ear had gone missing.

"What have you done!" he squealed. "What have you done?" His reaction almost seemed pitiful from a man his size. He just stood there, saying the same words over and over again. I looked at him, blinking, unable to understand his reaction.

Next to me, Angie lay gasping for air, along with an expression of surprise on her face at the big man's wailing. I pushed myself up onto my elbows and reached for Ash, who crawled toward us. She eyed the squealing man curiously before she switched to me with a frightened look on her face.

William changed his mantra from what have you done to, "You killed me, bitch." His words caught me off guard, but as I wiped a sleeve across my mouth and saw the blood that still exuded from my mouth and their meaning clicked. A glance at Angie told me she had come to a similar conclusion.

Commotion stirred where the soldiers and the men in black had their standoff. Questions were raised about what was happening. Mars turned to the direction of the men but kept his mouth shut.

William's chest seemed to belong to a wild beast. It rose and fell so fast I doubted he'd be getting any air inside his lungs. His eyes were locked on mine and were terrifying to look at. They carried an intensity that grabbed me by the throat. Moments seemed to transcend into hours, but not even a minute had passed since he had thrown me off his back. William's body jerked. His hands fell limp to his side. The rise and fall of his chest ceased. The crack of a gun drew my attention to the men still quarreling at the end of the hall. It seemed as if Sergeant Tyler had fired off a warning shot.

When I returned my gaze to William, my breath caught. White fog swam in front of his irises. His nostrils twitched, and his head shot up. The same ticks and jerky movements I had seen in every zombie rose to the surface of William's body language.

Ash had caught on, and as she moved closer to my side, grabbed my arm. Angie scrambled back when William's head snapped to the side, facing the direction of the men facing off. In an instance, he bolted to his feet. His nostrils flared, sucking in the smells around him, searching for the fresh blood that he needed to quench his hunger.

Without explanation, Angie crawled on hands and knees and grabbed Mars's legs. He was standing with his hands raised, watching the scene unfold. One of the men holding a gun on Mars lowered his weapon and stared at a roaring William. With a nifty move, Angie took Mars down and covered his body with hers. She needed to hide his scent before William had a chance to trace it.

William didn't even turn to Mars. He ran straight for the group of men.

The soldier he hit from behind had no idea what was coming for him until he felt the pain of William's teeth digging into his neck. Blood spurted from the wound. The soldier screamed, and all heads turned to the bloodied bodies of the two men on the ground.

William didn't hesitate to sink his teeth into the ankle of the soldier who stepped in next to him. The man screamed and jerked his foot to a side. The men in black rushed over to their leader, but William wasn't their leader anymore. He didn't care about anything anymore. His arms tore through the air at anything that came near him. Panic followed when one of the men in black was brought to his knees. This time William didn't even bother to go for the neck. He tore a piece of flesh from the man's cheek. Blood ran freely. William chewed and smacked as if his life depended on it before he lunged for the next. For a moment, it all seemed to happen in slow motion. Everyone standing in the hallway seemed to be stunned. We all knew of the zombie threat, but within the safe confines of this mountain, it all must have seemed as if it were a distant memory until reality kicked in.

Shots were fired. Bullets ripped through William's back, sending a mist of blood into the air. His body wouldn't stop moving—instead he threw himself onto his next victim.

I watched in horror. *Had I done that? Was I responsible for those deaths?* Around me, I sensed movement. Mars had retrieved Ash's chair while Angie had lifted her of the ground and seated in her chair. I, however, still sat on the ground. I caught Mars's glare. I couldn't tell whether the shocked look on his face had been one of disgust or concern.

Angie kneeled down in front of me, blocking my view from Mars. She called my name, but I couldn't respond. Thoughts, feelings, and words they all collided inside my head at light speed. This was not happening.

"Mags!" Angie shouted before she slapped me in the face. The burn-like pain triggered enough sense in me that I lifted a hand to my face. She raised her hand again, and I held it off.

"Stop," I said. My eyes focused on hers, and she cocked her head a little. *Was that pity?* I couldn't stand pity, not after what I had done. I turned away and got to my feet. Unable to ignore it, I watched the men fighting for their lives. William seemed to be unstoppable. He also seemed faster than any zombie I had ever seen.

One of the men in black who had been one of the first to go down, started to twitch, first a leg and then an arm, before he lifted himself off the ground. It didn't take him long to find the smell of blood, and he stormed into the crowd.

"We need to go," Ash said. "Soon there will be too many, and Mars is unprotected." She meant that the three of us carrying the cancer gene weren't interesting for the zombie's taste buds, but Mars didn't have that luxury. If we didn't get him out of here, he would end up like one of them.

Ash turned her chair in the direction we had initially intended to go before we'd run into William. Making sure Mars's scent was masked by standing between him and the zombies, Angie and I followed. The growls, moans, and screams of pain faded as we jogged and Ash rolled her chair along the hall. Ash had the lead, Mars followed, and Angie and I took up the rear.

I felt sick to my stomach. The taste of my own blood lingered in my mouth. I couldn't get rid of it. *What had I done? Stupid!* I hadn't thought it through. The infection coursed through my veins; I knew that. I knew the possibility of me infecting someone existed. My own blood must have run from my mouth and mixed in William's open wound that I had caused in the first place. *What had I done?* Thoughts hammered inside my head, giving me a headache, and then Ash pulled on the brakes.

26

I glanced around but didn't see or hear anything. "Why did you stop?" I asked Ash. She faced me with a raised eyebrow.

"Does anyone know where we are going?" she replied. That seemed like a fair reason to stop. Mars overtook Ash and headed further down the hall. He opened a few doors, checked the rooms, and moved on to the other. He didn't look as if he knew where to go.

I turned to Angie who had a similar *I'm-trying-to-get-my-bearings* expression. She lifted her shoulders in a shrug before shaking her head. Tyler's soldiers had us on a detour from the moment we'd encountered the voices of William's—or should I say Dr. David's—men. I hadn't set a foot in this part of the base before.

A sharp whistle screeched my ears, and I found Mars waving at us. He stepped inside a room and disappeared. After exchanging glances, we followed him.

As I stepped into the dimly lit room, my eyes fell on the abundance of monitors bolted to the wall and on the desks, creating a row on each side. Mars stood at the end of the room, hovering over a desk, with a computer centered between the two rows. I followed Ash and Angie along the middle lane, passing five desks on each side. The screens on the desks were filled with images of the rooms and hallways I might have visited over the past few days. This seemed to be some type of security station with an overview of the entire facility.

We joined Mars at the desk, his hands clicking on a keyboard, his gaze locked on a screen. It took him a while, cursing in the process, but he managed to find what he was looking for. A screen flickered, and the image changed to the boardroom. From having been there, I knew the room connected to General Whitfield's office. The room with the large boardroom table sat empty. General Whitfield's office also sat empty.

Mars clicked another set of keys, and the imaged switched to the lab. I sucked in a breath at the sight. The images were in black and white, but the layout of the room was visible—the people inside the room perfectly recognizable. The camera zoomed in on a group of people standing near Dr. Matley's work table.

At first, his back faced the camera, but it couldn't hide who he was. His posture, sleek haircut, and the gesturing with his hands immediately told me who he was. Dr. David Warren stood over Dr. Matley's limp form. Matley, who still wore her biohazard suit, had removed her protective mask. She lay on the floor and even in black and white, I could tell the pool of liquid spilling at the back of her head had to be the dark red color of blood.

Dr. David waved his hand to the men standing around the fallen body of Dr. Matley. Three men dressed in black coats and suits stepped into action. I hadn't seen them before, or at least I couldn't remember them, although they looked a lot like the men we'd faced earlier in that hallway. It seemed Dr. David had gathered quite a bunch of broad-shouldered, thick-necked muscle men.

The men honed in on the computers standing around the lab. One sat down at a station, clicking at the keyboard while another rummaged through the papers on the desk. The third man held a hand to his ear, and I could see his mouth move.

"Do we have audio on this?" Angie asked. Mars didn't look up from the screen but started tapping keys. He flipped a switch, and a crackled voice came over the speakers.

"Copy that," the man spoke before he lowered his hand.

"Dammit," Angie said under her breath. With that, she voiced my thoughts. I would have liked to know what he was talking about and to whom. The man moved to Dr. David. It made me hopeful we still had a chance to find out. We needed to know Dr. David's plan—what did he expect to find here, and more importantly, what was he willing to leave with or without? Maybe we'd get lucky and all he wanted was Dr. Matley's research. Maybe he would leave without pursuing us.

Dr. David raised his head at the man's

approach. "What is it?" he asked.

"We have a problem," the man spoke. His voice was deep, and I imagined it would make his message sound even more eerie. I had a feeling I knew what he would say. "There has been an outbreak."

Dr. David let out a deep sigh. "Where now?" The man cleared his throat, and his head shifted, looking everywhere except at Dr. David.

"Here," he said. Dr. David chuckled a laugh.

"Don't be ridiculous," he said amused. "There hasn't been a sighting on this side of the river. This is a safe zone."

"I'm sorry to say, sir," the big man said, "but I just received word from one of the teams. They barely escaped with their lives."

"But how, dammit," Dr. David snapped while he slammed a fist on the desk. The big man started to look more and more uncomfortable. His black-gloved hand rubbed the back of his beefy neck.

"They think it started with Mr. Darrell," he said. At the mention of the name, my brows furrowed. *Who the hell was Mr. Darrell?* Dr. David's shoulders tensed. "He had reportedly captured both subjects 101 and 102," the big man said. I glanced down at Ash, who looked up at me with a frown. "Something happened, soldiers interfered, and all we know was that within seconds, Mr. Darrell attacked the soldiers along with our own men in a violent matter."

Dr. David seemed struck by the news. He pulled out a chair and sat down.

"He's infected," Dr. David said in a distraught voice.

"Yes, sir, and it is spreading fast."

Without further acknowledging the man, Dr. David waved a hand. The big man distanced himself while Dr. David seemed to be staring off into space for a moment before he spoke. His words came out in a soft-spoken whisper. "You should have known better, William."

William Darrell—I hadn't even known William's last name, but now the name would forever reside in my head as the man I'd killed. The thought made it hard to breathe, and my knees weakened. I pulled out a chair and sat down. Ash moved in next to me while Angie watched me with careful eyes. Mars avoided looking at me. I couldn't bear to think what they thought of me, although Ash tried to reassure me with a faint smile.

While his men searched the lab, Dr. David spoke on the phone. It seemed that losing William hadn't hit him hard for long. He spoke with someone about sending a helicopter. Dr. David wasn't a man for staying around zombies for too long—at least not if they were running around freely.

The three men converged on the middle of the lab and spoke with each other for a moment before the big man addressed Dr. David.

"Sir, the data is not here."

Dr. David's head shot up, as did mine. If the data he was looking for wasn't there, then Matley must have destroyed it. Surely, the information had to be invaluable to Dr. David. It seemed Dr. Matley had signed our death warrants. The man wasn't a fool. He knew we were here, and he knew we must have been inside that lab. While he spoke into the phone, he inspected the sectioned-off room inside the lab where the bed sat surrounded by those plastic sheets. He also must have spoken with Dr. Matley before he decided to kill her. *What had she told him?* Either everything, and he shot her, or nothing, and they shot her anyway.

Dr. David's head lowered to his chest, and then he took in a deep breath and straightened his shoulders to stand straight.

"Find them," he said. His voice sounded cold and harsh. The three men glanced at each other before they returned their attention to the doctor. "Are you deaf?" Dr. David fumed. His hands balled into fists at his side. The big man took a step closer to the doctor.

"Sir, please forgive me, but ..." the man said, hesitating, "we have no protection against the infected, and by now there might be a hundred of them. Attacks have been reported all over the base."

Dr. David stepped forward. He stood about a foot shorter than the big man but didn't seem bothered by it. His eyes bored straight into the big man, who had a problem keeping his head from shifting away.

"You knew what you signed up for, and it was all fine when you got to sit in an office and cash a big check," Dr. David spoke in a calm but pressuring voice. "Now, this is what I have been actually paying you for."

One of the other men took a step into the doctor's direction. He stopped when Dr. David snapped his head to face the man. "But, but …" the man stammered. Dr. David cut him off.

"They are slow-moving brain-dead zombies; as long as you don't let them bite you or get their guts and gore into your mouth or eyes, you'll be fine. Use your guns, dammit. I don't care. Just get me 101 and 102."

I guessed these designations were meant for Ash and me, and we weren't his favorite subjects anymore; he had given us a number.

Dr. David stared at the men some more before they resigned, and they left the lab with him in their wake. After they left the room, Mars's fingers rattled the keyboard. Images on the screen flipped from one area to another. Some were empty; others, like the mess hall, were the basic scenes from a horror movie. The big man was right—the virus spread fast. I didn't know how it had gotten from that hallway to almost the other side of the mountain, but it had. Tables we had eaten at stood on their sides. Chairs and trays lay scattered across the floor, along with half a dozen or so bodies. A handful of zombies roamed the room as if they owned it.

Mars clicked through different images and found a bunch of survivors. A couple of them had locked themselves in one of the offices. Others had made it to the open area to where those massive doors were located. About two dozen soldiers had set up a perimeter at those doors and refused to let anyone pass who seemed to be infected. Anyone who came close without adhering to their commands got shot. The ones who did comply were checked before they were allowed to exit.

It looked as if more would survive than I had thought. Still, every single one who didn't would be on my head. I had done this, and I was to blame for every death that occurred here or anywhere else on this side of the Mississippi. The thought made my stomach turn. What if they got out?

General Whitfield and Colonel Cornwell appeared on one of the screens, and I was glad to see they had both made it to the open area. Mars looked from the screen to face us.

"It seems we need to get down there," he said. Angie rested her butt on the desk and let out a breath.

"Yeah, but how are we supposed to do that?" she said, pointing a finger at the screen. It showed the different hallways that I presumed would lead us to the open area. "It would mean we have to get past them." She indicated the zombies that roamed the halls. Although soldiers were making it out of here, this place employed over two hundred and fifty people, and we had definitely not seen all those in the open area. There were still a lot of them inside. No doubt some would be zombies by now, and others might follow soon.

"That is exactly what you will do," Mars said. We all looked up at him. "All three of you, you can just stroll past them."

"And what," Angie and I said simultaneously. The combined response made us glance at each other for a moment before we returned our gazes to Mars. I held my mouth so Angie could speak. I wasn't sure if my words held any meaning for Mars anymore.

"We will not leave you behind," she said. "That is not how this works."

"Well, there shouldn't be any zombies inside the mountain either, but I guess shit happens," he snapped at her. It was a cheap shot, but it hurt as if he had rammed a fist into my stomach. I bit the inside of my lip to keep it from shaking. No one blamed me more than I did myself, and I could understand how he felt, but that didn't mean it didn't hurt coming from him.

"Don't be an ass, Mars," Angie said. "We couldn't have known this would happen, and you were the one who wanted Mags and Ash here in the first place. You even told them your family lived here, just so she would come."

"Don't you think I know that," Mars said aloud slamming his fist on the table.

Ash's mouth dropped open as I closed my eyes. Tension started to claw at my chest. I opened my eyes and found Ash glancing nervously from one of us to the other.

"You lied to us," she said, puzzled. Mars's gaze softened and focused on her. He shook his head.

"It's not what you think," he said, but before he could say anything else, Ash broke in.

"You lyin' bastard," she said, "you're just as bad as Warren." Ash set off in a rant about how Mars had tricked us, inserting a curse word in every other sentence. The news hadn't come as a shock to me; Mars had practically confessed it the moment he had handed me that note. The fact I had read it days later wasn't his fault.

"Was that the reason you sprang us out of jail?" Ash said, fuming. "So you could trade us to Matley? Mags trusted you!"

"Ash, it's not like that," Angie said, trying to overrule the kid's rant. She obviously sat torn between Mars and us.

"You don't understand," Mars said even more loudly.

I stood up from my chair and walked down the row of desks, leaving the bickering behind. My jaw hurt, my tongue hurt, and my head, in general, hurt, and I could do without the shouting.

In the reflection of one of the monitors, I

noticed smears of blood around my mouth. I sat down behind a desk and grabbed a bottle of water of the tabletop. Using the water, I cleaned the blood away and rinsed my mouth. Without anyplace else to put it, I spit the water out on the floor. It didn't wash away the taste of blood, but my tongue seemed to have stopped bleeding and felt better.

Around me, I noticed the room had gone silent, and I lifted my head up. The three of them stared at me as if I had turned into a zombie. The sight of them made me smile. It all seemed so close to home, the bad language, the fighting, but somehow in a way that I had never understood before, never noticed in arguing with my family back home, I could feel their intentions. They all tried their best in the interest of the ones they loved. It seemed so strangely clear now. These people had become my family as well.

It had definite signs of a dysfunctional family, but what else was new.

"I think I get it now," I said as I focused on Mars.

Those pale jade eyes that had caught my attention from the moment we'd met, took me in. What I saw in them ranged from suspicion to confusion as he asked, "What?"

Ash and Angie glared at me as I replied, "That thing you accused me of." He strained and opened his mouth as if to defend himself, but I wouldn't let him.

"You were right," I said. "I get it now."

With that his lips curved upward at the corners and his face lit up.

"It's about time," he said.

"Huh," Ash said after a moment of silence.

"I already knew about his family not living here," I said as I stood and made my way to them.

"Including ..." Angie said, shooting Mars a hesitant glance.

"Yeah, he told me about Rowdy," I said.

Angie let out a huff of air in apparent relief.

"Okay, I'm starting to lose track here," Ash said. "What's a Rowdy?"

"He is Mars's son," I replied.

"Mars has a son," Ash exclaimed.

"Maybe we should talk about this later," Angie said, exasperated. "We still kind of have to get out of here."

I glanced up at Mars, who hadn't stop staring at me.

"All of us, right," I said.

He didn't reply immediately, but it wasn't hard to read that brilliant smile on his face as he said, "We'll need a plan."

27

We divided ourselves between the different stations to keep an eye on the monitors. There seemed to be a distinct movement in the newborn zombies. For some reason, they all managed to stumble their way in the direction of the open area. I didn't know whether they sensed that people were alive there, or they somehow remembered where to go. From our last encounter with Dr. David at his lab in Florida, we had learned that he had done something to make the infection by Mortem worse. He had done something that gave awareness to the flesh-eating creatures, something I had seen myself, fleeing from that lab, something I had seen in their eyes. A struggle raged behind those eyes as if they were fighting for control of their own bodies.

The cruelty of doing something like that seemed unimaginable to me at the time, but then so had knowingly infecting someone. That was what had started all of this, with Dr. David releasing a virus in the middle of New York, and now I had done the same. It gnawed at me that maybe we weren't that different after all.

"Why can't we just make a circle around him and walk out?" Ash asked. She, too, sat behind one of the monitors and clicked at a keyboard. She seemed more efficient at it than me, even though I had worked with a computer for most of my life.

"We did it for Jonesy back in Brooklyn," she added.

"I don't know if you remember, but that didn't work out to well for Jonesy, or Chuck," Angie shot back. I noticed Ash's shoulders slacken, and her face went pale. Angie immersed into the camera footage on her screen. If she hadn't been sitting three tables over, I would have kicked her in the shins. Jonesy had been Angie's partner when they'd raided the hospital where Ash had been admitted. The loss of Jonesy hadn't turned out to be a great miss. The man had taken following orders to the letter. It hadn't mattered that those orders had come from Dr. David, and he hadn't cared who had stood in his way.

Chuck, on the other hand, had become a friend to Ash. She had reluctantly told me about the old one-time soldier with a habit for booze and smoking while carting around an oxygen tank. Although it was hard for me to picture the two of them, I could tell Ash's eyes sparkled at remembering the old man's antics. Still, she didn't like to talk about it and certainly didn't wanted to be remembered of the old man's death. I reached out and tousled her scruffy blond hair. She faced me with a half-smile.

"That's it," Mars said elated. "I've had it. This shit is getting worse by the minute. I say we take the direct route back."

"Don't be stupid, Mars," Angie said.

"You do know I'm still your superior," Mars replied with a questioning look.

"Yeah well, if we get out of here and there is still an FBI, you can berate me."

I pressed a finger to the screen and tapped it. "I think B12 looks clear enough," I said, "and this maintenance duct leads directly into the open area."

"That's a hell of crawl, but I agree," Angie replied. "We should take the safe route and I doubt we'll run into zombies down there."

"Maybe we should shove Mars in a box," Ash said.

"I like your thinking," I said, chuckling, although Mars didn't seem amused.

"Could we be serious for one minute?" he said.

"Oh, I am, mister. I've been lying through my teeth—son of-" she started to say until I slapped a flat hand over her mouth. She mumbled away, but the words diffused. Angie still grinned as she got to her feet.

Although not everyone seemed happy about it, we came to an agreement to take the corridor, and the maintenance duct I had suggested.

The door creaked as Angie opened it a crack so she could listen. We couldn't hear any of the familiar moans, and she opened it further. She poked her head out and announced the all clear.

Ash and I had cramped up behind her while Mars stood at the other side of the room. We tried to mask him with our scents. We all knew it was a vain attempt if we ran into a bunch of zombies, but it might fool the odd few. We stepped out, and Ash rolled her chair into the hallway.

"Where to?" she asked. Mars followed and searched both directions. Left had been where we came from, and right was new to me. He pointed his finger to the left.

"We have to get back to the point where we encountered William," he said. "It connects with B12." My stomach dropped at the thought of what we would find in that passage, and I think he must have read it on my face. He touched my arm and gave me a confident smile. I tried to draw in some of that calm he radiated and took a deep breath. It didn't work.

Mars took off down the hall. Ash followed him and eventually over took him.

"You can't go wanderin' off, and you have to stay in the middle, so we can mask your smell," she said with a scowl.

"Hey, kid," Angie said as she stepped in alongside me. "You okay?"

I glanced at her sideways. "You calling me kid now," I said. "I'm like, what, five years older than you?"

A wide smile brightened her face when she said, "Yeah, I can't take on Ash, but I think I can handle you." The smile transformed into a smirk, and she nudged me with her shoulder. "Come on."

In a line, we walked down the hallway, making our way back to the place where it all went downhill. Everything seemed the same as I followed Ash while Mars walked behind me, and Angie took up the rear. Gray walls and doors lined the hall. Inside the rooms, monitors and screens cast different colors while it all seemed eerily quiet. It wasn't that long ago when these corridors were buzzing with people focused on surveying the skies and gathering information to fight the outbreak. They'd fought a war that seemed so far away then, and I had to go and bring it to their doorstep.

Deep in thought, I almost tripped over Ash as she suddenly stopped.

"Watch it," she whispered. I perched myself up on her shoulder. As I steadied my feet, I caught the reason she'd stopped. We had arrived at the T-junction where William had ambushed us. Blood covered the floor as if someone had dragged a body from one side of the hallway to the other. I squeezed Ash's shoulder and motioned her to stay.

I couldn't hear the moans of zombies or the sounds of screams or gunfire, so I figured it would be safe to take a look. Mars joined me as I eased forward. Although what I saw wasn't life-threatening, my eyes weren't ready for it, and I felt grateful for Mars's presence. A handful of bodies lay sprawled across the floor. Blood covered the ground and walls. Piles of what I suspected to be entrails shimmered in the fluorescent lights. The back of my hand shot to my mouth, and I gagged at the smell of coagulated blood along with the gruesome display of intestines.

The bodies were unrecognizable, mangled to a degree that the virus wouldn't be able to sustain them, although a name tag betrayed one of them as Donovan. The poor bastard's torso had been ripped to shreds. Among the bodies of four soldiers lay two men in black. I couldn't be sure William wasn't one of them, but they didn't seem big enough. That could mean he was still out there. Mars placed a gentle hand on my shoulder and guided me to the others.

"It's not a pretty sight," I warned. "Don't let your eyes wander." With a hard look, I faced Ash. She sneered at me. "Don't give me that tough-girl routine," I said. "This will give you nightmares for the rest of your life, trust me." She bit her lip as if she was considering it, and I shook my head. "Suit yourself."

I eased around the corner with careful steps. Slipping on blood or guts wasn't something I was eager to experience. I sensed the others behind me as I moved to the other side of the hall. Halfway down the hall, I heard several curse words. Over my shoulder, I saw the reason. The blood that covered the floor had coated Ash's wheels and had seeped on to her hands. Her hands looked as if she had clawed at the bodies herself. Mars bent to reach for a body.

"Stop," I called out. Shocked, he looked up at me.

"What?" he said.

"Don't touch those," I said stepping closer.

"I wasn't going to touch the blood," he said defensively. I, however, wouldn't take the chance.

"Just don't," I said and grabbed the body myself. I pulled at what was left of the man's collar and pulled him aside so Ash could fit her wheelchair through the gap. Mars shook his head and moved further down the hall. Exchanging glances with Angie, I could tell she was starting to get annoyed. We needed Mars at close proximity if we ran into any zombies. I sprinted ahead and overtook Mars. It seemed useless to argue with him, so I just took the lead.

As I closed in on the next turn, I could almost sense the presence of zombies. There was barely a sound, but somehow I knew they were there. I pressed my back against the wall and urged the others to do the same. I slid closer. My heart picked up speed with every step I took. Holding my breath, I peeked around the corner. Within the same second, I pulled back. The others looked at me expectantly. I shook my head. No way we would be able to get past the dozen or so zombies that lumbered in that corridor.

We had to figure out a different route, but which one? On the monitors, they all looked similar to this. I took another peek and saw that some of the zombies had found a dead spot out of the camera's view. That's why we had thought this route would be clearer.

"Shit," I said under my breath.

"That bad," Mars whispered. I looked up at him and nodded. My gaze shifted to the connecting hall. It ended in a dead end. A couple of closed doors might serve as an escape, but without knowing where they went, it might as well have been a trap. It was the end of the hall with the zombies where we needed to go. I eased my head around the corner and saw the maintenance duct we needed to reach. It sat low by the ground, covered by a grid, and looked big enough for a grown person, although Mars could run into some trouble squeezing into the tiny space because of his size. Still, it was the only option we had. I stepped back and ushered the others down the hall. I could think of one way to get Mars past the zombies, and although I didn't like it, I knew it had to be done.

As quietly as possible I moved to a door and wiggled the handle. It was locked. I moved to the next and found it unlocked. It clicked open, and I eased the door at a crack. Another office-like space lay beyond it. I waved for the rest to follow and entered. The room sat empty except for a single desk in the corner, a couple of chairs, and a painting of an F16 fighter plane. Not that I would have known that if it weren't printed on the bottom.

Angie closed the door behind us. Her eyes

narrowed as she waited for an explanation. Ignoring her, I moved behind the desk and started opening drawers. It took me a minute to find what I was looking for. Although a pair of scissors wasn't the best option, they would have to do.

"What are you doing?" Mars asked. I held the scissors out to him.

"The way I see it," I said, "we have one option."

"And that is?" Angie asked curiously.

"We need a distraction." They all glanced at each other, and the looks on their faces told me they didn't like where this was going.

"So," Ash said. I took a breath to gather my nerves. There could be only one scenario, and I needed them to agree.

"Mars, take your shirt off," I said.

Ash smirked. "I don't think this is the time for that," she said. Mars frowned at her but addressed me.

"What are you planning?" I noticed an edge of worry in his voice.

"You need to cut yourself with this," I said, "and get the blood on the shirt." He took the scissors from my hand and inspected them.

"You what to use my blood on the shirt as a distraction."

I nodded and replied, "It is the only way to get those things to move away from the duct."

"Wow, wow," Angie chimed in. "And you just want to wave a bloodied shirt at them as some kind of treat." I answered with a shrug.

"And then what?" she asked.

"Run and hide."

"We're not leaving you behind," Ash snapped.

"I'm not staying behind," I said with as much confidence as I could muster. "I'll just wait for them to settle down and follow once you get out."

Angie shook her head but didn't say anything. She knew it was our one chance. As we had seen in the control room, zombies blocked the routes to the open area. This was the only way to get past them. It wouldn't matter where we planned to do it.

"What if they catch up on you or there isn't a place to hide?" Ash asked.

"They won't and there will be—I've seen doors at the other end of the hall."

"You can't know that." Ash's voice raised an octave—the usual tell that she'd started to freak out a little. I moved around the desk and knelt to face her.

"We have to try," I said in a soft voice and looked up at Mars.

Ash shook her head. "We could just wait for the cavalry to show up."

I smiled at her. I guessed she still had faith. Mars answered, so I didn't have to.

"Remember the last time we ended up in a facility crowded with zombies?" he said. Ash looked up at him, and her face paled.

"They blew it up," she said with barely a

whisper. Mars placed the scissors on the desk and unzipped his flight suit to remove his shirt. Heat crept up my neck when my eyes roamed over this toned physique. Angie cleared her throat, and it pulled me out of my haze. I took the shirt from Mars and glanced around the room nervously until he zipped up his suit. Then he moved to the corner of the room where I joined him as he rolled up his sleeve.

Without hesitation, Mars pulled the sharp edge of the scissors into his skin. He didn't even flinch. I stood by to catch the blood. He glanced nervously at my hands before his eyes flickered to my face. Although I had cleaned my face, blood still coated my flight suit while flakes of it covered my hands and crusted under my nails.

"I'll be careful," I said with a whisper. He met my eyes with a hurt look I couldn't interpret.

The scissors left him with a deep cut and blood flowing freely. I caught it with his shirt and made sure not to touch him. Mars glanced over his shoulder where Angie had taken a seat on the desk. She and Ash were conversing in hushed tones.

"I'm sorry," he said in low voice. "I shouldn't have said ... you know, the things I did." Without looking up, I folded the shirt so the blood could spread, afraid to face him.

"I wasn't ready to hear it ... but it had to be said, I guess," I whispered. "Besides, I don't respond well to subtlety".

Mars grinned as he said, "I promise I'll never be subtle again."

"Does that mean you aren't fed up with me?"

He raised his uncut arm to place a hand on the part of my face that had caught the brunt of William's blow. I winced, afraid it might hurt, but his soft touch didn't allow for pain.

"I care about you," he said. My breath caught in my throat, and it became harder to breathe.

"But?" I said under the breath I managed to let out.

"But nothing."

I clumsily wrapped the shirt again, my brain spinning into directions it feared to go.

"I don't know how to make this work," I said. I hadn't been able to maintain a decent relationship with my direct family; how would I manage it with a boyfriend?

"Does anyone?"

I smiled at his remark but refused to look up. I could sense tears threatening my eyes. In an attempt to hide them, I focused on the shirt, which looked adequately soaked. My hands were coated with Mars's blood. Unsure what to say, I cleared my throat and turned to Ash and Angie.

"Do we have anything to wrap his arm up?" Ash rolled forward, reaching for the backpack that still hung off the back of her chair, and removed a shirt. They were leftovers from the clothes she had gone off to find for Angie.

"Here," she said, "pack it up good." Mars grabbed the shirt and wrapped it around his bleeding arm.

Ash pulled up her nose at the bloody rag that used to be Mars's T-shirt. It didn't hide her concerned expression. It turned out old habits died hard as Ash held on to the mask she wore to protect herself from being hurt. With my hands covered in blood, I bent to kiss the top of her head.

"It'll be okay," I whispered into her ear. She nodded with jaws clenched so tightly they wouldn't allow a reply. Angie stood by the door, blocking it.

"I should do this," she said.

"Probably," I said and grinned. "But you're a lot more valuable." There was no need to explain. She had been the first to survive a zombie bite without a natural high hormone count. Angie was proof the serum could work, and we needed to get her to Alaska in one piece.

Besides, the plan was set. Mars had to wait inside the room until Angie gave the all clear. I feared his cut wrist might attract the zombies into this hallway when we needed them to follow me.

"Wait until I've drawn them down the hall and past this hallway," I said as nerves started to rattle my voice. "Then wait for Angie's signal and get the hell out."

"Okay," Ash said when Angie stepped into the hallway, "be careful". She waited for me just outside the door. Ready to follow her, Mars took me by the arm.

"Just remember, okay," he said. Those pale jade eyes bored into me as they had the first time we'd kissed on that parking lot in front of a burning lab.

"Remember what?" I whispered

"It's not just about the people you need to be safe."

Our eyes met, and I felt unsure what to say. This whole thing was kind of about the people I needed to be safe.

"They need you as well," he said, "so you better get your ass back to us."

Mars looked over his shoulder where Ash sat in her chair, the mask she wore about to shatter. I wasn't far from choking up at his not-so-subtle reminder. He leaned in to kiss the top of my head.

"If you don't, I'll come and kick your ass."

I chuckled, unable to keep the nerves out. Fear of what I was about to do seemed to catch up, but I refused to let it get to me.

"You get your ass to that duct," I said. "I'll be right behind you." Ash raised a hand in good-bye as I clicked the door shut.

28

A tremble ran through my legs as I stepped into the middle of the hall. I turned to face Angie. She stood by the door with a determined look on her face.

"You've got this," she said.

I managed a half-smile. "Be careful," she added as I turned.

I stopped for a moment to take a breath. If I wanted to do this, I needed a cool head. With a tight fist I squeezed the bloody fabric to stop my hand from shaking. With careful steps, I moved to the end of the hall. At the corner, I stopped and glanced over my shoulder. Angie nodded and then crouched in front of the door. She needed to make sure not to attract the zombies' attention so she could alert Ash and Mars when they had to make their move. I nodded and took another deep breath before I stepped into the connecting hall.

I counted six of them. This wouldn't have scared me before. Zombies had ignored us enough for me to know they weren't interested in us, but we've had some hairy situations where agitated zombies didn't really see or smell the difference between regular people and us.

None of them reacted. I didn't know how long they had been standing there or how newly turned they were. Maybe they weren't hungry. That thought vanished when the nearest stuck its nose in the air. Dressed in green camouflage, which in itself wasn't a surprise—most of them were—the woman shifted her gaze to me. Her hair had been put up in a bun but, since then, had jumped in all kinds of directions. Blood ran down her cheek where a big chunk of flesh was missing from her face. I could see through it and out the side of her mouth when it stretched open and her jaw widened. Her head snapped my way.

Other zombies seemed to notice, and their eyes landed on me. I swallowed hard and remembered my job. Holding the shirt by the hem, I started to wave it. Noses shifted upward, and nostrils flared.

A zombie's head jerked as it took a step. He sniffed as if he couldn't place it. I figured my own body odor might be interfering with the smell of Mars's blood, and I held the shirt out. Several teeth snapped, making me jump. The zombie with the jerking head took another step forward, and others followed. In sync with them, I took a step backward. It worked. I started waving the bloody shirt in a frantic manner.

Growls sounded in unison. I had gotten their attention. In a slow-moving procession, they started to follow me. Moving backward, I glanced into the connecting corridor where Angie knelt by the door. She looked tense. Not that I wasn't feeling it. It was all I could do not to drop the rag and bolt. Walking among the brain dead was one thing, but trying to make zombies follow like the pied piper an entirely different one.

The lead zombie with the jerking head stopped as if he had changed his mind. Not that he had a working brain to change it with. He let out a growl that had me jump before he started to move, and I mean move. His slow shuffle turned into a more rapid pace. I backed up with quickening my steps, but he adjusted to my pace.

"Oh shit," I said under my breath.

As if they had heard or understood, they all growled. I almost stumbled, ducking for an arm that lashed out. Turning on my heel, I sprinted down the hall. I passed the T-junction, and from the corner of my eye I saw Angie siting crouched by the door but had to ignore her otherwise as I ran for the first door. I wiggled the handle, but it remained locked. *Why hadn't we checked the doors before we did this? Stupid!* A bloodied fist slammed into the wall next to me. They had gained on me. Never since the outbreak I had seen these things move this fast. How was this possible?

Unable to delve further into the why, I bolted for the next door. It too sat locked. I cursed and turned for the next one when a hand touched my shoulder. I yelped and turned to face the woman with half of her cheek missing. She opened her mouth to stretch her jaw. It snapped shut just inches from my face. Then a searing pain ran up my arm. A zombie had dropped to its knees and had gotten a hold of my hand holding the bloody shirt. I tried to pull it from him, but its teeth had a firm grip. As the zombie's teeth hit bone, I screamed and yanked harder. With my other arm, I pushed the woman to the side. I lifted my foot and planted my boot into the torso of the zombie biting my hand. It let go.

I turned to run. The zombie on its knees grabbed my leg, and I stumbled and crashed to the ground. On hands and knees, I crawled across the floor. As if the others had waited for their cue, they moved to follow me. Catching momentum, I got to my feet and slammed into the final door. This was it. If this thing didn't open, I would end up a zombie snack. I wrapped my hand around the handle, and a burst of pain shot up my arm. Along with the bloodied shirt wrapped around my wrist, everything about my hand looked like a bloody mess. I shook my hand to drop the rag as I tried the door with my other hand.

It clicked open just as a zombie slammed into me. With it, the door swung open, sending me tumbling inside the room. In a reflex, I kicked the door. It swung close, clocking another zombie in the head. It stumbled backward, and I kicked the door again. This time it clicked shut.

The zombie at my side moaned. I scrambled to my knees and crawled into the corner. Pain seared through my limbs as if they'd been gone through a shredder. In the corner, I reduced myself to the tiniest pile of human as I could manage. My heart hammered inside my chest on the brink of jumping out. Breathing hard, I watched the zombie that had entered the room along with me clamber to its feet.

In the hall outside, other zombies were pounding and scratching at the door, trying to get in. The zombie inside noticed and moved toward it. It pressed its nose against the door and sniffed. After a moment, it shook its head, and white milky eyes roamed across the room. Irises swimming in fog fell on me. For a moment, I feared it might attack. *Could Mars's smell still be clinging to me?* I inspected the bloody mess that used to be my right hand. It occurred to me I might be missing a finger. Blood ran from the wound where the zombie had bitten me—my blood.

The zombie shoved its nose into the air searching for the meal it had been chasing. I let out a breath when it shook its head. It seemed confused, as if unsure of what it was looking for. With the bloodied rag on the other side of the door, it had lost the scent of a potential snack. A tiny bit of relief washed over me until I remembered where I was. I had to get out of this office and out of this mountain.

My hand started to throb as took in my surroundings, and I cradled it to my chest. With the help of the desk that stood near the corner I was hiding in, I climbed to my feet. It turned out I was in one of the observation rooms. Computer screens decorated the walls with blinking lights and tons of graphic images. Desks filled the rest of the room.

As it ignored me, the zombie regained its idle shuffle and started to make its way to the back of the room. It seemed like as good a time as any to make my exit. I took the first step to the door when my vision started to blur. Blinking, I tried to focus, but it didn't work. I wanted to rub my hands over my eyeballs, but the blood on my hands kept me from doing so. It would probably make it worse.

I stumbled on my second step and sank to my knees. Pain shot through me as though the blood in my veins had caught fire. Without feeling the cold, my body started to shiver. I couldn't stop it. Fear took over when my eyesight worsened. *What was happening to me?* It seemed a stupid question. I had seen it before, but I refused to believe. *This couldn't be happening to me, could it?* Not after all this shit.

I curled up on the floor, shaking. My groans of pain must have alerted the zombie because it started to make its way to me. With slow, shuffling steps, it closed in. Gathering my strength, I forced my body into a sitting position. Every muscle ached, and the chatter of my teeth wasn't funny anymore. I crawled across the floor until I reached the wall next to the door.

The zombie seemed enticed by my efforts to get to my feet. The former soldier opened its mouth wide. A moan combined with a hiss rose from the deepest bottom of its throat. Its head dropped to a side after it sniffed the air. Except for some blood that ran down a sleeve from its shoulder and those damned milky eyes, it seemed so human. Nothing resembled the shredded bloodied forms that a zombie was supposed to have, but then these hadn't been around for that long. Although, even the eyes that must have made her stand out as young woman before she turned screamed of fear—this wasn't a run-of-the-mill zombie.

Her irises appeared wide behind the fog and showed a childlike curiosity. It stopped a few feet in front of me and raised an arm. A pale hand stretched its bony fingers. I squeezed my eyes shut in an effort to clear my vision. When I opened them, the fog hadn't disappeared. *Had I turned into one of them?* The fact that I asked myself that question should mean I hadn't, or was this what it was like to be trapped inside your own body? Thought upon thought collided inside my mind until it became impossible to hold a coherent thought. I strained to get air into my lungs, but the pain in my chest made it hard to breathe, while darkness crept up on me.

I woke with a jolt, unsure of what had happened or how much time had passed. As I glanced around the room and saw the zombie milling in a corner, it all came back to me. Sitting up, I noticed the shakes running through my body had faded, and I found a way to gather my thoughts. I hadn't turned. From what everyone had been telling me, and from what the tests had predicted, I couldn't turn. Still, the fear of it wasn't easy to subside.

With a hand on the door handle, I forced myself off the ground. The zombie clacked its teeth and then raised its arm a little as if it wanted my attention. I looked away as its pleading eyes met mine, unable to face the horror behind them. This had to be one of the new strain virus zombies that Dr. David had created. Somehow that new strain must have been introduced to my blood. How else would this type of zombie show up here? It seemed Dr. David had done more to me than just collect samples for his research. A small flicker of her remained present inside that body. My eyes fell on the name tag stitched to its chest. It read *Schumer*. I felt sorry for it or her, and felt ashamed that I was the one that had caused this, but I couldn't stay. With a turn of the handle, I opened the door and slid out.

29

More like her greeted me in the hallway. The six or so zombies that had chased me into this room crowded the hall. They all stood there in their army fatigues, watching me with blank stares. None of them made an attempt to attack. Instead, they all raised a pleading hand. It appeared to be a similar gesture as I had witnessed with the zombie inside the office. Teeth clacked and heads shifted to the side, resembling curious puppies.

The sight of them made something snap inside my head. I couldn't be here. I had to get out, away from these people whose lives I had destroyed. I took a step, hoping they would disperse, but they all kept their positions, blocking my way. Shoulder first, I tried to push myself past them. They wouldn't budge. I shoved harder until one of them lost its balance and tumbled against another one.

Using the last remaining strength left in my body, I shouldered my way through. Cold, sticky hands ran through my hair and along my face. They held on to my flight suit, but I pushed through— determined to get as far from them as possible. Half stumbling and flailing my arms, I fought my way past them. I came to a halt at the corner where I had last seen Angie.

My mind kept wandering to what had remained

viable inside the heads of the former soldiers. Even with my vision blurred, I could make out raised arms and pleading stares as they stumbled in pursuit. The sight of them tightened my throat and made it harder to breathe. I slid around the corner, steadying myself against the wall until I found the office where I had last seen my friends. It didn't seem right to think of them as friends, for they had become my family, and I felt relieved when I found the room empty. They must have made it to the maintenance duct as planned. I closed the door a crack, hoping the zombies wouldn't spot me. Eyes closed, I focused on my breathing. I needed to shut them out. Nothing could reverse what I had done. My resolve started to fade, and I felt my legs grow weak to the point I doubted they'd carry me far. I needed to get my head on straight.

You better get your ass back to us. Words spoken by Mars right by this door found their way to the forefront of my mind. If I were to find any kind of redemption for what I had done, I needed to find a way out of here. I needed to get back to my family and not just the one in this country. For the first time in my life, I realized I needed both families as much as they needed me, and I had to find a way to let them know.

I forced myself to focus on the faces that mattered. I couldn't help the ones who had turned, and it wouldn't do me any good to let myself be haunted by them. It was Angie, Mars, and Ash I needed to get back to. I balled my fist and flung it at the wall. The pain caused by the hit didn't even compare to the pain that radiated from my bitten hand that still bled profusely. For some reason, I welcomed the pain—as it kept me on my toes. As I opened the door, I couldn't see any of the zombies that had followed me, and I stepped into the hall. My hand throbbed, and I didn't see myself crawling through that maintenance duct the others had used to get out. Besides, on my own I didn't have to worry about anybody, and I decided to find the exit in a regular fashion. Cradling my bitten hand and using the wall for support, I took one step after another to get to the open area.

Finding the open area was slow going. Something was still wrong with my eyes, and rubbing them didn't help. The zombies I encountered didn't help either. Instead of shuffling in their idle position, they sought me out. Every last one of them either came toward me or followed me. Fortunately, they didn't attack, but it started to resemble a creepy Halloween parade.

I cornered a hallway with about fifteen zombies on my tail when I heard a shot. On instinct, I sank to my knees. I raised a hand to signal my companions, but then thought the better of it. The gesture made me want to laugh and cry at the same time. Maybe I *had* turned if I'd started to see them as my own.

Shaking my head to lose the thought, I focused on the shots being fired. The noise came from behind a set of double doors at the end of the corridor from what I presumed to be the open area.

Automatic gunfire reverberated throughout the hallway in rapid succession. But in a way, they seemed controlled and didn't sound like the panicked trigger-happy fingers of someone on the run from zombies.

I got to my feet and, sticking to the wall, eased myself to the doors. The weapons fire stopped for a moment, only to be replaced by the *click, click* of reloading the weapon before it continued. I stopped when it seemed to come closer. My heart hammered inside my throat. Blinking ferociously, I tried to clear my vision. There wasn't an alcove or anywhere for me to hide in the hall between the double doors and me. The zombies behind me made me eerily aware that whoever might step through that door would shoot first and ask questions later.

Another step took me closer to the doors. One of the zombies behind me moaned. The others joined in as if they had started their own little choir. I wanted to turn, as if a finger to the lips would shut them up, when the double doors swung open.

In a reflex, I dropped to my knees, wrapped my arms around my head and made myself as small as possible. Every muscle in my body tensed as I squeezed my eyes shut and waited for the inevitable.

Instead of the rapid report of automatic gunfire, words filled the hall.

"Holly shit," Angie said in loud voice, "are you planning a shindig?" I didn't react to her words and stayed huddled down on the floor. Angie hadn't pulled the trigger yet, but that didn't mean she wouldn't. One look at my eyes could change that.

I sensed the uneasy shuffle of the infected behind me as if they cleared a space around me. I heard Angie's footsteps closing in.

"Mags," she said in a low voice. I didn't know what to do. My body seemed frozen in place, and I didn't trust my voice to speak. *What if a zombie growl would exit my throat? Would Angie put a bullet in my head?*

A hand touched my shoulder. Without opening my eyes, I tilted my head. "Hey," she said, "It's me. It's okay." I shook my head. With a deep breath, I gathered my courage, and opened my eyes into a slit.

"I don't think it is," I said. The sounds that came from my mouth were rough and a mere croak, but it was my voice. I raised my head to face Angie. To her credit, she didn't flinch. Had she expected this?

"It's not as bad as it looks," she said, "but I think we should get out of here."

I hissed in pain as she took my arm to throw it over her shoulder. She stopped and inspected my hand.

"Jeezes, you're missing a finger or two," she said.

I replied with a groan. Angie's hands rummaged through her pockets and removed some bandages along with a plastic vial. My stomach turned at the sight. This wasn't going to be good.

"Clench your teeth," she said. My hand shook as she grabbed my wrist in a tight hold. She didn't wait for a reaction. Instead, she poured the liquid from the vial over my hand. It burned as if she had cut off the rest of my fingers. I jerked my hand to get it out of Angie's grasp, but her hold was too strong. The hand on my wrist clamped down like a vice. I screamed out in pain. Angie grabbed the bandages and started wrapping them around my hand. I slumped against the wall, overwhelmed by the pain. As she worked, her eyes kept darting to the crowd that had gathered in the hallway.

The zombies who had traveled at my back down these halls had created some distance. They seemed to watch us with interest. I tried to focus on Angie. I couldn't let myself think of the people that used to work these halls in their former capacities. It reminded me too much of what I had done to them.

Angie finished her work and let out a breath. Her hand reached up to touch my face, and I winced.

"It okay," she said. "Just …" She didn't finish her sentence and continued to move her thumb to my lower eyelid. She pulled the lid down and peered into my eyes. With a shake of her head she said, "Great, now we won't be able to take you *anywhere*, forget Disneyland."

My throbbing hand occupied my brain, and I couldn't think of a single word to say, so I raised an eyebrow.

"Maybe we can hide the zombification with some shades, say you're blind or something," Angie said as she thoughtfully eyed me.

"Zombification?"

"Well, you look like them, but you're not, right?" she said, "You're sort of coherent, so I'm thinking not."

Great, I have zombie eyes. Angie didn't give me time to voice my discomfort. "Maybe it'll subside like they did with me," she said. "We'll see. Come on, we have to go."

Angie pulled me to my feet, this time by the other arm, and she pulled it over her shoulder. As we moved to the double doors, the zombies behind us stirred. Angie looked over her shoulder and raised an eyebrow.

"They are following us," she said in a hushed tone.

"Yeah, I'd noticed that."

She turned us to face them and paused.

"What the ..." she started to say, but broke off. A little over a dozen pale-faced foggy eyed creatures stood watching us in their green uniforms. Pleading arms stretched out in front of them as if they wanted something from us. One of them took a step. In a reflex, Angie's hand went to the rifle that hung strapped to her shoulder. The zombie's mouth opened, and both hands raised palms up.

"I think they want to die," I said.

"What!" Angie exclaimed. "Zombies don't act like that."

"Well, these do," I said. "They're like the 3.0 version of Dr. David's variation on the virus. He made them aware, remember." Angie looked at me wide eyed before her head shot back to take in the pleading zombies. Their faces looked nothing like the blood-drained, decrepit sacks of bones we had encountered before. These almost looked like the human beings.

Angie released my arm, shouldered her rifle, and pulled the handgun from its holster. She extended the handgun.

"You're helping," she said in a hard tone. This was my mess, and I was obligated to help her. I appreciated that she didn't point it out.

I took the gun from her with my good hand and nodded. Not waiting for Angie, I walked up to the first zombie. This was my mess. I raised the weapon to point at his forehead. Its pleading arms dropped, and its eyes closed. A sickening feeling rose up in my throat. Before I could puke all over this poor man, I pulled the trigger.

30

None of them attacked us. They all just stood there waiting for the bullet that would put them out of their miseries. As if they were at peace with their fate. One by one, bodies fell to the ground until none of them were left.

With a combination of regret and relief raging inside my gut, I handed the gun to Angie. Instead of keeping it, she reloaded and handed it back. I had hoped it would be over. That these would be last to die by my hand. This time it really felt as if I had killed human beings instead of taking out zombies.

"We can't leave yet," Angie said as I started to walk to the double doors. I turned to face her.

"Why not?"

"Whitfield wants me to walk the halls," she replied. For a moment I wondered how it had been possible for Angie and the others to get out, talk to Whitfield, and then for Angie to come back in such a short time, but then I remembered passing out. I must have been out longer than I had thought, I realized as Angie continued. "Zombies aren't as much of a threat to me, so he wants me to take out what I can, before he sends in the cavalry."

I swallowed hard to force down the barrier in my throat. Besides the fact that this place was an enormous area to cover for one person, the job itself

I knew to be horrendous. I swayed a little on my feet but quickly regained my balance.

"Listen, you stay here and wait for me. You look paler than Ash," Angie said as she stepped closer, "and I don't trust those guys at the door. They might shoot you on sight with those eyes of yours."

"Trigger-happy soldiers," I said with a smirk.

"Something like that."

I squinted at her as if that would help to get her face into focus. "I think I'll come with you," I said. Angie didn't say it, and even though her face was still a bit blurry, I could tell she was worried.

"I'll be fine," I said to reassure her.

"All right," she replied, but I knew I hadn't convinced her.

My legs had reclaimed their function, and I followed Angie down the halls without her support. We took out the zombies as we went along. If you turned your mind off, pulling the trigger didn't seem to come as hard; also, the fog impairing my vision helped. After a while, I started to fall behind and Angie needed to stop at the end of each hallway so I could catch up.

"Let's take a break," she said after the tenth or so stop.

She didn't have to tell me twice. As my back hit the wall, I slid down in a crouched position. I wanted to focus on my breathing, but all I could do was watch the gun in my hand. How had I gotten from being an office worker in my dad's company to shooting zombies in a high-security facility? The thought reminded me of my mom and the messages she had left. I still hadn't listened to all of them. Maybe I shouldn't listen to them anymore. The person they were spoken to had ceased to exist. The thing that had remained of that already-broken person was less than a shell. A half shell that saw through the eyes of a zombie and killed the things she had become.

Angie touched me on the shoulder. I hadn't even noticed her kneeling down next to me. Unwilling, I forced myself to face her. If we managed to get out of here, I knew I would have to face some judgmental stares for what had happened to these people, and I might as well start with her. Angie hit me with that dark gaze she had managed to perfect. I might have been mistaken because of my funky vision, but I didn't sense the resentment I expected.

"Here's the thing," she said calmly, "Whitfield kind of wants you dead."

I blinked and almost chuckled a laugh at that. She didn't waste time sugarcoating it.

"I guess that shouldn't be a surprise," I said.

"Yeah, he thinks you've gone zombie." She said without hesitation. "The footage of you lumbering down the halls with a bunch of zombies on your tail seemed to have him convinced."

"They have footage?"

"Well, you know these places. They have backups for the backups for the backups," she said.

"They've had the place evacuated pretty quickly to a secondary facility. It didn't take them long to start monitoring the internal systems."

"Are they watching us now?"

"Probably," she said as she sat down next to me. I guessed that would mean I was screwed. If Whitfield wanted me dead, then he would just have someone wait for me at the exit. I didn't know of another way out. Or maybe he had already sent me my executioner. Would Whitfield be so callous to send my friend to kill me?

I rested my head against the wall and watched Angie from the corner of my eye. She seemed relaxed as if she was sitting with a friend in the park.

"So ... what are you waiting for?" I asked. As if she hadn't heard me, she clicked out the empty magazine from the rifle and replaced it with a new one.

"Why haven't you shot me already?" I added. Angie stopped what she was doing to look at me.

"You have some serious trust issues, don't you?"

I glared at her.

"You said Whitfield wanted me dead," I said as a matter of fact. Her mouth twitched into a slight curve. If I had blinked I would have missed it.

"I said he kind of wanted you dead, but the man isn't an idiot. He needs us to get that data to Alaska —they need us to go there, so they can create Divus juice, and two is always better," she said. "Besides, that skinny doctor we met in Matley's lab became all excited when he found out you had gotten yourself bitten again."

She placed emphasize on the last word and grinned.

"They are curious of the effect and, therefore, still need our participation." She climbed to her feet and grabbed my good hand. "That said, this means you should probably shut up and don't start acting all zombie and shit," she said. "And for God sakes, keep your eyes down."

I let her pull me up and watched her in silence for a moment. Unable to hold her gaze, I dropped my chin to my chest.

"Come on," she said, "let's get out of this mountain."

When we reached the main entrance where General Whitfield waited for us behind a barricade of soldiers, my hand throbbed like a bitch. I did as Angie said and kept my head down. It didn't seem to matter, because Whitfield was bent on ignoring me anyhow. Unfortunately, Colonel Cornwell had a different idea. He threw a tantrum like a spoiled brat. It added up to something like we could have lost the entire base because of you, but my head couldn't process his words. It might have been because of the blood loss, but anyhow they didn't hit home. All I could do was scan the crowd for familiar faces, the ones I knew that might not judge me, but I couldn't find them.

When Cornwell finished spitting in my face, medics rushed in to place me on a stretcher and shoved me into a vehicle where one of them started to inspect my hand. Everything after that became a blur, and it wasn't just because of this white mist swimming across my eyes. The needle that one of the medics stuck in my arm could have had something to do with it.

The blur changed into strange images. Faces of people I knew and loved crowded my mind. Eyes with colorless irises engulfed by a white mist peered at me from every single person. My mom, dad, brother, and sister, even Mars, stood in the mob with stretched arms out to get me. It wasn't until something jerked my body around to face William's dead eyes that I woke with a start.

It took me a moment to orient myself in the darkened space. Light filtered in from what looked like a door, but I couldn't tell whether it was day or night inside this windowless room. At the sound of a soft click, a light standing on a small table switched on.

I squinted against the brightness and wanted to cover my eyes. Pain shot up my right arm as I tried to raise it and found it heavily packed in a thick layer of bandages. Three fingers peeked out the top.

"Zombies ate your fingers," a soft voice said. I recognized Ash, and lowering the bandaged hand, I found her sitting at my side. The lamp cast a shadow across her face, hiding her features, but I could tell she looked tired. I blinked after I noticed the blur fogging up my eyes had vanished and color had returned to my vision. Feeling relieved Ash didn't have to witness my zombie eyes, I shifted onto my side to face her. Muscles in my limbs ached and my hand, along with my head, throbbed, but otherwise I felt all right.

Ash wore a new flight suit without the spatter of blood, and her combed hair looked damp as if freshly showered. I glanced down at what I was wearing and noticed a brand-new flight suit. Glad to see Ash, I smiled.

"Where are we?" I asked. My voice came out more or less as a croak, and my throat felt as if I'd smoked a pack of cigarettes.

"Above ground," Ash said in a tiny voice, "Whitfield set us up in some kind of improvised housin' while they are makin' sure the base is zombie-free."

As she spoke I glanced around the tiny windowless room, but it was the quaver in her voice that drew my attention back to Ash.

"You okay?" I asked.

Ash shook her head no and rolled her chair closer to the stretcher I was lying on. Light fell on her features, and the sight of her took me aback. She looked so fragile and small. Tears glistened her eyes, and her lower lip trembled. This wasn't the fake pucker she used to get her way.

"Hey," I said, reaching out with my good hand. "It's okay."

My fingers raked through her damp hair before I pulled her closer. She leaned in, wrapping her arms around me and burying her face between my neck and shoulder. Within seconds, her tears dampened my skin.

"It's okay," I repeated. "We're both okay, right?"

Ash gripped me tighter before she spoke into my shoulder, "You didn't follow ... we waited but you didn't come ... it took so long and you didn't come." Her words rolled out almost frantically—the voice of a little kid. Angie had been right, earlier in the lab. Ash was still a kid, and she needed to be reminded about that fact herself, once in a while. I gripped her tighter, wrapping both arms around her and ignored the throbbing in my hand.

"It's okay, baby," I said without thinking of the repercussions. "I'm here." This time there weren't any.

It turned out to be night, and by the time Angie showed up, Ash had crawled onto the stretcher with me and lay curled against my side. Without any room to move on the narrow stretcher, I raised a hand to welcome Angie.

She also wore a fresh flight suit, and her wet, braided hair rested on her shoulder. A newly molded Mohawk perked on the top of her head. She plopped down in Ash's wheelchair and let out an exasperated breath.

"Zombie ate your fingers," she said.

"Tell me something I don't know," I said with a chuckle as I raised my bandaged hand. The loss of my fingers hadn't hit me yet, probably because I felt glad to be alive; besides, I preferred my left hand, so I should be able to survive.

"How's our kid doing?" she said, placing emphasis on the word *kid*. Angie rolled closer, looking surprised at the lack of retort, but Ash was out cold—hopefully sleeping a dreamless sleep.

"She's out," I whispered and wiped a couple of stray hairs from Ash's face.

"Probably a good thing," Angie whispered. She rolled the chair back and forth. I watched her for a moment as she occupied herself, an aching question on my mind. Although I had no idea what time it was, it felt as if it had been hours since I'd woken up and there hadn't been a sign from Mars.

"Where's ... I mean, have you seen Mars?" I asked hesitantly. The same shadow from the lamp that had helped hiding Ash's face now covered Angie's. Her hands stopped rolling the chair, and I felt her dark gaze fall on me.

"He's been here, but you were out," she said. "Now, it seems they've been planning for most of the night and will be for some time." Something in her voice told me she didn't agree or maybe didn't like the fact of being shut out.

"You mean with Whitfield and Cornwell," I

said.

Angie nodded as she replied, "And some others."

"You know what they're planning," I asked and hesitated before I added, "for us?"

Her hands wrapped tighter around the wheels of the chair and started moving it back and forth. It started to make me nervous, and it occurred to me she might be nervous, too.

"I don't know," she said. She kept her gaze on the ground as if she didn't want to face me.

"What's wrong?" I asked. I had known Angie long enough to know something was up. That woman lacked the capability to be nervous in normal circumstances. She stopped shifting the chair and stood. She leaned in, and her hand came down to gently caress Ash's cheek.

"You should get some sleep," she said and gestured to an extra stretcher on the other side of the room. "You want me to take her? I doubt you'll get any sleep like this."

I shook my head. "No, it's fine. I don't wanna wake her."

Her hand shifted from Ash's cheek to my shoulder and squeezed it.

"Then I'll take it," she said and took the two steps it took to cross the room. The stretcher creaked as she sat down. She grabbed the blanket on top and draped it over her legs.

I waited for a moment for the silence to return.

Outside I heard the sounds of wildlife and the occasional pair of boots slushing through the mud. In the distance, I could hear an engine or two rumble before they took off.

"You haven't answered my question before," I said after a moment and had realized she had diverted my question when I had asked her what was wrong. Angie's breathing had turned shallow, but I knew she'd be awake. Her head shifted to face me after a long moment.

"I don't like being kept in the dark," she said in a low voice. "Now sleep. You're gonna need it."

I watched her for a moment and then said, "But you've been out there, right, and talked to people. You must know something, like what happened to Dr. David."

Angie rolled to her side and looked straight at me. Even with the dimmed light, I could tell her eyes held me with a venomous glare.

"For as far as I know, Warren is missing in action. No one has seen him, but it seems I am no longer in the service of the FBI, because my condition," she said, making air quotes around the last word, "makes me a security risk, so it's not like anyone is telling me anything—even your boyfriend won't talk to me." Her words came out in a hard tone, but nonetheless she tried to keep her voice down, so she wouldn't wake Ash. It wasn't difficult to decipher the hurt expressed on her face. Angie huffed out a breath in frustration and plopped down on her back.

"I'm sorry," I said. She turned her head to face me

"We used to be friends you know—went through training together and everything," she said, and from her words I presumed she was talking about Mars. "Now he just looks at me with a pained expression as if he's got the whole world on his shoulders."

"He must have told you something."

Angie nodded and placed a hand on her forehead and rubbed it as if to fend off a headache.

"The big plan is to vaccinate large groups of soldiers who'll be sent east to eradicate the zombies," she said, "but they need to be sure the vaccine works. We are to meet with Whitfield in the morning, and maybe we'll get some more details."

"So they wanna keep us around for that?"

"Yep," she said and dropped her hand at her side.

I gaze up at the ceiling, not sure how I felt about that. "You think we'll have any kind of say in whatever they're planning?" I asked. On the other stretcher, I heard Angie shift and I directed my gaze toward her. She had regained her position lying on her side, her head perched on her hand.

"I doubt it," she said, which wasn't exactly what I wanted to hear. "But we kind of owe it to the world to try and help."

"I guess," I said with a sigh and looked down at

Ash who lay nestled at my side. "The kid stays out of it, though."

"I think we can all agree on that, even Whitfield," Angie said. "The general might be a hard ass, but he's not callous."

"I'm not so sure about that," I said under my breath. The room fell silent after that, and my thoughts shifted toward home. I wondered if I would ever get to see my family again and felt the urge to call them, but I had left my phone inside my pack somewhere inside that mountain.

"Listen," Angie said, pulling me from my thoughts, "I'm not going to roll over and do whatever they want, but let's not freak out before they have a chance to explain themselves, and if it turns out to be something we can't agree to, then we figure out something else."

"Like what?"

"Like get the hell out of here, find a nice place, and ride out the apocalypse," she said. "Now get some sleep."

I could read the determination on her face, and as I held her dark gaze, I felt this nagging feeling that it was going to be a long time before I would see the rest of my family again.

"It's going to be okay, and no one is going to touch the kid," Angie added as she pulled a blanket over her shoulder, "right?"

"Right," I said at a mere whisper. Although I didn't have much faith in tomorrow, I knew we also didn't have much of a choice. I reached for the lamp, which wasn't easy without waking Ash.

With a click, the room was bathed in darkness.

"Good night," I whispered into the dark and soon felt the world around me disappear.

31

It hadn't been a good idea to let Ash sleep on my stretcher, because I woke from a fitful sleep. Ash stirred and perked her head up. I groaned as I tried to shift my body and lifted my hand. Pain shot up my arm, and I hissed in agony.

"Son of a ..." I moaned. Ash quickly pushed her legs over the side of the stretcher and sat up.

"Sorry," she whispered as she pulled her chair closer and slipped into it. I sat up, cradling my arm and grinding my teeth to bite through the pain.

"Not your fault, kiddo," I said through clenched teeth. Realizing my mistake, I looked up at Ash. She sat unmoving in her chair with a scrunched-up face and biting her lower lip. From the other side of the room, Angie glared at me as if I'd just kicked a puppy or something.

"Back at ya," Ash said after a moment of silence.

Angie burst out laughing, something I didn't hear too often. The sound together with the expression on Ash's face made me smile, while I leaned forward in the same instance. I felt sick and sucked in air to keep myself from throwing up. My hand felt as if someone had been whacking it with a hammer.

"Here," Angie said as something landed on my

stretcher. A plastic bottle lay next to me, and I grabbed it with my good hand. I fumbled to get the cap off and set the bottle to my mouth.

"Just two," Angie said. "Take two every couple of hours."

Taking her advice, I let two pills drop into my mouth and dry swallowed them. I took a moment, hoping the painkillers would kick in fast, and let out a long breath of air.

"What time is it?" I asked no one particular.

"Time to get up," Angie said. I scowled at her. The pills hadn't kicked in yet, and the pain was killing me. I wasn't in the mood for fun and games.

"About eight" she added.

"You think they'll let us out?" Ash said as she rolled her chair to the entrance. What I had thought to be a regular door last night turned out to be the opening to a container. I had figured it had to be part of that of makeshift housing Ash had mentioned.

"Huh," I said blinking at the sunlight coming in through the door. "Out of what?"

Angie stood from her stretcher and walked over to me. She helped me stand and then said, "It's time you find out what we've gotten ourselves into."

I frowned, not liking were this seemed to be going. Angie's face looked strained as she maneuvered me to follow Ash out the container. As I walked out, I cradled my arm tightly to my chest —afraid someone would bump into it. My eyes needed some adjustment to the light. The sun had barely found its way up into the sky, but already shone brightly. I blinked and found the meaning behind Ash's words.

Our container sat in the corner of an enormous parking lot. About four meters from the metal box stood wooden fences that surrounded the container on all sides. They weren't the threatening barbed wire kind of fences that stood seven feet tall, but more like something used at a construction site. They wouldn't have stopped us from an attempted escape if it weren't for the three guards walking around the perimeter. At a significant distance across the parking lot, I could see an area with buildings and people bustling around. I glanced down at Angie who shrugged.

"Wanna explain?" I asked.

"Well, you had those funky eyes and everything," she said and shrugged again, "so they thought it better to keep us from general population for the time being."

"Great," I said before I considered Ash might have seen my eyes after all. I glanced at her, but she didn't seem fazed by the mention of them.

"They said it would be a short isolation to be sure you wouldn't turn," Ash said. "And you didn't eat us, so you passed."

"So why are you in here then?" I asked.

"Moral support," Angie said.

"We volunteered," Ash said, looking up, "to

keep an eye on you."

I managed a hesitant smile. While I appreciated Angie and Ash's gesture, the fact that they thought I needed to be separated didn't make me feel any better.

"Thanks," I said, despite the twisting feeling in my gut.

"Good, you're awake," a man said in a loud voice. I looked up to see the geeky-looking beanstalk of a man with the black wide-rimmed glasses who we had glimpsed inside Dr. Matley's lab. The man entered our makeshift isolation area. Ignoring Ash and Angie, he pulled out a penlight and directed it at my eyes. I flinched at the bright light, but the man seemed satisfied. Then, while he guided us past the barricade, he started talking about how excited he was that I not only had survived one but two zombie bites. It took about a minute for me to feel exhausted by the man's chirpiness, and my shoulders slumped as I followed him. Two of the soldiers who had been standing guard at the container followed us, and as I glanced at them, one of them rolled his eyes at his colleague while he nodded in the direction of the geeky beanstalk. His gesture made me smile. Guess, I wasn't the only one jaded by the rambling man.

The geeky-looking beanstalk didn't notice as he kept blabbing away about my medical significance while we followed him across the parking lot to a two-story building. Everywhere I looked, trees surrounded us, and to our left, the mountain that I presumed held the military complex rose over the roof of the building we approached. The thought of Dr. Matley and her lifeless corpse lying on the floor of her own lab, along with all the other lives lost, sent a cold shiver down my spine.

Not at complete ease, I glanced over my shoulder at the two soldiers following us. It wasn't any different from what I had experienced inside the mountain. In there they wouldn't let us walk around on our own either, but somehow it felt daunting out here in the open sky as if our lives weren't our own anymore.

The beanstalk, whose name I couldn't remember—or maybe he had never mentioned it— flashed a card at the entrance of the building. One of the two guards posted there nodded, and they both turned to open the door for us.

Angie had taken the lead behind the beanstalk, Ash stuck to the middle, and I took up the rear as we walked along a corridor that reminded me of a combination of a hospital and the office spaces inside the mountain, but with windows. The beanstalk guided us past a secretary's desk and through a pair of glass doors. It was when the doors fell closed that I noticed that Beanstalk hadn't followed us inside. The room behind the glass doors had a similar boardroom feel to it as the one inside the mountain, except this one looked a lot brighter.

Light filtering in from the outside reflected on to a mirror, which I decided to avoid, but it added more light to the sand-colored interior. Big leather chairs that seemed to beg for my attention stood around a mahogany table. My hand throbbed, although I had a feeling the pain medication had started to do its work, and I debated whether to sit down.

Al those thoughts faded into the background when, beyond the glass doors, I saw Mars approach us. If it weren't for the serious expression on General Whitfield's round face and Colonel Cornwell with his permanent frown at his side, I might have been tempted to make a short sprint to greet him. It wasn't until our gazes met and I registered his expressions that my heart sank. Something was wrong—I could see it in his eyes.

I moved to stand alongside Ash while Angie stood behind her. We exchanged glances, and I think we all knew something was up as we waited for them to enter. The three of them took up the side of the table near the door while the three of us remained standing on the other end of the room.

Whitfield gestured for us to sit, but I hesitated. As the general and Colonel Cornwell took a seat, Mars lingered behind them. He changed his expression to something more comforting, but his glance toward Ash made me feel nervous. I didn't understand what he was trying to tell me, but it raised the uncomfortable feeling already stirring inside me to a new level.

"Please, take a seat," Whitfield said, lifting a hand in invitation. Then he turned to Mars, who was still standing behind them. "Agent," he added. Mars flinched, but quickly composed himself and joined the men at the table.

Unsure what to do, and, in fact, unsure of the entire situation, I froze until Angie spoke.

"We'll stand if you don't mind," she said as a young man knocked on the glass door and entered without pause. The young man handed the general a stack of papers and left without a glance at us.

"Let's see," Whitfield said as he rummaged through the papers. "Our final count is forty-two dead including five of Dr. Warren's men and six are still missing."

His words felt like a stab through the heart. The look of disgust Cornwell directed at Whitfield before he turned his accusing face my way felt even more painful. At that point I wished I had taken the option to sit.

"This isn't fair," Mars said appalled. "You cannot put this on her—" Before Mars could suck in a breath to continue, Cornwell interrupted him.

"We aren't here to lay blame," he said, "but we can't ignore the fact that the three of you pose a certain threat."

"A threat that you added to," Angie chimed in, referring to herself.

"True," Whitfield said as he flipped through a few more pages. Then he released the pile and sat back in his chair. I tried to gauge the man, but he had the unreadable face of a poker player.

He sucked in a breath, and it made me fear the words he was about to utter. "Colonel Cornwell here has suggested that we should ship the three of you off to Alaska on a prisoner transport where you would aid us in finding the means to fight Mortem," Whitfield said in a casual tone as he lifted a hand to indicate the colonel. "Wasn't that how you had put it, Colonel?"

A shock ran through me jolting my heart into overdrive. *Had Angie been wrong about the general?* Cornwell nodded with a satisfied look on his face. My good hand balled into a fist as Ash spoke up.

"You can't do that," she said in a loud voice.

Cornwell chimed in, pointing an accusing finger at us and said, "You are a danger to our society and —"

"Who put us in this situation in the first place?" Angie said interrupting Cornwell.

"Enough," Whitfield said, lifting a hand in a gesture for everyone to shut up.

"Fortunately for you, that is not the way we operate here," Whitfield said.

"But, sir," Cornwell tried to interject, but Whitfield shot him a hard glare. The room fell silent for a moment, and we all stared at the general, who resumed sifting through his papers as if we weren't even in the room. He stopped on a page and laid it open. The letters were upside-down and too small for me to read, but I recognized the logo on the top of the page. It was an orange V with, underneath it, black and bold letters—my father's company logo. My muscles tensed as my eyes shifted from the logo to Whitfield.

"We've been in contact with your father," he said. "He is very eager to get you home, Ms. Vissers."

I released the breath I was holding and felt a shimmer of hope ignite inside me. Maybe home wasn't that far away.

"I have spoken with him in great detail concerning the current situation," Whitfield continued. "He explained that your country has maintained a stable situation—meaning that they have managed to slow the spread of the outbreak and are now working on containment."

I felt my legs wobble as Whitfield continued to explain what my father had told him, how the first outbreak started at Schiphol airport and many people had died. He also explained how the Dutch had made use of the hundreds of miles of canals to help contain the spread, but I had no idea how that would work. Whitfield continued announcing the counted death toll as if he were reciting the numbers of a lottery ticket, but as he started naming places like Amsterdam and Haarlem, it started to hit me, names that sounded so foreign coming from the general's mouth, but felt so dear to me. Although my hometown of Rotterdam wasn't among the cities mentioned, it became difficult to keep myself upright.

"I think I'll take that seat after all," I said as I pulled the chair back and sat down. Angie pulled another chair from the table on my left to make room for Ash and then found a seat of her own next to Ash.

I glanced around the table, and except for the red-faced anger coming from Cornwell, and Whitfield, who was reading from his papers, all eyes were on me. Mars, Ash, and even Angie gave me sad looks, which seemed ridiculous because this was happening to all of us. Unable to hold their stares, I glanced down at the bandaged hand resting in my lap. Only my thumb and two fingers stuck out, and I wiggled them. It started to throb again, and having heard enough of the atrocities happening around the world, I just wished Whitfield would come to the point. He might have not wanted to lock us up, but I was sure there was an angle to his story.

When he finished, Whitfield looked up to face me and folded his hand on top of his papers.

"You see, Ms. Vissers, this outbreak is as much of a concern to you as it is to us," he said. Whitfield paused, and I looked up from my hand to see whether I had missed a question, but as soon as our eyes met, he said, "I have explained your condition to your father."

I had to fight the tears threatening my eyes as

Whitfield told me how relieved and grateful my father had been when he heard that Mortem had stopped my deterioration from cancer and that he couldn't wait to tell my mom.

"Your father is not a fool," Whitfield said. "He knows the stakes and what your assistance might mean for the fight against the zombie threat."

Before he could start to use my family to swindle me into doing something I probably didn't want to do, I spoke up.

"What is it that you want?" I asked, trying to keep my voice steady. I knew the stakes and I didn't need him to drag my family into this, at least not the one back home.

"We need you to accompany Ms. Meadow to one of our medical facilities," he said, sounding casual. "Ms. Meadow is our best chance to finding a solution to our problem, the key to unlock phase three."

I glanced sidewise to look at Angie. She shrugged. Nothing new there. We knew from what Matley had told us that another phase of testing would be necessary. They needed to reproduce the accelerated growth of cells along with something to induce hormone levels. Those two combined with the vaccine would prevent women and men from getting infected. Although I had no idea why they wanted me there—except maybe as a backup.

"Why me?" I asked. Whitfield sat back in his seat with an audible sigh.

"We've seen what happened to you inside the mountain after ..." he said as he gestured at my hand. "We need to verify our solution is stable—it wouldn't be wise to start inoculating folks if it meant they would eventually turn."

"Is this the medical facility in Alaska that Matley mentioned?" Angie asked.

"It is," Cornwell said.

"What about Ash?" I asked.

Cornwell glanced at Whitfield with a contented smirk on his face.

"Ah, yes," Cornwell said, "ever since the outbreak, a child of her age would have been placed in one of the refugee camps for children. Many kids have lost their parents, and they stay in these camps until proper caregivers can be found."

For all I knew, Cornwell had just hit me with a sledgehammer and it made me feel sick to my stomach.

"Like hell you are," Ash said, raising her voice. "You can't tell me what to do."

I glanced at Ash, and she looked at me expectantly as if she wanted me to speak up, but I couldn't. My mouth wouldn't form the words.

"This is bullshit," Angie said. At Angie's words, I glanced at Mars, and he caught my gaze. Those jade eyes bored into me as if they were trying to reach inside my head and tell me something.

Ash had started throwing a colorful range of words as Whitfield cleared his throat.

"That's enough," he said in a booming voice. Although the others remained silent, Ash didn't seem impressed and kept venting her thoughts. I squeezed her shoulder and shook my head as she looked up at me. She clamped her mouth shut but couldn't hide the hurt look in her eyes.

Whitfield cleared his throat again and shot Cornwell a glance of disapproval before he turned to Ash.

"Considering the situation and the fact that you have the same virus coursing through your veins as these two ladies, I believe that might not be such a good idea," Whitfield said. "Besides, we are well aware of the fact that the child has created a bond with you, Ms. Vissers. Therefore, we have come up with a different solution."

"Ash will come with me," Mars said. My head perked in his direction at the sound of his voice. It seemed as if I hadn't heard his warm voice in ages, and now they spoke the words I wanted to hear. "For the time it takes you to do what you need to do in Alaska, Ash will stay with my parents and my son."

"Yes," Whitfield said, "considering Agent Marsden's intimate knowledge of the virus, I thought this would be best."

"I'll arrange things with my parents," Mars said. His lips curved into a faint smile that started to light up his eyes. Afraid his gaze would distract me too much, I turned to Whitfield.

"What happens after we come back?" I asked, trying to keep my wits.

Whitfield nodded and said, "If you want, we'll do what we can to help you gain custody of the child."

The word *custody* sounded official, and for a moment I felt the anxiety of being responsible for a child, but it wasn't anything different from what I had dealt with the past year or so.

"What do you mean 'help get custody'?" Ash said, sounding suspicious. Probably for the first time since I had met the man, Whitfield smiled.

"I think you know what I mean," he said. From the corner of my eye, I could see Ash's grin grow, which made me smile.

"There is still a matter of international travel," Cornwell stated.

"So," Ash piped in, sounding annoyed. It was pretty obvious she didn't like the, man and I would have to agree with her.

Cornwell shot Ash an equally annoyed look before he said, "Europe is bound by a treaty that only accepts nationals to enter their territory."

"Then Ms. Vissers might have to stay in the United States a little longer," Whitfield said elated.

"Oh," Ash replied, glancing up as if to check I would be okay with that. I nodded and smiled at her faintly. I doubt my family at home would appreciate it and knew it would be hard, but I could do that. Also, it would give me time to work on other things.

A sliver of hope rose inside me. I glanced at Mars expectantly, and he met me with a smile.

"We'll leave you to talk it over," Whitfield said as he rose from his seat.

"What if we refuse?" I asked.

Whitfield grasped for his papers before he straightened and faced me. Cornwell, standing next to him, crossed his arms over his chest and gazed at me with that permanent frown he carried around as if I had it coming now.

Whitfield scratched his temple at the edge of his gray hair and said, "We might lose our best chance to defeat the zombie plague, and we'd have to send you home—alone. But if I should believe your father, and he sounded pretty convincing, then I know you'll make the right decision."

With that he nodded and turned to leave the room. Cornwell looked disappointed as he followed him.

32

As the two men closed the door behind them, silence fell over us. Outside I could see Whitfield talking to Cornwell, and although I couldn't hear them, the fact that Cornwell's head was turning bright red told me he'd be the one getting it.

Mars took up a seat at my right while Ash and Angie still sat at my left. No one spoke for the longest time, as if we needed a moment to digest the information given to us. Although it hadn't been a surprise, I still felt a combination of relief and anxiety: relief because it could have gone much worse. As Cornwell had implied, they could have just handcuffed us and dragged Angie and me to Alaska while shipping Ash to some kind of camp for orphans; anxiety because a trip to Alaska meant I would have to leave Ash behind.

I glanced at the frail kid sitting in her wheelchair by my side. Her face looked as confused as I felt. Mars was the first to break the silence.

"Are you guys okay?" he asked as he placed a hand on my arm. I wasn't sure if I'd be able to find my voice and nodded. But as I looked up and saw the smile on Mars's face, some of the tension fled from my body.

"Sunbathing in California," Angie said in an upbeat tone. We all turned to face her. Her mention of California, the place where Mars's parents lived, and the look she gave me told me she had made up her mind. I guessed we all had. We had ever since we had taken those flash drives that Dr. Matley had handed us. We had managed to get them out of the mountain and out of the hands of Dr. David, and now we would take them to Alaska.

Angie shook her head and said in exaggerated voice, "Yeah, that's gonna be rough." Ash raised an eyebrow.

"What's in California?" she asked.

"That's where you'll be staying if Mags and Angie agree to go," Mars said. "It's nice. You'll like it."

"Maybe you can finally learn how to swim," I added.

Ash gave me a hard look before she shifted her gaze between Angie and me.

"You guys will come back for me, right?" she said in a soft voice that nearly broke my heart. Over the course of her short life, too many people had left her and had never come back.

"That's kind of the point to all this," I said. My gaze shifted to Mars. "How long is this trip going to be anyway?"

Mars pursed his lips and thought for a moment. "Depends on how Whitfield is going to let you travel," he said, "but shouldn't be more than two weeks at the most."

"Well, I'm not coming back," Angie said. I shot

her a suspicious glance. "I'm thinking of becoming Canadian," she said. "Things are way too hairy for me here."

Ash's fist shot out and hit Angie in her upper arm.

"All right, all right, I'll come back," Angie replied, throwing an arm around Ash and pulling her in for a hug, "but only for you."

"What about Dr. David?" I asked Mars as Ash and Angie still goofed around.

"It seems he has been summoned back to Washington, DC," Mars said. "The president still resides in the White House, surrounded by an army to fend off the zombies, and he wanted a personal update after General Whitfield had informed him how Warren almost destroyed his base and the potential solution Matley had discovered."

"But I did that!" I said, a bit shocked. Mars shook his and squeezed my arm.

"It would have never happened if Warren hadn't shown up," he said. I couldn't detect any doubt in his voice, but still my chin dropped down to my chest.

"Maybe we'll get lucky and a zombie bites him in the ass," Mars said. He probably wanted to lighten the mood, but I couldn't laugh at his joke. Even though it seemed we had found an ally in General Whitfield, the thought of Dr. David still sent shivers down my spine.

Mars placed a hand on my left cheek and traced

the scar with his thumb as he lifted my chin.

"You don't have to worry about him anymore," he said. Before I could reply, Ash spoke up.

"Finally," she said. I turned my head to face her, and she continued. "But like Mars said, I hope a zombie bites him in the ass." This time, I could laugh at the joke.

"So now what?" I asked.

"I'm kind of hungry," Angie said with a shrug.

"Can we have pizza for dinner?" Ash asked.

"We should probably start with breakfast," I said. A round of laughter filled the room.

Mars got up from his seat and said, "I'll see if I can find something for you to eat." As soon as he had said the words, Ash and Angie applauded him. Mars responded with a bow, although instead of rising, he moved closer to me and then leaned in for a kiss. Shock quickly turned to heat flowing to my cheeks. His five o'clock brushed my skin as he moved his mouth to my ear and whispered, "Can I get you anything?"

I had to clear my throat before I could answer. "Any ... eh, thing will do," I managed to say. He smiled that great smile of his and then turned to leave the room. My gaze followed him through the glass walls until he turned a corner.

When my attention redirected to inside the room, two sets of eyes glared at me.

Angie shook her head and said, "This is going to be two long weeks."

The tension had been broken, and although the world lay in turmoil, it seemed our little corner of it had found some relief. I had almost forgotten that it had been no more than a day ago that the virus we were trying to fight had also stopped Angie's cancer, but the smile on her face said that she had not. With its lethal side effect for others, Mortem wasn't the miracle cure one would wish for, but at least we were alive. Maybe things weren't all bad, at least not for us.

At my side, Ash nudged my shoulder. I turned to face her and frowned at the worried look in those big blue eyes.

"What's up?" I asked and noticed her slender fingers fiddle with the fabric of her flight suit.

"That thing Whitfield mentioned ..." she started to say, but hesitated, "the custody part ..."

I had a feeling where this would be going, but waited patiently for Ash to finish.

"Would you do that?"

I couldn't help but smile at the nervous glances she gave me before I replied, "If you want me to."

She watched me for a moment, but then her face morphed into a grin. "Yeah," she added for reassurance.

"Yeah," I replied.

AGROUND

Book Three in the
Wheels and Zombies
series
By M. Van

Thanks for picking up this book and I hope
you've enjoyed it. I would really appreciate it if you
left a review.

If you would like to find out more,
visit www.42links.net and join the mailing list.

Also available in the Wheels and Zombies series

Book #1
Ash: a novella in the Wheels and Zombies series

Book #2
Brooklyn, Wheels and Zombies

www.ingramcontent.com/pod-product-compliance
Lightning Source LLC
Chambersburg PA
CBHW030552260626
47157CB00006B/2289